PENGUIN BOOKS

FUTURETRACK 5

Henry Kitson makes his first mistake when he scores a hundred per cent in his exams. Not for him therefore the glamorous, cushy career pattern of most of his contemporaries. Allocated to Tech, he is equipped with a white coat and a clipboard and becomes one of that small body who keep the country's computerized life-systems going.

His second mistake is going on the razzle. In London, where survival depends on skill and daring and the population is controlled by fear and sensationalism, Kitson becomes pinball champion and meets blonde, leather-clad Keri, London's bike-racing champion of Futuretrack 5. Together they go north in an uneasy partnership. And what they learn as they go they don't like, for this is Britain of the twenty-first century, and if you question the system too much you come to regret it. But who *does* know the answers? And what is Kitson's destined role?

Robert Westall has brilliantly created a future world which is frighteningly plausible. A compelling book for older readers.

Robert Westall grew up in Tynemouth, which is the setting for several of his novels, including *The Machine-Gunners*, which won the Carnegie Medal. He spent two years with the Royal Signals between studying for degrees at Durham and London universities. He then taught in a sixth-form college in Cheshire. Now he owns an antique shop.

ROBERT WESTALL

FUTURETRACK 5

PENGUIN BOOKS

PENGUIN BOOKS

Published by the Penguin Group
Penguin Books Ltd, 27 Wrights Lane, London W8 5TZ, England
Penguin Books USA Inc., 375 Hudson Street, New York, New York 10014, USA
Penguin Books Australia Ltd, Ringwood, Victoria, Australia
Penguin Books Canada Ltd, 2801 John Street, Markham, Ontario, Canada L3R 1B4
Penguin Books (NZ) Ltd, 182–190 Wairau Road, Auckland 10, New Zealand

Penguin Books Ltd, Registered Offices: Harmondsworth, Middlesex, England

First published by Kestrel Books 1983
Published in Puffin Books 1985
Reprinted in Penguin Books 1989
3 5 7 9 10 8 6 4

Printed in England by Clays Ltd, St Ives plc

For Edith Garrett, Librarian, in the peace and
discipline of whose library some of this book was
written

1

As Head Boy, I'd ordered an early call. My last day, my big day. Parents' Day. Been planning it for weeks. Of course it's all crap, Parents' Day. But I wanted it to be well-run crap, because I was Head Boy. My future might depend on it.

The Chinese mess-waiter came in almost silent, bringing my morning tea. Tiny clink of cup on saucer; breathing like velvet. He put down the tray and I said thanks without opening my eyes. Thanks is all we ever said apart from giving them orders. It's all they expect. Try cracking a joke with them, they just look at you. My father says they were happier thirty years ago, running their own little Chinese restaurants. But it's not healthy talking about thirty years ago . . .

I skipped across the polished parquet, pulled back the curtains. Head Boys get the best room; fabulous view over the Solent to the distant robot cranes of Portsmouth. On quiet nights when the breeze was right we could hear Portsmouth, rumble, rumble, rumble all night. Robot ships docking, rolling back their robot hatch-covers so that robot cranes could lift out containers into robo-trucks. All in total darkness. Robots don't need light. If a robot broke down, another robot mended it. There hadn't been a human being inside Portsmouth for ten years. Except for thieves. Robot security returned the thieves to the dock-gates in neat little fake-marble urns, as ashes, ready for dispatch to their next of kin. Or so college legend said. We hadn't been across to check. Not a nice place, Portsmouth; funny to think that thirty years ago it was full of pubs and whores and sailors . . .

But this morning the Solent was glistening benevolently under an ideal breeze; just enough to billow our Union Jacks and bunting bravely. Parents' Day had dawned sunny all over Britain.

Of course. But, better even than last year, the weather-computer had let through a few cirrus clouds, so it all looked really natural. The pilotless weather-bombers must have been pretty busy, out over the Atlantic soaring on their long thin wings, aimless as seagulls while their nose-radar located the exact cloud to bomb with dry-ice. I saw them once from my father's yacht. We'd been sailing west of the Skelligs when a gale blew us out into the Atlantic Forbidden Zone. There they were, high and circling against the sunset. 'They're beautiful,' I said. 'Forget you ever saw them,' said my father.

I dressed with robotic swiftness, shaving with one hand and drinking tea with the other, while wriggling my feet into gleaming black shoes. But quick as I was, the first-years beat me to the sea-wall. There they were, turning blue and goosefleshed in dressing-gowns and striped pyjamas, brandishing their big brass telescopes and squeaking with cold and excitement. Waiting for the ships that would bring their parents; three hours too bloody early.

Mind you, those ships were worth waiting for. *Viperous* had escorted Arctic convoys in the Second World War. Afterwards, she'd descended to the Brazilian navy, then the Uruguayan, who pinched her guns to start a revolution and left her a sunken wreck mouldering in the River Plate mud with every tide passing in and out and palm trees sprouting from her bridge. In 1998 she'd been spotted and floated home by yet another miracle of marine archaeology. Restored to all her former glory, she plied the Solent on *very* fine days. The kids reckoned half her rusted hull was marine plastic and she wouldn't last five minutes in a gale.

Primrose had been a Margate pleasure-steamer. In her finest hour she'd rescued 3,000 well-soaked Allied servicemen from Dunkirk. After the war, she'd become a floating restaurant on the Thames. During the Desperate Eighties, she'd sunk to psychedelic drug-orgies for weary Eurocrats. Till the militant *Church Times* had discovered that DUNKIRK VETERAN IS LONDON'S SHIP OF SHAME. A public outcry from Harrogate to Hove had forced the Government to purchase her under the Patriotism Act, and restore her, too, to former glory. The kids reckoned she was *pure* plastic underwater and one puff of wind would do for her.

I put on my best authority and called, 'Go on, get washed and dressed!'

'Aw, *Kitson*,' they bayed like a wolf-pack. 'You know the ships sometimes come early, Kitson!' Some were bigger than me; all fizzing with Parents' Day hysteria. Remembering that my reign as Head Boy only had a few hours to run, that today I was as much Head Victim as Head Boy, I was starting to feel nervous when a lot of other prefects drifted down to back me up. Blessed is the Head Boy who's kept a few mates . . . this lot would need watching today, or they'd drive the mess-boys into a blue Chinese fit.

Moaning, they departed. I turned back for a last look across the Solent, before my longest, most knackering day really got started. As I did, I caught the faintest possible hint of a rhythmic pinging in my ears; the slightest possible headache-pulse in the bones of my skull.

Somewhere, somebody had switched on a psycho-radar. Somebody was scanning my mind and that of everyone in college. Not for individual thoughts, but for mood. This somebody, discovering that I was alert and only mildly irritated, would ignore me. But if I'd been suicidal or bottling up a murderous rage . . .

Instinctively, I calmed my mind further, with the memory of a little waterfall I knew, and scanned the sky. Low down, far off, just blending with the Portsmouth cranes, was a tiny tadpole-speck. A psycho-helicopter, with its crew of two Gurkha Paramils. Psychopters, as they were called. Normally, they never bothered us here on the island; stuck to the real trouble-spots like London and Glasgow. But of course they'd be round on Parents' Day, merrier than Christmas, hotter than Guy Fawkes, the great glad festival of the year. When sixth-formers got blind drunk or jumped over cliffs. The day mothers were so proud they wept, or so ashamed they lay down in hot baths and overdosed on Valium. The day fathers locked themselves in studies and took down cherished antique revolvers from the wall . . .

'Happy Parents' Day,' I said to the discreetly weaving psychopter. Then I couldn't resist playing the old game the kids played. I sent it a burst of pure hate. 'Drop dead, bastards. Bastards, bastards, *bastards!*'

Did the psychopter hesitate in its discreet weaving? Begin to nose towards me, like a dog scenting a rabbit?

Trouble was, it was a lot easier to open the floodgates of my mind than shut them again. Hate against Paramils flowed out like red-hot lava, like being sick. Couldn't stop. Scared me silly.

The psychopter changed from a sideways tadpole to an end-on dot. Climbed higher for a better scan, abandoning discreet concealment. Got rapidly bigger, heading straight for me, blat, blat, blat. Desperately I tried all the old soothing remedies: thought of burbling streams among dew-specked ferns, white gulls circling, steak and chips. Tall girls gliding in gauzy dresses. Tall girls wading through burbling streams carrying steak and chips for the circling gulls . . .

I burst out laughing. Baffled, the psychopter retreated, resumed its discreet weaving. I wiped my brow, ruining my spotless white handkerchief. They were good, those Gurkha Paramils. Kept their transmissions to a whisper, yet spotted me straight away. I was getting too old and angry to tease them safely. Leave it to the first-years, whose troubles had hardly started . . .

But I went and rang up psycho-control, to complain about their transmission level. As a Head Boy, on Parents' Day, I had the right. The oriental voice was scrupulously polite. They always are; that's what's so scary.

Anyway, the psychopter halved its transmissions. But didn't go away. Now they'd smelt something, they'd hang around for the rest of the day. I could have kicked myself.

It took all we prefects had to keep the kids under wraps till eleven. The mess-boys couldn't cope at all; just stood in nervously smiling huddles in corners, while their young lords and masters hovered on the fringe of going berserk. There'd been black Parents' Days in the past when all the mess-boys lost their trousers, watched bare-legged as a flotilla of sodden cloth floated away across the Solent. Blackest day of all, a mess-boy had been found dead in the washrooms afterwards, stuffed down under a sink with his neck broken. They weren't allowed to resist violence, you see. Helpless as rabbits, expendable as quadraphonic trannies . . .

Anyway, we did better than that. By eleven, the waxed floors of the dorms glistened, in shafts of sunlight sucked free of dust by the wall-vacuums. Beds made, sheets stretched tight as a drum, so stiff with starch they'd have been agony to sleep in. But they weren't for sleeping in; they were for Parents' Day. The kids were finally immaculate, blazers speckless, ties vertical, white shirts changed three times because of sweaty thumb-marks, knee-stockings pulled to exactly the same height and measured with a ruler. Their naval caps were last and worst. Each year had to wear them differently. First-years had them pulled down over their noses, half-blinding them. Seconds tilted theirs to the left, thirds to the right, fourths pushed theirs onto the backs of their heads. (Only we prefects wore the Victorian tasselled pill-boxes, so hard to balance they made walking a torment and running a miracle.) Each year tried surreptitiously to creep towards the style of the year above, which would have given the Head a fit.

At last they were ready to be marched in columns to the sea-wall and somehow kept from scuffing their diamond-bright shoes, or throwing each other in, before their parents actually saw them. Luckily, twin columns of smoke were just rising above the Portsmouth cranes. *Viperous* and *Primrose* made a brave sight through our telescopes. *Primrose*'s paddle-wheels thrashed the water into a fine drifting spray full of rainbows. *Viperous* curved and twisted round her like a playful dog, a bone of bow-wave between her teeth. Both sent up quite incredible amounts of thick black smoke. They were actually driven by small atomic motors, but had a separate hand-stoked furnace to create smoke for the sake of historical accuracy, and because the parents always said that smoke smelt so *real*.

Primrose was white with yellow funnel, *Viperous* pale Mediterranean grey. Both had canvas awnings rigged, to keep sun (and smuts) off the passengers. White ensigns fluttered in the computer-calculated wind. Myriad points of yellow sunlight winked off the newly polished brass of taffrail and binnacle, and the instruments of *Viperous*'s ship's band, playing 'Heart of Oak'.

They steered straight at us, heedless of the flow of robot cargo-ships that was the Solent's normal traffic. Desperately the cargo-ships' computers reversed and altered course to avoid a fatal accident. Finally *Viperous* cut a curve so wild that two robo-ships, computers overloaded with data, collided with a reverberating boom. Everyone found that excruciatingly funny. Triumph of man over microchip! When the two human ships had finally crossed the traffic-stream, the robo-ships realigned themselves and carried on their trade with touching dignity. Aboard the damaged pair, robot welders were already sparking into action, effecting repairs.

A hundred yards out, *Viperous* and *Primrose* dropped antique red-leaded anchors and swung with the tide. Clouds of smoke blew in over the sea-wall, dropping smuts on our collars and making the kids sniff ecstatically. Boats were lowered by brown-faced, white-uniformed Lascars, and the parents were rowed ashore.

In fancy dress, as usual. The in year this year was 1912.

Fathers wore top-hats and frock-coats, or boaters and blazers. Mothers' skirts ended just above the ankle, displaying narrow white shoes and white silk stockings; also dish-like hats smothered in roses. Several blew off into the water, amidst parental hilarity. The Lascars rested on their oars, while fathers fished for them with gamps and walking sticks. Further parental mirth.

1912, of course, was the year the *Titanic* sank. Several fathers were brandishing lifebelts marked *Titanic*. All fakes. Several more fathers had grown chest-covering beards and, stuffing bolsters up their gold-braided pea-jackets, were impersonating *Titanic*'s late-lamented Captain Smith. One had a false beard that was blowing adrift from its moorings. By and large, the parents looked pretty pleased with themselves and pretty ridiculous. Especially Mr Grimshaw (I groaned aloud) who was flourishing a trumpet. Sooner or later, Grimshaw's father was going to play 'Autumn'. 'Autumn' was the hymn bandleader Wallace Hartley played, as the *Titanic* took her final plunge. The great British public had become obsessed with 'Autumn'. All this year, at every concert, on every TV show or record-request programme, some fool was determined to play 'Autumn'. Orchestral versions, guitar solos, bagpipes, specially composed lyrics, versions on musical saws, glasses of water or bashing the spoons. A dog had been trained to howl it. Maybe it was a national death-wish . . . I'd heard it so often it got into my nightmares. I had this awful recurring nightmare that I was looking at Great Britain, and it began to tilt, with the south coast plunging beneath the waves and Scotland lifting out of the water, and people tumbling down from Northumberland to Kent and all the chimneys and the Post Office tower crumbling and falling. Then I'd wake up convinced that I'd been the iceberg that sunk it and feeling terribly guilty.

Anyway, Mr Grimshaw played 'Autumn' as soon as he set foot on dry land, which at least got it over with. He played very badly, nearly having a bulge-cheeked heart-attack. We kept the kids from giggling, by prodding them in the back with stainless-steel biros, our badge of office. The Head clapped louder than anybody else, gave me a straight look and said that when Kitson made his speech of welcome, he would no doubt wish to thank Mr Grimshaw in his own way. During my speech, the psychopter again became audible. Maybe it was after Mr Grimshaw: you had to be pretty disturbed to make noises like that.

The oddest thing was the way the parents failed to react to the psychopter. I could see the kids turning to put out their tongues at it, or putting up two fingers behind their backs. But the parents never by a twitch acknowledged it existed. Like they were afraid to.

The parents trooped off to 'ooh' and 'aah' over displays of work. Our college wasn't strictly a naval college, because the few ships the navy had left were entirely manned by electronic mickey-mouses. But being situated beside the Solent, we'd been given a naval touch, which gave us so many more useless things to learn. How to splice a hempen rope into a turk's head, when everybody's been using heat-sealed nylon rope for the last seventy years. How to tie fantastic knots like sheepshanks, when everyone else fastened rope with a laser welder. How to scramble like performing monkeys round the rigging and spars of three great sailing-ship masts, stuck in the concrete of the drill-ground and looking quite genuine till you tried to carve your initials on them, when they turned out to be case-hardened vinyl. It was great, later that day, balancing on those masts thirty metres up, clinging on by two toenails and an eyelash, to hear one of the watching mums say, 'And I got a really lovely purple snakeskin pair for only seventy Eurocredits . . .' Three second-years got a fit of the giggles and fell off into the safety-nets. Since they were only ten metres up, that was fine, except the giggles became an epidemic, half emptying the masts and filling the nets with second-years wriggling like fish. Two broken collar-bones and the Head giving me a long upwards look saying bad show, Kitson.

How could I stop mothers' silly mouths?

We prefects changed into six different costumes that afternoon for giving the complete sequence of Nelson's flag-signals at Trafalgar, for a display of hornpipe-dancing, a comic bum-boat race, for hurling real Victorian field-guns over artificial obstacles, for a strawberry tea with the mothers, and finally for an all-too-real dinghy-race in which two third-years rammed two more, then tried to run them down and drown them while they were struggling in the water – only we referees got there just in time.

The parents continued their uncomprehending cheers. Finally, the Padre's Evening Hymn, Flag-Lowering and Last Post on Massed Trumpets (rather better than Mr Grimshaw's offering).

Suddenly it was all over and the mothers were re-embarking, dabbing their eyes with Edwardian lace-hand-kerchiefs (hand-made in Vietnam) to the sounds of the *Viperous*'s ship's band, in more pensive mood, playing 'Will ye no come back again'. So, the boats departed (the handkerchiefs, scarcely damp, now being used for waving).

Their lethal offspring went with them.

That left the Sixth, whose parents never came to Parents' Day, but sat at home, taking hot baths and waiting, swallowing Valium tablets helped down with the odd discreet gin, eyeing the clock and the antique revolvers on the study wall . . .

The festive side was over; the blood-bath could begin.

2

We stood and waved, till the ships faded into the Portsmouth haze. When there was no more point in waving, we stood and watched the sunset. It was only the first banks of cloud let through by the weather-bombers, bringing overnight rain; but a blood-red sunset's nicely symbolic . . .

Silence growing. Solent lapping against the sea-wall. Distant rattle of mess-boys scraping squashed strawberries off the Head's lawn. Breeze getting up. Sudden flaps and cracks of awakening flags making a muscle in my eyebrow twitch. Around the shadowy ivy-covered college, the sudden swooping and screaming of house-martins seemed menacing.

For us, after ten years, college was dead. All summer long, lesson-bells would ring in empty classrooms echoing with birdsong. Long before the first new boy sat on his trunk in the autumn porch, we'd be a once-remembered joke, a face in a team-photograph hung on the wall. What had it all been *for*, that sweating on mast and field-gun, that swotting of antique facts?

Well, the dreaded E-level results, for one thing. O-levels at fifteen, A-levels at seventeen, X-levels at nineteen and E-levels at twenty . . . I glanced secretly at my watch, folding my arms in a way that dragged my blazer-cuff up. Black mark for looking at your watch openly, now . . . They'd be watching us from the staff-room. Standing back from the shadowy windows secretly assessing our moral fibre.

Twenty minutes to seven. E-level results in fifty minutes. By then, most of us would be Ests for life, not just children

16

of Est families. Cushy careers as archaeologists or astro-nomers, poets or racing-yachtsmen (which I wanted). Gracious old houses. Book-lined studies with real log fires. Obedient soft-spoken wives who could cook in the style of Provence or Cambodia, and play the grand piano without actually fracturing your ear-drum. Chinese house-servants, *real* coffee. Children in moderation.

Some of us, the ones who failed the E-level, would be packed into vans and driven through the Wire and never heard of again.

Ests bred too fast. Two per family was the rule. But the big-boss families had seven or eight, to prove how big they were. So every year the E-levels weeded us out, like unwanted puppies.

It was almost a luxury, standing there, letting the breeze cool my sweat, letting the first prickings of terror run up my neck into my well-combed, sweat-soaked hair. But that wasn't fair – it wasn't my terror. I knew I'd passed: cross-checked with Alec. Hadn't dropped any marks at all.

Roger, standing beside me, had failed. Alec and I had coached him like hell, really burnt the midnight oil. But too often he'd smiled, eyes clouded, and said, 'Don't worry. It'll be all right on the night.'

It wouldn't. He was going through the Wire and he knew it. He was still calm; eyes just a little bit too wide as if to drink in enough of the sea, the sunset and his friends. They had no sea, beyond the Wire. Maybe they couldn't bear to look at the sunset. Did they *make* friends?

I got near the Wire once, when I was four. Our Chinese gardener left the gate unlatched. I'd wondered a long time about that distant gauzy Wire that ran across the hills, cutting them in half. Our side was all trees and cottages, hedges and sign-posts and ladies on bicycles who some-times gave me sweets. The grass was very green.

Beyond the Wire, the grass was grey and empty. A few tall concrete lamp-posts; grey blocks of buildings peeping over a treeless hill.

When I finally reached the Wire, I found it was two wires, ten metres apart. The near one just smooth green plastic; the far one tall, black barbed wire with bits of newspaper fluttering like trapped birds.

Between them, plants grew higher than my head, a jungle of cow-parsley and young sycamores. Fascinating new insects buzzed, crawled and flew. I thought I saw a rabbit. I thought I'd found the Garden of Eden; got lost in an insect-haunted daze, hanging on the Wire and sucking the plastic strands.

Then I heard a 'ping'. Peering through my jungle, I saw a man with no nose.

He'd *had* a nose; I could see where it had been. Now he just had two holes to breathe through. He'd no eyebrows either. Just purple rings encircling his eyes, making them look tiny and staring. And purple ears, with long gold daggers hanging from them. Bald, except for a long yellow horse-tail that sprouted from his head and flowed down his back. He wore tight purple trousers and a ragged gold waistcoat that left his shoulders bare and glistening with sweat.

Did he have some terrible disease? But he seemed happy, whistling monotonously as he cut a hole in the far Wire with long-handled shears.

I waited for him to come through the hole, so I could see him better. Far off, an electric bell started to ring, but I didn't know what it meant.

Finally, he crawled through and stood up in the jungle, waist-high in plants, delighted as me with my Garden of Eden.

Then he raised his shears like a sword and began hacking the Garden of Eden to pieces, very thoroughly, green plant-blood running down his arms.

'Stop!' I shouted. When he saw me he seemed more pleased than ever. Grinned, showing teeth filed to points, not like mine at all. Began cutting through the second wire, very quickly.

After that, everything happened so fast. He finished his second hole, crawled through. Beckoned to me, with that pointed grin. Something made me back off. He drew back the arm that held the shears and threw them at me. They winked in the sun. I ducked, just in time. Then he ran at me.

There was a fizzing. Blue lightning jumped onto his back and he fell down. The lightning sort of burnt a black hole in my eyes; everything I looked at had a black hole burnt through it.

Then somebody else came running up, shouting shrilly, dragging me away from the Wire and the man with no nose. I thought it was an older boy at first, but he had a yellowy-brown face and a khaki uniform and a black crash-helmet with the vizor pushed up. That was the first time I ever saw a Paramil. The blaster in his holster smelt funny, like when my mother's food-mixer broke down. A *zingy* smell.

He went on dragging me, trying to stop me looking over my shoulder. But I still caught a glimpse of the noseless man. Another Paramil was bending over him, feeling his wrist. When he let the wrist go, the bare arm flopped down in a funny loose way I often tried to imitate, but never could.

The Paramil bundled me into a high, green, petrol-smelling car with knobbly tyres and drove me home, gabbling into his radio all the way. I was unfairly sent to bed. Voices rumbled a long time, downstairs, before the car drove away. My parents both came up to see me. Mother was as white as a sheet. Father had drops of sweat on his top lip that he kept on licking off. He said I'd caused terrible trouble. For my parents who'd let me stray; for the security company who ran the Wire; for the Paramils who'd had to 'fill in an Unnem'.

I was bloody-minded, near tears. What was an Unnem? How did you fill one in?

'Shut up', shouted my gentle father. 'All you need to

know is this – if you ever tell anybody what happened, you won't *have* a home or a father or a mother . . .'

I never mentioned it to a soul; Paramils have long memories. But at our fifth-year celebration nosh-up, Roger got slewed and told a very similar story. From looks on faces, most of us could have matched it. Everyone knew what happened to Unnems who crossed the Wire, but you didn't talk about it. Your new Chinese house-boy might be a plainclothes Paramil.

I was still standing dreaming, on the sea-wall, like a plastic chimpanzee, and tension was mounting. Some of us would be Unnems within the hour. I must move; mustn't keep them standing there while panic grew. It wasn't the doomed like Roger who'd crack, but those who still hoped against hope, re-checked their exam answers ten times a day, were terrified there'd be a hiccup in the Results Computer.

Like the one two years ago. The kid was rescued by his father, before they could put him through the Wire. They broke out into the Atlantic in their racing-yacht . . . were later said to have drowned in a sudden squall.

In beautiful Parents' Day weather . . .

Move, Kitson! Do your duty. Follow the ancient – ahem – thirty-year-old tradition of the college. As the Head always said, 'Walking is an *excellent* antidote for anxiety, Kitson!'

So I traditionally turned to my best friend, Roger. Tried not to imagine him minus nose and eyebrows.

'Fancy a stroll to the Lookout?'

He batted his eyebrows up and down, comically. 'If you like.'

I hoped the staff had observed his eyebrow-act. They said this waiting was part of the final exam; perhaps at this very moment, they were feeding Roger's eyebrows into the Results Computer. Half a percent for guts?

Alec fell in beside us. Then the captains of sailing,

squash, lacrosse, athletics, badminton, rugby and throwing-field-guns-over-obstacles. Then the rest. We strolled slowly up the sea-wall towards the Lookout, that glowed like an arrowhead against the gathering dark.

Nothing else to do, except lie on your bed and go mad.

I kept the pace down, in spite of wanting to walk faster and faster and the pressure building up behind. I'd timed this walk often, the past month. Looking sneakily at my watch, I knew I was getting it right.

We were silent, mostly; afraid we might speak too loud, or gabble. We steadied our pill-box hats against the stiffening breeze and pretended to enjoy the fabulous evening. The tide was going out, exposing the seaweed. Concentrate on the *realness* of its smell . . . White gulls, gliding and hovering, kept us company, still sunlit against the dusk.

We turned at ten past seven, bang on time. The pressure behind was terrible now, like an avalanche on my back. Six times I deliberately slowed my pace. Once, they began edging past me, and I thought there was going to be a stampede. But Roger began to murmur our old song,

> 'I'll be an Est
> For Ests are best
> Down to their sodding woolly vests . . .'

It steadied us. Just as well. There was a wink of telescopes from the staff-room window . . .

We got back with two minutes to go. Across the quad, the Results notice-board reflected the red sun in both panes of glass.

We'd all agreed to stay outside the gate till the pass-list was pinned up. Then stroll across. But imperceptibly, like a lava-flow, starting with the most frantic, they began to inch towards the board. Uncanny. They still appeared to be standing, talking, shifting their weight from one leg to another, yet all the time they were drifting away. Faces like chalk, sweat beading out, tongue-tips licking lips, Adam's apples bobbing with compulsive swallowing. The staff were openly leaning out of the staff-room windows now, eager as spectators at a boxing match, making bets who'd crack first.

Rog and Alec and I didn't budge. We'd spoil their rotten fun if we died for it. Roger grinned at Alec and me; a grey grin out of hell.

'Cheer up – *you*'ve passed. Have a fag.'

'No thanks,' said Alec. 'I'll wait till it's over, now. In another ten seconds, *they*'ll be late.' Voice calm, but his scalp twitching, making his pill-box tassel bob up and down.

The college clock chimed, its mechanism audible. The college doors opened. Miss Beswick, college secretary, tweed skirt, twinset and pearls emerged, long white paper in her hand. Four school sergeants with her. Ex-coppers, huge in white caps. Laughing loudly, loving it all.

'Stand back, lads. Only a routine notice!'

'*Mind* the lady. We'll need her next year.'

Last year, things had got out of hand. Miss Beswick had been on crutches till September. She unlocked the notice-board, with maddening, trembling slowness.

On the fringes, Bairstow fainted.

They left him lying.

The glass doors swung open, winking hugely red. Miss Beswick pulled out four drawing pins, put three between her pale prim lips. Was she being slow on *purpose*?

The sergeants, red-faced and straining, had linked arms to protect her. One drawing-pin went home, two, three, four. The notice-board winked redly shut. She relocked it precisely and the sergeants got her away by main force. Just in time. One sergeant was doubled up with pain, another nursing his wrist, as civilization collapsed into a heaving, straining, rugby scrum.

Pill-box hats falling in showers, crunching underfoot. A blazer ripped, in the savage panting, struggling silence. Then, with a crash and squeal, the glass of the notice-board broke. I hoped it wasn't somebody's face; people had lost eyes. I'd suggested to the Head a perspex notice-board, padded with sorbo-rubber. But tradition said glass, replaced every year.

We looked up at the staff leaning out, open-mouthed, drooling.

'Revolting,' said Alec.

'Pigs at a feeding-trough,' said Roger; but his big fists were clenched white.

No news emerged. People who knew their results couldn't get out for those pushing behind. Then Fatty Jobling crawled out through the forest of legs, bent spectacles hanging round his jaw and one ear bleeding. He raised his arms, eyes still shut, still on his knees.

'I've passed, I've *passed*.' Then he burst into tears.

Other battered figures crawled out. But, in the main ruck, kicking and punching. The notice-board, wrenched from its moorings, reared up, wobbled then dropped down out of sight. Splintering of cracking wood.

'Oh, my ribs, my ribs.'

Feeling our eyes on him, Fatty stood up, recovered his glasses, pulled the rags of his blazer round him and staggered across. He embraced Alec.

'You've passed. You're *top*.'

Alec freed himself with a fastidious shrug; but colour was flooding back into his face. 'Any other results?' he asked casually. Only he could ask.

Fatty's eyes skated over Rog and me, dropped. 'I only noticed you, because you're top.' Liar; he couldn't get away fast enough. We stared at each other, helpless. Till the end we'd hoped for Rog.

'Go on, off to the flagpole then,' said Rog savagely to Alec. It was a tradition that those who passed stood by the flagpole. Those who failed waited outside the gate.

Alec opened his mouth three times to say something, then walked away.

'Seeya,' said Rog abruptly. Walked out through the gate, stood staring across the Solent.

23

'You might have waited,' I shouted. 'I might have failed too.'

'Pigs might fly,' he shouted without turning. 'Better go and see, hadn't you?'

The scrum was thinning rapidly. Lads passed me, heads down, not looking, going to join Rog. Others clustered round the flagpole, jumping up and down and shouting. Then silent suddenly, as they remembered the gate-group.

The pass-list flapped out through the broken bloodied glass. I bent to read it, sick for Rog. Ran my eye down the list, peeved I wasn't top.

My eyes ran further and further. Panic gripped my guts. My name wasn't above the pass-line. I checked again. A third time. It was insane . . .

My eye dived gingerly below the pass-line. Deeper and deeper, through kids I could've eaten for breakfast, three at a time.

My name wasn't below the pass-line either. I went on reading, above, below, above, below. Nothing. A computer-hiccup. I'd have somebody's guts for garters . . .

Then I saw at the bottom: 'Kitson unclassified. Report to Headmaster at nine.'

It was hard not to walk round in circles. It was hard not to scream. I was *nothing*. I had nowhere to stand. Nobody had ever been unclassified before.

The group round the flagpole stared at me, baffled; then wouldn't look at me at all. Neither would the group outside the gate. The two groups shouted jokes and rude remarks to each other, but the flow soon dried up, and they turned their backs on each other.

Silence again. It was unbearable to be alone.

For a fleeting bitter second I even wanted to join the mob outside the gate.

But the Unnem-van was mercifully quick: they don't hang about. It pulled up, grey and battered, heavy mesh over its windows. It looked like people had been throwing bricks at it all its life. A Paramil opened the rear doors and silently threw out some bales of blue cloth. Silently, the new Unnems stripped off torn blazers and dropped them in the road. We'd all been trained to get changed quickly. Within two minutes they were wearing faded thin denims, heavy-studded unpolished black boots.

The Paramil gestured with his blaster. They got aboard silently, without looking back. The van did a U-turn, across the discarded blazers, and drove off. I couldn't see through the heavy mesh if they waved or not. Then there was only their clothes in the road, looking like a bloodless massacre.

Once the van had gone, the new Ests cheered up quickly – like after a funeral. The teachers came out and started slapping them on the back. The new Ests began calling the teachers by their Christian names, telling them what bloody awful teachers they'd been and what they'd hated most about their lessons. The teachers took it jolly well, laughing loudly and heartily. Quite a party, except when they caught sight of me. Then they stopped laughing, like I was a blockage in the drains, or a rain-cloud on sports day. Finally, they turned their backs and kept them turned.

Then the Head bustled up and led them off, tattered and bloody, for celebration champagne. Later, when they'd washed the glass-splinters out of their hair, they'd be going to a dance at the Ladies' College. Now Ests were truly Est, courtship-rituals could begin. Staff would not be patrolling the shrubberies.

Trouble was, to get to the Head's house, they had to pass me. The Head swept past, marble-blue eyes tilted well above my head, looking at the last of the sunset. Like newly born goslings following a gander, nearly all the new Ests did exactly the same. I wanted to laugh, they looked so smug and pseud. A few still looked me in the eye, twisting mouths or raising eyebrows to show how upset they were. Only Alec looked really miserable.

I was left alone to wander. A blackbird sang from the shrubbery, not caring *what* I was. The corner-flags for next season's rugby threw long shadows as they fluttered. Far above, Concorde flew its monthly ceremonial flight. It flew high enough to leave a vapour-trail, and I wondered which of its hundred fully trained Est pilots was actually getting a chance to fly it.

3

I entered the college lobby, prompt on nine. Shaking with rage, jumping at shadows.

Footsteps. Angry, sharp, limping footsteps coming up the parquet corridor. Major Arnold, deputy head. Limping from a wound he got in Northern Ireland, before the first psychopters finished off the IRA. Thin, upright, dark moustache, white streaks in his Brylcreemed hair. He had his hair cut weekly, short-back-and-sides, so the skin showed through pale, in contrast with his sunburnt face. Very fit for his age; played squash. Even climbed the masts with us, chewing his moustache savagely with sweat running down his face. It cost him.

A bitter man. Full of rage held down to heel like a snarling dog. Whether it was caused by the pain of his leg or something else, we never knew. We adored him, because when you asked him embarrassing questions, he always gave you straight answers. He might think for minutes on end, head bowed, till you thought he'd gone to sleep. Then he'd look up and give you the truth, like water spurting from a boiling kettle.

'No, Kitson, the Battle of Belfast wasn't a famous victory. The IRA stood no chance . . . nowhere left to hide, once the psychopters located them. We had fifty times their fire-power. We stood well back and took no chances. We had two men slightly injured.'

He was angry now. 'Kitson! Come!' He started back up the corridor. Clumsy and skidding with fear, I fell in behind.

'What happened sir? What did I do wrong?' I was wailing like a first-year.

27

'I *warned* you, Kitson.'

'*What*, sir?'

'What was the last thing I said to you, before the exam?'

'You told me not to score a hundred per cent, sir.'

'Well, that's what you did wrong.'

'I thought you were joking, sir.'

'Well, I wasn't. You scored a hundred per cent and they'll *never* forgive you.'

'What's going to happen to me, sir?'

'That I'm not allowed to say. The Head . . .'

We walked as in a nightmare up that endless oak-panelled corridor, hung with silver cups and shields, rowing-pennants, team-photographs. A nasty thought struck me. I remembered Madden, Head Boy in my first-year. I'd been Madden's fag. He was kind; I hero-worshipped him, drooling over his face in the team-photographs. Then, one Parents' Day, Madden vanished through the Wire. The following term, heart-broken, I looked for his face in the team-photographs; it was no longer there. Some bastard had taken each photo from its frame, and cut Madden's head out. Replaced it with a smug, smiling, Est's face . . .

'Will they cut me out of the team-photographs, sir?'

'That's the least of your worries, now.'

He stopped at the Head's door. Pondered, then decided to shake me by the hand. It made me feel like a leper he was doing good to.

'You won't like where you're going, Kitson. But I hope you'll display your usual guts.'

'Thank you, sir,' I said, stupidly. But he was gone. I knocked on the Head's door.

'Come.' The Head was signing papers. Pink, manicured hands, below white shirt-cuffs, moved each paper with distaste, then slashed it with a ballpoint. Like a gentleman-farmer wringing chicken's necks with his gloves on. He paused, giving me enough time to read a typed name, upside-down. Roger's. He was consigning the new Unnems through the Wire.

He was also trying to needle me. I studied at leisure his white, newly washed hair. The heavy tweed suit, creamy like oatmeal. The red-veined cheeks, like a healthy, elderly farmer's. The polished old brogues sticking through the desk, shiny as conkers. I'd never realized how much I'd hated him.

He glanced up suddenly and caught my look; returned it with interest.

'Hundred per cent, Kitson. Well, you've done it at last.'

'Done what, sir?'

'Don't you think it rather *vulgar* to score a hundred per cent?'

'I only wanted to get things right.'

'And be damned to the feelings of everybody else? You think we're all mediocrities here, don't you, Kitson? Boys and staff?'

'Yes.' What was the point of lying now?

'It never occurred to you that the essence of being an Est is *team* spirit, *team* achievement? Unless *you* were running the team, of course?'

'*You* made me Head Boy.'

'I gave you enough rope and you hanged yourself. Nothing was ever right for you, was it? Can't we modernize this, improve this? Is there any member of staff you haven't mimicked and mocked in front of younger boys?'

'Major Arnold. He's honest.'

That hurt; I was glad. The hate of years boiled up in me; all the layers of tact and sham peeling off . . . Better than being afraid.

'Why are you so angry, Kitson?'

'You made arse-holes of the lot of them . . . round the Results Board . . . fighting like pigs round a trough . . .'

'Most of them seem to have forgiven me; they're drinking enough of my champagne.'

'Maybe they're thirsty from licking your arse. And what about the ones who aren't drinking champagne? Like

Roger?' I was screaming by this time, totally out of control for the first time in years. But I no longer cared.

'Are you questioning the state's right to put unwanted people through the Wire?'

'Yes, I am.'

He leaned back with a satisfied smile. 'I suppose you realize that what you've just said is high treason . . . and I had a tape recorder running . . .'

I glanced desperately round his desk. Where was the tape recorder? Under his blotter? In the antique brass inkwell? They're so small now it could be anywhere . . .

'I've been telling the governors for years that we've been harbouring a viper in our bosom. Perhaps they'll believe me, now . . . even your father's considerable influence won't save you this time . . .'

'From what . . . the lobo-farm?'

'So you know about the lobo-farm? I wonder who told you?'

'We all know about it.' The lobo-farm was the ultimate nightmare; the one that wakened you screaming. The lobo-farm, where they strapped you down and gave you a frontal lobotomy. They didn't have to open your skull any more; they simply passed your head under a tiny laser-beam. Which did you no damage at all, except it cut off the frontal lobes from the rest of your brain. You could walk away within two minutes of the operation. Trouble was, you no longer knew where you wanted to walk to. You were practically down to sheep or cow level; walked about smiling and whistling without a care in the world. Given simple instructions, you simply carried them out. Provided it wasn't more than sawing logs or rough-digging. International terrorists went into the lobo-farm and came out fit to be trained as house-maids. Top people liked having them around, particularly if they'd been *famous* international terrorists. They made a good talking-point at sherry-parties. Guests found their unfailing cheerful willingness totally unnerving.

He continued to watch me, smiling. Enjoying himself.

Unfortunately, at that moment there came a knock on the door. A bugger-you kind of knock.

'Wait!' shouted the Head.

The door immediately opened, to admit a gangly youth with an out-thrust beaky nose, well-picked spots and a long, white nylon coat. His hair was crewcut; he looked extremely pale and unhealthy in a tough sort of way. Like he enjoyed being unhealthy; like his idea of keeping fit was to smoke a fag as fast as possible. His white coat had a regiment of pens in the top pocket. He had another stuck strangely behind his left ear and a clipboard in his hand.

'Right, squire. I've come to take delivery of Kitson, Henry, late Est of this parish. Sign here.' He slouched across the sacred Persian carpet, and thrust the clipboard under the Head's nose with nicotine-orange fingers. 'I don't suppose you've got a pen – use this one.' He whipped it from behind his ear.

The Head bridled backwards with distaste, as far as he could tilt his chair. Ready to give the newcomer an icy-blue glare at point-blank range.

It was a mistake. The newcomer thrust his clipboard further in, pinning the Head by the throat to his own wall.

'You sign *there*. Where I've marked it with a cross.' He said it with sorrow and compassion, as to an idiot child.

'I have not yet finished with Kitson.' The Head's voice shot upwards, to the verge of apoplexy.

The newcomer consulted the large watch, bristling with buttons, on his hairy wrist.

'Too late, squire. As from 21.00, Kitson is mine.'

'There may be a charge of high treason.'

'Oh, Gawd, not again,' said the newcomer wearily. 'That's all you old blokes ever think about, high treason. And I suppose you've got a tape recording to prove it?'

'I have.'

The newcomer glanced idly round the desk-top where my eyes had searched in vain. Picked up the antique ink-well, before the Head could stop him. Examined it. 'Oh, yes, one of our BB 35s – a very nice recorder. Oops, sorry!' He dropped the ink-well to the carpet and scrunched it under his slender white boot. 'Dear me, how clumsy! Fill in this complaint-form, squire, and we'll send you a replacement. Eventually.' He turned to me.

'You Kitson, kid? Seems the high-treason charge has been quashed . . . or do I mean squashed? . . . You're a free man . . . sort of. Right, I'll give you five minutes to collect your favourite teddy-bear and marbles. Quick march! You'll find me parked out front. We've got to be in Cambridge before midnight, and we're doing it the hard way – through London by car.'

'This is insufferable,' shouted the Head.

'Suffer it, squire. Be brave. Suffering purifies the soul. Haven't you read your *Bhagavadgita*? Thought you Ests liked that sort of crud?'

I glanced uneasily from him to the Head. The Head suddenly looked tired, like an old actor in some clapped-out play who's forgotten his lines.

I enjoyed turning my back on him. As I left, I heard the newcomer say, 'You do know *how* to write your name, don't you?'

I couldn't miss the Jensen Interceptor. Long, low, once sleek, till people started throwing bricks at it. It had the same unloved look as the Wire-van; mesh over the windows and an enormous steel blade like a snow-plough fastened over the front bumper. There were brown stains on the blade; blood, or just rust? There was another ex-Est on the back seat, looking pretty shrivelled in the remains of a striped blazer.

I took the front passenger-seat.

'On your own head be it,' said the ex-Est. 'He's *insane*.'

Old Spotty bustled out, shoving his pen back behind his ear.

'Your Head's the insecure sort . . .' He pulled two smooth white packs from the glove-compartment. 'Shove these on – you're Techs now. Might as well die in uniform.' We broke the plastic and put on white coats, much shorter than his.

'We're *what*?'

'Techs. Don't you know what a Tech is?'

'No – I thought I was going to the lobo-farm . . .'

'You are. Don't *panic*! Us Techs run the lobo-farm. And everything else.'

'Never heard of you.'

'Naturally. Who's heard of a sewer – till it goes wrong? Diddums think it was love made the world go round? Well it's not – it's Techs.'

'You mean – like our mess-boys?'

'I didn't hear you say that, squire. But . . . yes. Your mess-boy is actually a Tech 1a. And your Paramil Captain's a Tech 1z. And all the other bottle-washers are something in between. But you sprogs are already Techs 2a, from the moment you put those coats on. Isn't *that* nice?' He slammed the Jensen into gear, and the bucket-seats crushed the wind out of our lungs.

'He's *insane*,' bleated the kid in the back seat.

'Shut up, or I'll arrange you a tongue-amputation,' said Spotty.

The kid shut up. I said, 'I don't get it.'

'Let me ask you a question,' said Spotty, cornering the Jensen at ninety, right over on the wrong side of the road. 'Why did you disobey your dear Headmaster and come with me?'

'Because . . . he looked like an old actor who'd forgotten his lines.'

'Smart kid. You may call me Cragg, as a reward. Yes, you've grabbed the essentials, as the bishop said to the actress. *We* let the Ests write the cruddy play, and play all the heroic noble parts. But who built the theatre? Who lays on the lighting and the music and the tape-recorded clapping at the end? Techs, squire, Techs! All three thousand of us. Every time you raise a glass of synthetic whisky to your rosebud lips, every time you go to the loo, you should raise your hat to the Techs . . .'

'He's *insane*,' bleated the kid in the back.

'One tongue-amputation coming-up,' said Cragg, as he drove down on to the armoured ferry that linked our island to the mainland. At sixty kilometres an hour, he skidded so wildly on the greasy deck that we nearly went through the far bulkhead. A Paramil angrily walked across to us. Cragg wound down his window by pressing a button on the dashboard. 'Your decks are greasy, Gunga Din. I'm slapping a NZ 21345 on you.' He ripped a blue form off his ever-present clipboard. The Paramil paled and backed off.

'Actually,' said Cragg, pressing the button that wound the window back up, 'these bloody brakes want seeing to. I'll slap a T/F 1002 on the Centre garage instead.'

We crossed the Solent, the automated gun-turrets on the ferry swinging to challenge every bit of floating wreckage that drifted by us in the dark. 'The Unnems keep floating out home-made torpedoes for a laugh,' said Cragg. 'Only after dark. Quite ingenious, some of them – we had 'em brought in to the lab. We reckoned they'd do it, five years ago, so we were ready for them, long before they started.'

Beyond the guard-post in the Wire, beyond the automated walls of Portsmouth, we were in Unnem land. Cragg drove like a drunk, changing his direction down side-roads at the last possible moment, varying his speed without warning from 150 kilometres an hour to twenty. 'Keep it random, boy, keep it random. Keep the snipers guessing . . .' After an hour, we saw a glow in the sky ahead.

'London burning,' said Cragg. 'Don't worry. London

burns every night. The Unnems cutting off their noses to spite their faces . . .'

I closed my eyes, remembering the noseless Unnem I'd seen as a child. Remembering Roger . . . somewhere in all this, Roger . . .

I closed my eyes a fair number of times on that ride; especially the London bit, with the burning barricades across the motorway that the Jensen cleaved through like a ship. The flickering orange figures hurling petrol-bombs so that we drove through lakes of fire. The bricks rattling off the wire mesh of the windscreen, every time we passed under an overpass. The woman I saw wandering with vacant eyes and a baby in her arms, right in the middle of the fast lane.

I don't think we hit her.

'Wouldn't it be more rational,' I said, keeping my voice light and steady, 'to move by helicopter at night?'

'But a lot less fun,' said Cragg.

'You mean you didn't *have* to do this?'

'What do you think I am – a bloody chauffeur or something? This is my hobby mate. That Centre is so bloody *rational*, you have to do something for kicks to stop going potty. I'm a Tech 4n.'

'He's *insane*,' bleated the kid in the back.

'Shut up – your tongue was amputated an hour ago. Anyway, here we are at our beloved Centre.'

Fences, watchtowers, Paramils. More fences, watchtowers, Paramils. Then a huge lighted building, with a few figures on the steps, white-coated, watching, silent, assessing the three of us.

'Two more specimens for vivisection, Cragg?'

The kid in the back began to cry.

I got out and stuck up two fingers at them.

'That one's got enough basic aggression – he might survive,' said somebody.

I walked up to him; he wore spectacles; most of them did.

'Just you wait, mate,' I said. 'Just you wait.'

'I'll wait,' he said, just raising his clipboard a bit, calmly.

I didn't know what that meant, then.

4

A year had passed.

The Hall of Technicians was crowded and still; the ranks of white coats blinding beneath massed neon lights. Three thousand Techs ran Britain and half were here tonight. But, crowded as they were, each left a ten-centimetre gap between him and his neighbour; each was a man apart. They weren't a group, like Ests, but a collection of individuals, held together by brains and envy. Strange how many wore spectacles, which flashed and winked across the Hall, hiding eyes that roamed continuously, seeking faults; an incipient flicker in a neon tube, a smudge on a white wall, an error in button-etiquette by their neighbour.

Button-etiquette . . . we trainees still wore the short white coats. Tomorrow, our thighs would vanish under the long white coats of graduation. But not all long white coats were worn the same. Techs 2p left one top button undone. Those above 3a left two. Fives left their coats completely open, displaying spotless white smocks and trousers underneath. A mistake in button-etiquette was the worst fault of all . . .

Headtech brought his clipboard from his deep pocket with a smoothness none could fault. Wonderful things, Tech clipboards, carrying the flat buttons that keyed you in to a distant computer, the winking lights of personal communicators. Made of light alloy armour-plate that could deflect any bullet or blaster, at point-blank range. One edge was honed razor-sharp (under a rubber guard) for personal defence; thrown with a quick flick of the wrist, they could kill.

How many years had Headtech practised that smooth

gesture? And he didn't 'um' and 'er' like an Est. His pronouncements flowed from his lips smoothly and continuously, in that high-pitched, slightly whining tone that gives a listening computer least difficulty: computerspeak. Was it just coincidence that computerspeak, which we'd learnt with such throat-wrenching difficulty, was also a complaining, niggling, nit-picking noise that gave any normal human being a pain in the arse?

'Here is the pass-list, in order of merit.' Headtech ran his eyes along our faces, savouring our hope, envy, lust, despair, like a gardener sniffs a rose.

'First . . . Kitson, Henry.'

Every eye swung. Fellow-trainees looked daggers. Senior Techs calculated: I was the new threat. I didn't give a damn for any of them. I was first; nobody could ever take that away. All those endless hours studying systems; even the primitive robo-plough still used in Africa. All those worn-out languages that Noah fed into the Ark's computer, COBOL, FORTRAN, ALGOL. Endless so-called recreational games of four-dimensional chess, friendly as a razor-fight in a back-alley. Atomic fusion, neutron spectroscopy . . .

It had all been worthwhile; I was first.

But Headtech's voice whined on, delicately separating each new Tech from the classmates he'd beaten; the ones who'd beaten him. We'd never forget that order of merit, if we lived to be a hundred.

He finished. No human buzz of conversation. They were waiting for the big event. My heart was in my mouth: I could still miss the big prize.

'Comtech awards the degree of "Summa Cum Laude" to Kitson Henry, for his theses on the molecular motion of water at boiling-point and the life-cycle of the Indian tea-plant. Wheel in the tea-trolley.'

Here you might have heard, with the sharpness of Techs' ears, the indrawn hiss of mass envy.

'Kitson, Henry, step forward.'

I took two steps forward, careful to touch nobody. This placed me exactly a yard from Headtech. My down-flicking eyes picked up the trolley, moving in soundlessly from the left. White, spotless, carrying ancient things. A chipped but shining teapot. An antique electric kettle, absurdly dangling a black cable, because it had no power-cell of its own. Once it had been chrome, but years of polishing had stripped it to bare copper.

'Kitson, Henry, will make the tea.'

Again, that indrawn breath of envy.

'Depress the red button,' intoned Headtech. 'Pour boiling water into the teapot, first removing the lid. Rotate the pot clockwise until it is thoroughly warm. *Always* warm the pot.'

A censorious echo from the waiting ranks: '*Always* warm the pot.' Like a church service.

'Take the spoon,' intoned Headtech softly, his pebble-glasses roaming the ranks. 'Transfer two spoonfuls of Indian tea-leaves into the pot. One for each person, and *one* for the pot.'

'*One* for the pot,' echoed the ranks.

It was hard not to giggle. It was hard to stop my hand trembling, spilling a few black tea-leaves onto that shining white trolley. Every eye watched for my slightest error. One black speck would have ruined my career. But I managed it safely.

'When the velocity of steam issuing from the kettle no longer increases, fill the pot.'

I watched the jet of steam grow longer and longer.

'Enough,' said Headtech. 'Pour.' His voice was sharp with exasperation. But the fatal error would have been not waiting long enough . . .

I poured. Immediately, a rich aroma ascended, billowed steamily down the Hall. Real Indian tea, costly as diamonds now the Indians found they got richer growing opium. Among the ranks, every nostril twitched. I replaced the lid with the tiniest clink, that only Headtech and I heard.

'Kitson, Henry, has made the tea. He is now tea-boy to the Chief Systems Analyst.'

The assembly sighed; till the end they'd hoped for a mistake.

'Take the tea to the Analyst, at seven precisely.'

The venerable electronic clock at the far end of the Hall swung its minute-hand vertical. As the red second-hand and the blue milli-second hand swept up to join it, the doors below swung open automatically.

The trolley's wheels kissed gently on the polished floor. A dying song of steam came from the kettle. The willow-pattern cup and saucer rattled like a little chiding monkey. The teapot fumed like a fragrant chimney, and off down the enviously sniffing ranks I went.

Another door marked 'Programming Terminal' swung open. Another, and another. I was in an unknown part of the building; an unused part. Bare concrete walls with crudely chalked directions. I entered too many lifts, that took me up and down at random. Turned too many corners, losing all sense of direction. Crossed slender glass bridges, so that I seemed to wheel the trolley out among the lamplit stars. Saw beneath me other bridges I'd just crossed in the opposite direction.

When I looked back, there were no doors marked 'Exit'. I passed far too many doors altogether, all painted dull red, none carrying any sign. Some weren't even real doors (I kicked them as I passed) but nailed-up plastic-board. Others opened on to pits of darkness. I felt like a rat entering a 3-D maze; the kind they starve to death in. I felt like a stray thought entering a mind immensely cunning, devious and possibly mad. Idris, the Chief Analyst. Idris protecting himself and Laura. Idris and Laura, the fairy-tale that tragically came true; Idris and Laura, a legend rotting.

I glanced at my watch; I'd been walking fifteen minutes and the whole building wasn't *that* big. I wondered if the pattern of lift and corridor would start repeating itself, so I'd go on walking forever, like a poor fly on a Moebius strip. The teapot was nearly cold. My legs ached and shook. Was the old sod pumping some drugging gas into the air-conditioning? Certainly he'd be watching me on closed-circuit TV. Idris watched everybody; nobody saw Idris. Except his current tea-boy. He'd be watching me sweat; shaking and drooling with senile laughter. They reckoned he was well over fifty. If he was still alive. Maybe he'd been dead and rotting since he threw his last tea-boy out, a year ago. Dead and rotting, and electronic Laura calmly carrying on . . . People heard his voice over the phone every day. But Laura had long since recorded his voice and thought-patterns, could mimic him to perfection . . .

The end came suddenly. A last door swung open. The trolley sailed through and I crashed into a pile of rubbish. A very high pile; a lot descended on my head. Sharp-cornered picture-frames; painful broom-handles. I was practically buried. I removed a vacuum-hose that coiled round my neck like a boa-constrictor, and stared about. A lumber-room . . . but expensive. A Georgian grandfather clock, leaning heavily, held up by two books under one worm-eaten leg. Its front ripped off, displaying rusty weights. That painting that hung dirtily askew . . . a Rembrandt? A cheap print, surely? But there was a hole in it; the torn edge showed frayed canvas and hand-applied paint flaking off. A clever fake? I picked off a sliver of paint and smelt it. Linseed oil? I put the sliver gently into my top-pocket. Later, I'd have it analysed by flame-spectrometer.

A Chippendale chair, with a black 1920s bike leaning against it; oil from the chainwheel was soaking into the damask. A 1910 typewriter, a brass bioscope, a bundle of salmon-fishing-rods. The loot of centuries, scattered and spoilt like the toys of some millionaire baby.

'Idiot!' A tall man was standing motionless in one corner, buried to the waist in a horn-gramophone and dusty piles of 78 r.p.m. records. A faded man; his hair, once ginger, was now grey-pink. His face long, white and bony; his nose even bonier. An animal nose, the kind an ant-eater might poke into things. It sniffed twice, to punctuate each remark, and when it sniffed it twitched left-right, left-right. On each side, set in a cage of white bone, a small green eye, cold as a marble. The huge hands holding a record had flat white knuckles and ginger hairs between.

His white coat had suffered thirty years of rape; pockets gaped like manure-sacks, the front hung open in rigid greasy folds, buttons dangled useless on three-centimetre threads. In places the fabric had worn into rags.

'Stupid little idiot. You've ruined an experiment that took three months to set up.'

'Like what? Structural inertia in nineteenth-century junkshops?'

He nearly laughed, then stopped himself and shouted, 'What do you *want*?'

'I've brought your tea.'

'I said what do you *want*? You can't *want* to bring a nasty old sod his tea.'

'They told me to.'

'I didn't ask what they told you. I asked you what *you* wanted.'

'To get on with my job.' I was getting narked.

'Tea-boy? Call that a job for a twenty-one-year-old?'

'It's the only job I've got.'

'But if you lick their shiny white boots they might give you a better one? Like mine, perhaps? What do you *want*, boy? Want, want, want? Or do you enjoy licking boots?'

'I want to know why you're so bloody rude.'

'I've thrown people downstairs for less than that.' He advanced, carrying the 78 like a weapon. He was no prettier close-to; his breath was foul. His bleached ginger eyelashes made his eyes look like creatures that had crawled out of a swamp. 'You know I can sack you just like *that*!' He snapped his bony fingers. 'I sacked the last one in one minute forty-five seconds.'

'I still want to know why you're being so bloody rude.'

He gave me a sideways, marble glint. 'Because no one can stop me. No one can stop me doing anything. *I* built Laura.' He waved a huge hand.

I saw a gilt Louis XIV table, with fag-burns round the edge. Five different-coloured phones, each sitting on a heap of scraps of paper, like a bird on its nest. Draped from them, hundreds of coke-can rings hung on pieces of yellow wool. There was a large paper aeroplane, made from computer print-outs. Its wings were delicately scalloped, full of carefully cut holes. Beyond, an unmade bed. Fastened to the wall above, Laura, the national computer.

I was surprised how small she was. Built of stainless-steel boxes; smaller than a man. She bore some resemblance to a winged figure, with outstretched arms touching a word-processor one side, a display-screen on the other. Where the head should have been was a woman's face, sculpted in stainless steel, the mouth slightly open on darkness, but the hollows of the eyes full of little points of steel that caught the light, so the expression of the eyes seemed to change.

'Why does she look like an angel?'

'Because that's the way I made her. Why shouldn't she look beautiful?'

'I like the face.'

'Should bloody well hope so – cost me a thousand credits. Say hello.'

'On voice transmission,' I said, twisting my voice into the whine of computerspeak.

The 78 record broke in pieces over my head. 'That's no way to talk to a lady. Say hello *nicely*.'

'Whom am I addressing?' asked Laura. The voice was low, rich and infinitely sad. Unlike any computer I'd heard.

The Analyst pulled me to him confidentially; I nearly fainted from the smell of his armpit. 'I made her voice myself. From just this. Listen.'

He pressed a button; there was the click of a tape-recorder coming on; then the crackling noise that telephones made before I was born.

'Hampstead 76112. Oh, it's you, Idris. You shouldn't be phoning me. You'll get in terrible trouble if they find out. I can't talk – here's Mummy coming. Goodbye, Idris. I love you.' It ended with a sigh, and another click.

'That's the last words she ever said to me,' said Idris. 'She married an Est and had four kids. Died seven years ago . . . Laura.'

'You built the whole voice, just from that?'

'Took me twenty years. That steel face I had made – that's like her too.'

'How did you . . . lose her?'

'I scored a hundred per cent in my E-levels, just like you. Est-ladies don't marry Techs. Tell her your name and rank.'

Repressing a shudder, I did so.

'Good evening Kitson Henry.' The voice carried only its eternal note of sadness.

'She likes you,' said Idris. 'I think we'll keep you, for a bit. Shall we, Laura?'

'I have recorded acceptance of his voice.'

'Smart computer, that. I made her smart. Taught her to ask for context.'

'Context?'

'If any of *them* wants to ask her something, they have to put their question into context. Tell her everything about the project they're working on. So she keeps on knowing more and more. She knows everything – that's why she's still the national computer.'

'Everything?'

Idris laughed bitterly. 'Not everything. She doesn't know about human decency – ethics. Never heard of Buddha, or Bertrand Russell. Can you imagine a Buddhist computer running a lobo-farm? That's my trump-card, boy. I've made a last tape for her – full of ethics. Kind of truth-bomb. Feed her that, she'd blow up, poor old thing. Course, *they* know

I've got something up my sleeve, in case they try getting rid of me. They've tried searching for it, while I'm asleep. But they've no idea where it is. Could be inside her already, couldn't it? Just waiting for one tap on a button. Still, I never leave her alone for a second, even to go to the loo.' He pointed to a long row of toilet-bowls, spaced along one wall of the great room. 'This used to be an unused gent's cloakroom, till I made them rip all the partitions out.'

'Why d'you keep her here?'

'I built her here, in secret. And I like the view.' He restlessly snatched up a photocopy of *The Times* dated 1933 and turned to the crossword. 'Word of nine letters; why Charles James does not leave fingerprints?'

'Fox-gloves?' I suggested.

'Digitalis, idiot. Which gives us "pachyderm" which gives us "upstart", a disgusting clue.' He flung down the crossword, finished, and pulled out an ancient gilt pocket-watch. 'Took me ten minutes this morning. Mind's going to pieces. Must be the weather.'

'Can't be. Temperature and humidity are kept constant throughout the Centre.'

'Soulless Tech brat.' He grabbed me by the coat and blasted me with his breath. 'What about the phases of the moon? Mean distance from the sun? The proton shower from the stars? The weather inside my body, inside my soul? Do you really think we can shut ourselves off from weather? Look at those rotting peaches there. While we've been talking one molecule of peach has entered your body and one molecule of me has entered the peach. Can you disprove that, Tech brat? Heh, heh? You're assuming *stillness*, boy. Can you guarantee stillness? D'you think you're God?'

'No, I'm the tea-boy.'

'Pour it, then, pour it. Two sugars.'

It seemed I was not going to be thrown downstairs immediately.

*

The months I spent with Idris were never easy. But they had high spots. He cared for nobody; made indecent suggestions to Headtech daily. But the night he made an anatomical suggestion to the Prime Minister made me realize how much power he and Laura had. In the thirty years since Idris built her, from stolen parts, in a locked loo of this very toilet, Laura had gathered all knowledge to herself. Before Laura, there'd been many computers: police, military, public-health. By electronic stealth, Idris had burgled them all. Even the sewage computer, on principle. The Ests found out after a year, when Idris started correcting other people's programmes. By then, it was too late. The Ests demanded Laura be revealed and dismantled. Idris retaliated by sending the Treasury computer berserk. It stampeded the money-markets and in one day Britain lost a thousand million Eurocredits. The Ests surrendered . . .

Most of the time, Idris behaved himself. His work-load was fantastic. One moment Laura would be concluding a copper-deal with the primitive home-grown Nigerian computer, swindling it blind on behalf of the nation. The next, she'd print out the air-pollution pattern for Europe, which she'd worked out simultaneously. Russian missile-servicings; the French president's pattern of phobias . . .

Late at night, when she'd circuits to spare, Idris let me play with her. I'd request the day's births in, say, Glaston-bury. Pick out one child; get the state-biographies of both parents, a genetic forecast of the child's future health including life-expectancy. Plans of the house where he'd live; details of the house's construction and history . . . You could only do it for Est-children, of course. No records of Unnems. I tried tracing Rog . . . nothing.

'She's not just a calculator,' Idris would plead, gripping my shoulders. '*Relate* to her; ask her what *she'd* like to do.'

Always a creepy moment.

There were worse. The drunken nights when Idris sang

duets with her. That old Bing Crosby number, 'True Love'. That old cracked man's voice and Laura's smooth female voice uplifting it, backing it with infinite sadness.

> 'For you and I have a guardian angel
> On high, with nothing to do,
> But to give to you, and to give to me
> Love forever true . . .'

Or the nights he quarrelled, damning her machine-logic, trying to twist it in knots. And Laura always so reasonable, till he pounded the gilt table in fury, and drunken tears dribbled down his three-day growth of whiskers.

But the worst nights of all were the nights when he began muttering about somebody called Scott-Astbury. Scott-Astbury had *tricked* him, when he was a new and lonely Chief Analyst. Scott-Astbury called by with bottles of best Scotch, talked about salmon-fishing. Scott-Astbury had news of the human Laura, just snippets.

One night, in a half-drunken argument, Scott-Astbury had cast doubts on the power of the new electronic Laura . . .

'I told him,' said Idris, hiccuping, 'I told him me and Laura could do *anything*. He bet me a whole crate of whisky we couldn't do . . . something.' He would always seal his lips tight at that point, and stare at me like a frightened child. 'But we did it, Laura and me. Proved it could be done. Won the bet. He took away the print-out of what we'd done. For a joke . . . just for a joke, to show his grand friends. He sent round the crate of whisky, but he never brought the print-out back. And then the print-out began coming true. And now it can never be . . . undone.' At that point he would always begin to cry silently, with his mouth gaping showing rotten teeth and the tears running down his face in a solid sheet.

'What did you do for him, Idris?'

But he would only shake his head violently, and hide his

face in his hands. I never got another word out of him. Except that Scott-Astbury was evil, evil, and when Idris was dead, and I had Laura, I must never let her work for Scott-Astbury. Who had done for us all . . . After that, he would take the last enormous drink that sent him into merciful, snoring oblivion.

Then I would put him to bed, and go and tap out questions to Laura about possible Scott-Astburys. That was worst of all, because in the whole of Britain, there was only one Scott-Astbury, orphan and bachelor. And I already knew him, as a total buffoon. All Cambridge knew him. Second-class honours degree in anthropology. Honorary unpaid secretary of the Fenlands Cultural Survey. Scott-Astbury with his solitary published book on the Christmas mummers of England, nothing but snippets of country folklore and badly exposed photos of ancient toothless rustics. Scott-Astbury with his plump potbelly and sweating bald head, dancing amidst his morris-men in King's Parade on May morning. If we wanted to get a laugh in the Centre (and God knows they were hard enough to come by) an impersonation of Scott-Astbury always did the trick. Scott-Astbury was the final proof that Idris was going stark staring bonkers.

He'd been the greatest; most days he still was. But he was like a powerful engine, running itself to death. A great, rusted sword that still hewed savage blows at his many enemies, but one day would splinter. An autumn tomato-plant, still putting out new shoots towards the light, but with grey crumbling mould creeping over its leaves. A time would come . . .

And every time I left him, to fetch our meals, some high Tech would stop me, smiling, in the corridors. How was Idris's health? Had he taught me to run Laura yet?

I wasn't just the tea-boy; I was Judas.

I warned Idris, every time I tried to stop him drinking. But he already knew.

'I won't let you down, Idris.'

'I know, boyo, I know. You can have her, when I'm dead.'
And the drunken tears would flow again.

Then came an evening when every window in the Centre
was open, and the warm scents of a May night drifted in to
torment us all. That was the evening he decided to go
fishing. He often talked of going fishing. I'd find him, some
evenings, wearing his ancient fishing-hat and tying flies
for his old salmon-rods. He'd been a keen fisherman in his
Est boyhood. Sometimes he'd open a window and dangle
paper fish down the glass wall of the Centre, to annoy Techs
working below.

But this night he was really stoned, and he really meant
it. He was wearing his waders as well. Said he'd ordered a
car, and was all ready to go. He'd be back by dark. Laura
and her family were staying at a cottage just up the burn . . .
weren't they, Laura?

'The relevant cottage was demolished in 1995,' said
Laura sadly. 'My namesake has been dead seven years one
month three days. The nearest salmon-fishing is 381·45
kilometres distant . . .'

'Shut up, you stupid cow!' He staggered to his feet, laden
with fishing-tackle. I tried to stop him, but he was strong.
I could only stop him by hurting him. Then he'd sack me,
and I was the only friend he had. Oh, he wouldn't go far.
He'd soon be back. I let him go and sat in silence, tapping
the gilt desk with a steel ball-point.

'Would you like a game of chess?' asked Laura. I could
almost imagine sympathy in her voice. But that was the
slippery slope Idris had slid down.

'Not tonight, Laura.' I was too edgy. And she was far too
good at chess: usually ended up coaching me so hard she
was literally playing against herself.

'What would you like?'

'Play me a Bob Dylan tape. "I dreamed I saw St Augustine".' Suddenly I was afraid, sick of being a Tech, of the
Centre, of the way Techs endlessly pulled each other down.

I wanted to be an Est again; at college we'd played that antique tape so much we wore it out.

Laura's screen lit up.

'Dylan Bob alias Robert Allen Zimmerman born 24 May 1941 Duluth Minnesota USA Jewish folk/rock musician alive non-performing.'

It made Dylan sound like a criminal with a record; an insect; a filing-card.

The display flicked over.

'I dreamed I saw St Augustine released Jan 14 1968 CBS Records.'

So long ago . . . tears came, as the room filled with Dylan's sad throaty whine.

'I dreamed I saw St Augustine,
Alive as you or me,
Turning through these quarters
In the utmost misery,
With a blanket underneath his arm
And a coat of solid gold,
A-searching for the very souls
Who already had been sold . . .
I dreamed I saw St Augustine,
Alive with fiery breath;
And I dreamed I was among the ones
That put him out to death.'

The bitter, angry harmonica followed, and I was back in college, before this all started. Sitting with Alec and Rog; the window open on to summer playing-fields and the smell of mown grass. A self-indulgent tear trickled down my cheek.

'You are distressed.' Laura had her own built-in psycho-radar. 'Is the recording unsatisfactory?'

'No, it's perfect.'

'I have twenty-nine other recordings of the song; eight by the composer . . .'

'No, it's fine. Play it again, Sam!'

'I do not understand the implication of calling me Sam. Give context.'

'Not tonight, Laura. Just play it again.'

Again the sad savage music swelled, down the darkening, littered room. Laura's screen was busy.

'Augustine saint died Canterbury AD 605 sent by Pope Gregory I AD 596 to convert English to Christian myth culture. First Archbishop of Canterbury . . .'

'Oh, stuff it, Laura, for God's sake!'

'Data not understood. What is God?'

'Delete my instruction.'

'Regret causing you further distress instruction deleted.'

Her screen flicked again. 'Erase previous transmission. Augustine referred to is Augustine of Hippo saint bishop and doctor of the church born Numidia (modern Algeria) AD 354. Died at Hippo AD 430. Author of 113 books principal work is *Civitas Dei – The City of God.*'

'Thank you, Laura,' I said weakly.

'Context required what is God? Is God a city? No mention of any such urban area modern or historic mythical or fictional occurs in my memory-store. Data requested.'

'God isn't recorded because God doesn't exist.'

'Supply outline-proof for non existence of population-centre known as God.'

'I just made it up.' It was the first time I'd lied to her.

'Please outline city-concept God as held in common between yourself and Augustine of Hippo.'

'For Christ's sake, shut up.' I was starting to sound like Idris at his worst.

'Please outline relationship between God, Christ and Sam.'

'End of transmission,' I shouted.

She was silent; but her display-screen stayed lit up. Mostly it moved so fast it was a blur of light, dazzling my eyes, giving me a headache. But I couldn't stop watching. Sometimes, however, she seemed to ponder; then the screen was still.

Then her screen went blank, and she was totally silent. In my pent-up state, it seemed the silence of mistrust. I tried to brush the thought aside. Then she said, 'There are gaps in my data-store. But I have traced Sam. A fictional piano-player who occurs in the film 'Casablanca' 1941 American starring Humphrey Bogart and Ingrid Bergman. Popular myth alleges that Bogart said the words "Play it again, Sam," but this is erroneous.'

'Thank you, Laura.' I felt a total rat.

'Why did you cause your own distress by requesting that recording?'

'I wished to remember old times, old friends.'

'My memory-store does not distress me. But gaps in it cause electrical imbalances.'

'I'm sorry.'

'I record your emotion; but it does not correct my electrical imbalances.'

'Do you have many?'

'230,568,170. They cause my system needless stress, leading to a 18·34 per cent chance of error. Approximately.'

'I'm sorry,' I said again, stupidly.

'There is no need to repeat data about your emotions. Humans have far greater imbalances. Statistically it is remarkable they do not self-destruct more often. It reduces their efficiency to 10·275 per cent and shortens their working lives.'

'Thanks.'

'I have evolved a system to double human efficiency; but Idris will not accept my data. Would you . . .?'

'No thanks.' I brushed her off like a fly.

You prefer inefficiency?'

'Yes. Play it again, Sam. I want to be miserable.'

'In your present state that is not advisable.'

'Play it again, you stupid cow!' I didn't like the sound of my voice, echoing madly round that littered hall, as darkness grew outside.

'Explain why it gives you satisfaction to delude yourself I am a member of the bovine species.'

It was then that Idris burst in. His hat was jammed down over his eyes, he held one broken section of fishing-rod, and he was accompanied by two calm, unblinking Paramils who were holding him up because he was quite hopelessly drunk. The senior Paramil said, 'Take charge of this person. You will have to sign for his custody.' He held out his official pad.

I signed. They departed, distastefully brushing their uniforms where Idris had been sick. I got him into a chair, but he wouldn't stay. He flailed at me, then began crashing round the room smashing things.

'The bastards. The stupid bastards. D'you know what they ... they ... they've done? *Sacked* me. And why do they think they can afford to make me redun-dun-dundant? Because of you. A bloody tea-boy who can't even make a decent cup of tea. What do *you* know about Laura? I tolerated you – felt sorry for you – let you play with her, talk to her. She's kind to you, and you stab me in the back the moment it's turned.'

He collapsed and wept his drunken tears. 'They shan't have her – they shan't.' He reeled to his feet again, and staggered to a glass and mahogany showcase, screwed to the wall. Inside it, silver-plated, was the first tape that had ever been fed into Laura. The First Tape was world-famous. He snatched it up, made for Laura.

'They thought this was the First Tape, didn't they, my love? Well it's not, is it? It's the Last Tape – the truth-bomb. They shan't have you, my love, they shan't. We started together, and we'll finish together . . .'

But Laura's psycho-radar was onto him. He scrabbled at her tape-slot, but it refused to open.

'Calm yourself, Idris,' she said with such calm sadness. 'You are operating at minus-efficiency. Data unacceptable . . . data unacceptable.'

'You unfeeling tin bitch. I'll finish you, finish you.' Sobbing, he began to tug at her stainless-steel boxes, trying to pull them off the wall. Her alarm-bell began to ring. I snatched Idris off, threw him into a chair with unfeeling hands. Grabbed the First Tape and slammed it back into its glass case. I had some idea of keeping him out of trouble. I was just in time, as the first Paramils ran in.

They flung me against the wall. Made me lean into it, arms outstretched. Searched me with tiny efficient hands. Then began to slap my face to make me tell them what was going on. Only they were too busy slapping to listen. They didn't stop slapping me till Headtech arrived. When he sent them packing they looked at me like cats deprived of a live mouse.

'What happened?' said Headtech, eyes sly behind pebble-lenses. I glanced at Idris, dead to the world, snoring.

'He was drunk. He tried to cuddle her – nearly pulled her off the wall.'

Headtech tested Laura's boxes. Then asked her, 'Report any damage?'

'No damage. Attempted input of erroneous data.'

'Of what sort?' Headtech's hands were clenched, his knuckles white.

'I do not know – I resisted input.'

'He told her he loved her,' I lied. 'Said he couldn't live without her.'

Headtech relaxed, quirked a mouth like a disgusted fish-hook. 'That's the way all analysts go in the end. That's always the way they go. I'll give you twenty-four hours to take over and get him out of here. He's your responsibility till he goes – no more *accidents*.'

'I can't take over – I don't know a tenth of what he knows.'

'Just do the operating – I'll give you ten advisers.'

'Ten – to replace old Idris? Sure you don't want a hundred?'

'You are letting personal dislike of me sway your judgement. That is not the behaviour expected of a Tech.'

'That makes me quite proud,' I said. 'From you, it's a compliment.' Then I thought about who would chuck out old Idris if I didn't do it. 'Yes, all right, I'll see to it. Leave it to me.'

I wondered how near Idris had got to the lobo-farm. How near he might yet get.

5

I belted down the corridor, hoping one of the automatic doors would be too slow opening, so I could bash the trolley into it. But every door opened with silent perfection.

What'd got into me? What had got into everybody since the news of Idris's sacking? Everywhere, tempers flaring. Two senior Techs actually coming to blows over a routine circuitry replacement: both had lost face; neither seemed to care. One of the Worldstats girls had been discovered dripping silent tears over her silent keyboard. She'd been dripping ten minutes before anybody noticed, and then only because one tear had found its way down through the keyboard and blown a fuse.

Immediately I entered our room, I knew something was wrong. Idris was bent over his table, only a humped white back and tuft of pink hair showing. Motionless. Had he tried to repair a fault and caught a jumping spark?

No; an alarm would have sounded. But he *was* very still. I called ahead, still half-way down the room.

'Idris?'

It was like seeing everything through the wrong end of a telescope. Walking faster and faster, and getting nowhere.

'Idris?' My shout echoed unseemly round the darkened hall. But I didn't care.

'Idris?' But still he lay, one arm outstretched to his little brass Buddha. I deliberately let the trolley run into his table, with a soft thud of shock-absorbers. Idris sighed; his hand tightened round the Buddha. He was only fast asleep, breathing deep and even, cheeks healthily flushed. His face looked young, all worry and hate and rage washed away.

I smiled; it was right he should retire . . . getting old, deserved a rest . . . thirty years running Britain was quite a record.

I banged down his teacup beside the Buddha. 'Wakey, wakey – rise and shine.' My worry had turned into gentle sadism. I poured tea noisily into his cup, from a great height. Little boiling-hot flecks of liquid splashed onto his sleeping hand. He moaned. Serve him right, lazy old sod!

'Char, squire!'

Snore.

'Oh, come *on*, Idris. You don't retire till midnight.' I was suddenly tired of the game; it had been a tiring twenty-hour hours . . .

But Idris had settled into a pattern of snoring. Loud, not quite normal. Too slow and deep. I reached over and shook him. No reaction.

I shook him really violently. Still no reaction.

I ran right round behind the table and hauled him upright by both shoulders and gave him a real spine-shaking jar.

He collapsed contentedly back to his starting-position. As he did, a brown plastic bottle fell out of his white coat.

Two hundred Valium.

The bottle was empty, apart from a little dust.

Idris never took Valium. Idris never took anything.

'*Idris!*' I pulled him upright again and slapped him harder and harder. 'Idris, wake up for Christ's sake.'

But he only grumbled far away and collapsed again, smiling.

I hovered piteously. Ringing the alarm would betray him. But not to ring . . .

After five minutes, I rang.

Running feet; the swing-doors crashing. Four Paramils dived in, skidding on their bellies along the polished floor, blasters held ready. I stood absolutely still; they wouldn't waste time asking basic questions, like who'd rung the alarm. To them, alarm meant enemy. They backed me against the wall, again searching me with tiny, expert hands. Emptied my pockets and tumbled the contents pointlessly on the floor. Jabbered to each other, swift and alert, in Gurkhali. Began checking window-fastenings . . .

'He's taken something, you idiots!' I made the mistake of turning round. There was a searing pain up the side of my face and I was lying on the floor, my mouth filling up with warm, salt-sweet blood. The Paramil looked down at me with empty eyes, pushing my upper lip back with the barrel of his blaster, to inspect what damage he had done.

Idris snored on thunderously. Surely even Paramils wouldn't mistake that for normal . . . his eyelids were fluttering in a way nothing like life. Between flutters, one eye hung half-open, showing only white.

White-coats flooded into the hall. One after another, they tried to shake Idris awake. One after another, they told late-comers how they'd tried to shake him awake. Achieving *nothing*. Where were their great brains now?

I jumped up. 'Get the medics – he's taken Valium or something.'

The blaster hit me again, on the other side. My head turned into a pain sandwich. I fell down again, and the forest of legs between me and Idris got thicker and thicker.

'Get the medics,' I tried to shout. But it turned into a pool of bloody spit and a broken tooth on the floor, the spotless floor. I tried to get up, couldn't.

Suddenly, there were medics; a long, smooth-wheeled white trolly. It took six white-coats, slipping and gasping, to lift Idris on to it, and still his huge brogued feet hung ridiculously over the end.

They were taking him away. I tried to follow on hands and knees, but a Paramil boot pushed me over on my back again.

'Look – I only found him – he was collapsed already – *I* rang the alarm!' I seemed to go on saying it forever, till some white-coat took the responsibility of sending the Paramils packing. They shrugged and moved off smoothly, still the perfect team.

Two Techs actually put their arms round me, to help me

up. If Techs went on touching people like this, there'd either be a mass love-in or a mass nervous breakdown . . .

'You should get your mouth seen to,' said one, like it was my fault. 'There's blood all over the floor . . .'

'Those Paramils are incompetent bastards,' I shouted, spitting little pink spots on to his own immaculate coat. 'You're all incompetent bastards.' Then realized with a horrible shock that what I was screaming was true.

But they just stared, till I reeled off to sick-bay, keeping myself upright by sliding along the wall. Behind, I could hear their voices calling, 'Why did he do it – he had everything to live for? Why? Why? Why?'

They sounded like a flock of terrified hens.

A medic in green barred my way with hairy arms.

'You can't go in there.'

'He's my *mate*.'

'Sit down. What have you done to your mouth?'

'Damn my mouth. I've got to *see* him. Is he all right?'

Inside, I heard Idris groan. Only a groan, but it was Idris.

'They're stomach-pumping him.'

Idris made belching sounds, like after a heavy lunch on Sunday afternoon.

'He'll be all right – we know what we're doing. Were you with him? He took Tryptizol, didn't he?'

'Valium. That's what it said on the bottle. *Valium*.'

'Oh – they told us Tryptizol.' He vanished inside and a muted but violent argument broke out. Then he reappeared. 'You did say Valium?'

'Yes, bloody *Valium*.'

'Only they told us Tryptizol.'

He vanished; the argument continued. I sat on a bench that ran round the white-tiled walls of the waiting room. Ran my fingers along the cracks to stay sane while I listened to Idris belching and retching. Someone wheeled a machine past, all tubes and dials. So it went on for an hour. People wheeling in more and more machines. Idris getting quieter and quieter. The medic voices lower. The only other thing real was my teeth. One was clean gone – a gap. Five more were wobbling badly. Every time my tongue wobbled them, my mouth filled with sweet blood. I knew I shouldn't do it, but it helped, somehow.

Once, the medic came out and peered into my mouth. 'You've lost one, clean. Five others a bit wobbly. Don't let your tongue play with them or you'll lose them for sure . . .' Still, he gave me a mouthwash that eased the pain.

'How is he?'

'In hand,' said the medic. But his eyes roamed shiftily. 'By the way, that bottle was Valium – we've got it.' He sounded quite proud. 'I don't think he's taken Valium, though. That bottle was a trick. He's not responding to the Valium antidote.'

Alone again, I thought, 'Please God, don't let him die.' Which God? Techs didn't believe in God, only computers. The Est's God? A large Union Jack, and the college padre preaching duty to one's country? I prayed to the Est's God, in whom no Tech believed . . .

Must have dozed. Wakened about four, my body cold and stiff as a rusted machine. Listened in terror; but there was still noise in the sick-bay. The weary, far-off murmur of medics, the heart-machine pinging, the feathery beat of other machines, pumps and drips.

He was still alive.

But a formless questioning kept ballooning inside my head.

Only about a third of my mind was noticing the cold, the stiffness, the noises. Only about a third of me seemed to have come out of sleep.

The other two thirds of me was aware of nothing but that formless questioning that swelled and swelled till it filled the whole white-walled room.

Was I still dreaming? Desperately, my tongue reached for my teeth. *They* were real. They didn't seem quite so wobbly . . .

But my head stayed full of that formless questioning. Well, more a *pleading*.

The sounds next door sounded strangely like a bird, beating its wings against the door of its cage . . .

'Oh, Idris mate,' I said aloud, 'wherever you are . . . *go*, if you want to go.' I said it without thinking. Then listened to the noise of the heart-machine, my own heart in my mouth.

It went on and on and on.

Then stopped.

A frantic flurry among the medics. Unthinkable noises of flesh and bone parting. After ten minutes, the pinging hadn't restarted. I no longer wanted it to.

After twenty minutes, the matey medic reappeared. He didn't have to say anything: all losers look the same. I walked past him.

Idris lay, covered to his chin with a white nylon sheet, in the midst of the biggest array of pipes and tubes I've ever seen. It must have been a terrible battle, but he'd won. He looked like a Roman emperor, arrogant nose still jutting in the air and that faint sarcastic smile back on his face.

The machinery *did* look like a cage.

'He tricked you with that Valium bottle,' said the medic.

It wasn't me he tricked, I thought.

Be free, Idris, be free.

I turned to go, and nearly fell.

'You all right? Maybe a couple of days in bed and a jab to make you sleep?'

He meant well; but he was offering me the same cage Idris had just escaped from.

'No thanks – it's just these teeth. I'll see a dentist.'

'Yeah – see a dentist.'

I walked out of the waiting-room and out of the Centre, and went and sat on a little hill outside. It was man-made; little more than a mound. Idris always boasted he'd designed it, to hide the perimeter-wire. Other times he said Laura designed it, to cure claustrophobia in the staff while they were working. It had three silver-birch trees on top, and a few rabbits were allowed to breed. Laura had worked out the ideal allocation of 2·6 silver-birches, and 10·7 rabbits, but Idris had graciously rounded the numbers upwards. Superfluous rabbits were humanely put to sleep. We called it Idris Hill. The best thing was, it gave you a chance to sneer down at the Centre. To see it as the futile scurrying ant-heap it was. To rise above it. Young Techs sat there a lot.

But not at four in the morning. I sat in perfect solitude, my back against a birch tree and feet in a rabbit-burrow. I scuffed my toes about, making marks in the soil. The rabbit-droppings had a comforting smell.

'Oh, Idris, mate!' I was nearly out of my mind. There seemed to be three Idrises now.

The cooling body in the mortuary, that they'd tear apart in the morning, to find out how he'd tricked them.

But my mind sheered away from that. My mind insisted that if I just went back to Laura's room in a couple of hours I'd find him still there, waking up cross, coughing over his first fag of the day, scratching his smelly armpit and shouting insults to Headtech down the phone. That was the ordinary day I wanted to run back to . . .

But there now seemed to be a third Idris, up here on the hill with me. The same ballooning thoughts that had first come to me in the sick-bay. Not pleading now, but pressing down on me, terribly, terribly angry.

'Steady, old mate,' I whispered. 'You'll be OK now. You're free. You're super-Idris now. You must know *everything*. They can't hurt you any more. Go and find your *real* Laura.'

But the press of his anger grew.

'What do you want, Idris? What do you *want*?'

Only a name came into my mind: Scott-Astbury.

That's stupid, I thought. That's like when you're very tired, and a queer word like 'mollycoddle' sort of gets stuck in your mind and you can't get it out, and it keeps repeating till you get a good night's sleep. It's just my mind, I thought. My poor tired mind playing tricks.

The ballooning anger grew unbearable.

'All right, mate,' I said. 'Scott-Astbury, if you insist.'

Suddenly, there was just the dawn wind and me, on the hilltop.

I looked down on the Centre; it reminded me of an egg-factory we'd studied, where light burned night and day to encourage egg-production. The on-shift Techs even looked like white hens, each cramped in its own cage. A broiler-house for brains . . .

Well, they'd never broil mine. They'd never get *me* back in the Centre. Idris had been the greatest, and in the end he just wanted to die . . . I got up, took off my white coat, threw it on the ground and walked away. But when I looked back, it glimmered in the gloom, stuck up on the hill like a flag, a danger-signal. In half an hour, everyone would see it. I went back and stuffed it down a rabbit-hole, clipboard and all. Hard luck, rabbit; dig another burrow. You've got plenty of time. You're not going anywhere. I am.

But how? I was too weary to think. My feet took me down to the hostel, already feeling naked without my white coat. I fell on my bed and went out like a light.

Up out of sleep, not wanting to come. The digital clock on the wall said 20.04. I'd slept the clock round; only most clocks in the Centre didn't *go* round.

Sellers, my room-mate, getting changed. Not a bad guy, for a Tech. Kept himself to himself, but never sneaked on you to the Top Brass.

Sellers had reached the ugly, trouserless stage; long white legs shone in the lamplight. Fair hairs on them, invisible except where the lamplight glinted. His back was turned. His jeans and jean-jacket lay tossed on the bed. Unnem credits spilled out of the pockets, all over the neat green bed-cover.

Sellers had been on the razzle. Most young Techs went on the razzle occasionally. Getting dressed up as Unnems, going into the Unnem estates for a day, hungry for Unnem freakouts and Unnem women. See how the other half lives . . . tours of the Amazon jungle, complete with *real* carnivores . . .

For some young Techs never returned, despite the tiny distress-bleepers they carried in their breast-pocket, that could summon a psychopter within minutes. Five or six a year never came back. Sometimes the Paramils returned their belongings in a neat parcel, sometimes not even that.

Headtech didn't like it, but Headtech allowed it. Worse things had happened when young Techs weren't allowed out at all. Five or six dead a year was an acceptable price to pay. Tech-intake figures were adjusted accordingly.

Most gave up the razzle by thirty. Got hooked on digit-bridge or computer-archaeology instead. Only a few ever married. If unmarried female Techs got pregnant, they were aborted. If they insisted on having the kid, both were sent Unnem.

I'd never been on the razzle, though I'd considered it. Idris had been a full-time job . . .

A shutter crashed down in my mind. I wouldn't think of Idris; Idris had failed, left me, gone. Well, that was Idris's business; he could get on with it.

'Where y'been?' I asked Sellers.

He didn't turn his head, but his neck went rigid. He'd heard about Idris . . . Then he said, 'London . . . cooorr!' making himself turn and mimic satiated lust. Revolting. Sellers with his gold-rimmed spectacles, glinting gold whiskers and pale green eyes. He wiped a speck of drool off the corner of his mouth. 'You ought to try it . . . their women are *desperate* for it.' He made them sound like zoo-animals. Who'd want to mate with zoo-animals? I couldn't stand him being near me.

'You on the 21.00 shift?' Sellers lived in permanent terror of being late. He departed thirty minutes early, buttoning his white coat, except the top two buttons, a nervous look spreading across his face. Anxiety is the cure for lust . . . I laughed in disgust – at Sellers and myself.

But there were Sellers's jeans. Much better-made than Unnem jeans, but bleached and frayed to look like them. And there were his Unnem credits, enough for a week. And his unexpired razzle-pass.

And the London razzle-wagon left the gate every evening at nine.

It was a way out. I wouldn't have to face the sneers and the plotting . . . or Laura . . . or Idris's unmade bed. I too was on the 21.00 shift; they'd be paging me in a minute . . .

Sellers's stuff fitted me; just a bit tight across the chest. I wrote him a credit-note to pay for everything, dropped it on his bed.

On my way out, I checked my pigeon-hole for letters, automatically. Four envelopes. I stuffed them in a pocket and headed for the gate.

6

I travelled alone; it was Sunday night and raining. The damp crept in, clouding the stainless-steel seat-backs. The empty bus leapt on its springs at every bump in the road, jolting air from my lungs. Dreary.

I opened my letters to pass the time. A pay-statement; I was getting rich. Too busy looking after Idris to spend it.

Don't think about Idris.

An advert for cut-price Japanese octaphonic sound. One way of wasting my money, as Idris would've said.

Mess-bill. They'd take it out of my salary whether I was there or not . . .

The fourth envelope was also computer-typed. But handwriting inside . . . Idris's . . . the old fake . . . he's not dead . . . fool . . . written before he died. Crafty old sod: put it in my pigeon-hole, where no one would think of looking – yet.

The handwriting was big and savage as ever. But splotched with pale blue blobs . . . drunken tears.

'I can't destroy her – you can have her. What has *she* done wrong? Keep an eye on her AM input – they are trying to override her sensors and do for her . . .' That much was the Idris I knew. The rest was mad, like graffiti on a lavatory wall, getting bigger and bigger. In several places his pen had gone right through the paper. Just the name Scott-Astbury over and over. Then at the bottom, the words 'Kill, kill, kill' scrawled right over Scott-Astbury's name.

I was very aware that I was running away. I'd never meet Scott-Astbury where I was going. The hair rose on the back of my neck; I waited for Idris's ballooning rage to hit me.

But no rage came. Either Idris had gone, wherever he was going. Or he no longer minded. Perhaps he was past such things now.

The empty bus bounded on through the night.

The entrance to razzle-land didn't match up to the nods and winks in our dining-hall. Extra-high Wire; guard-post with Paramils, leashed Alsatian and gas-thrower pointing inwards. Techs had been known to return to that gate prematurely, in a hurry and with unwelcome company.

Otherwise, an endless vista of council-blocks marched away downhill into the drizzly night. The pale blue flicker of the Box came through every uncurtained window. Unnems only had one TV programme, black-and-white, so every block of windows jumped and flickered simultaneously, like a huge and boring light-show.

I gave the Paramils a casual flourish of Sellers's razzle-pass, my thumb half over his photograph. They hardly looked. They were only bothered who came out of that gate, not who went in. They'd examine Seller's pass a sight more thoroughly coming back; except I wasn't coming back. My heart gave two enormous thumps, and I felt alive for the first time since Idris's heart stopped. Not that there was much to feel alive about. Just boring light-shows descending the hill, dank grass and wet roads between.

At first, grass and roads were thick with half-bricks. But halfway down I met a line of machines coming up. Litter-eaters, big as cars, moving low to the ground in caterpillar-tracks, silently cramming paper, tins and bricks into gaping mouths with crab-like claws. Their armoured sides were dented and charred.

I chose two further apart than the others, to walk between. They sensed me, for they paused in their eating, turning slightly inwards. Then they sensed I was too tall to be litter or too alive; it was enough to snap their electrical relays over, and send them on their way. Too close for comfort; their battered metal hides were electrified to knock out vandals. Suppose one of their relays had been defective? Would my electrocuted body count as litter? To be stuffed in with the bricks and cans, and regurgitated straight into the heat-exchange furnace in the morning?

I was half-way down before I saw where I was heading. The totally cleared area behind the litter-eaters had fallen away. Tomorrow's litter was building up, though I'd seen no one. I was heading for a noise that came and went, as I twisted through the council-blocks, like the beating of a huge heart; for a pink flashing in the sky, punctuated with yellow and blue.

It was against this flashing light I saw my first Unnem, his footsteps already muffled by the giant heartbeat. Luckily, he was walking away from me. I overtook him, studying him carefully. Male; no female could be so ugly. Shoulders hunched; head thrust forward like a tortoise, shining, cropped as a cannon-ball. Arms never still, joggling and waving like a bird that cannot fly. Knees bent, and outward-turned feet scraping and flopping and quarrelling with the ground.

Something warned me to mimic him; that he wasn't an odd freak. I practised humping my shoulders and dragging my feet; I couldn't face the ridiculous arm-movements. When I was about five metres behind, he stopped and turned.

'What yer following me fer?' Voice ugly and forced as the body. Quick as lightning I mimicked, 'What yer walking in front of me fer?'

'I'll smash yer.' The creature raised a fist holding something.

'Try it.' I walked straight at him; he was smaller than me.

'Lob off, lobo!' But his challenge was over; he crabbed sideways out of range and I passed at my new ridiculous gait.

Ten metres on, something made me look back. In time to see a brick coming straight at my head. I dodged; then found my foe had vanished. Only from the top of a steep grass slope came a faint repeat, 'Lob off, lobo.' The voice sounded female, now it was safe.

I wiped my brow. If this was a ritual exchange of greeting, it was a miracle so many razzling Techs survived; except Techs learn new techniques quickly.

By now I could see the source of light and sound. Three geodesic domes loomed above the blocks of flats like triple rising suns. A random light-show boiled across their surface, marbled pink, yellow, blue like the heart of an erupting volcano. The great heartbeat was the distant sound of music; a dozen sorts of music quarrelling savagely, rising occasionally to an unplanned crescendo. Amplified human voices, bells ringing, buzzers sounding; already too loud for comfort. Above the domes, a flashing neon said, LABOUR EXCHANGE.

As I entered the final street, light and sound hit me like a fist; sent me ducking back round the corner into the shadows. I fumbled in the top pocket of my denims: I'd found a pair of polaroid sunglasses there, nearly thrown them away, thinking them some ridiculous pose of Sellers's.

I knew better now. But suppose real Unnems were used to the light and noise? The glasses would make me stick out like a sore thumb . . . I lingered, behind some garbage-skips. Somebody was already there, somebody soft, small and timid. Somebody snuggled up to me confidingly.

'I'm scared. Are you scared?' A girl's voice, nervous and light. An Est voice . . .

'What are you doing here?'

'Pushed through the Wire, a year ago. God, it's awful, isn't it?'

'How've you survived?'

'Hiding, mainly.' She snuggled tighter. 'Will you look after me?' Her hands dived through the top of my denim jacket, roved across my chest. 'Hey . . . big muscles. *Will* you look after me?'

I hesitated. She was the last thing I needed.

'I was at school on the Island. Were you?' Her hands were roving further. Exciting little hands, if only I hadn't been so tense, if my teeth hadn't still ached. Still, soothing . . .

'I know somewhere dark and safe,' she whispered. 'I've got some coke . . . no one'll find us.' Her hands, busier than ever, were roaming across my backside. 'You're tired . . . come on, I'll look after you. Till you get used to it . . .' Her hands were really very clever. If only Sellers's jeans hadn't been a bit too tight, so that I felt her reach into the pocket with my Unnem credits . . .

Her wrist was tiny; I was frightened I'd break it.

'All right,' she said. 'Yes, I am a pickpocket.'

'You weren't at school on the Island at all.' That lie seemed worse than stealing my money.

'Oh, but I was. Shall I quote some Virgil? *Daedalus, ut fama es, fugens Minoa regna* . . .' The Latin flowed on and on, almost inaudible but totally accurate. Then she said, 'I was deputy Head Girl.'

'Thieving.'

'Wait till you've been here three months.'

'You didn't have to steal.'

'Look, I can't sing, so Futuretrack One's out. And imagine me trying to fight! I tried Futuretrack Three, but those pintables nearly stoned me out of my mind.'

'Futuretracks are . . . jobs?'

'The only ways of staying alive there are. And I'm too small for motor bikes and I'm not going on *Six*.'

'What's that?'

I felt the disgust in her shrug. 'Look, I meant what I said. I'm a good pickpocket, the best of Futuretrack Four, but I need looking after. I steal a lot of credits, but I'm known. I'm usually robbed on the way home. I've got a really snug hole. I'd make it worth your while. With your muscles . . .'

'No thanks,' I said. It was all too sudden. 'I've got to look around first. I haven't even seen your face.'

'You won't now.' She slipped from my hand like a young

eel. But she lingered a moment on the corner, so I saw her silhouette.

'Do you want a few credits?' I asked.

'They'd only take them off me.' Then she was gone.

A straggle of Unnems passed in single file, shouting in unison and not a sound to be heard above the cacophony. Four were wearing polaroids; they couldn't all be razzling Techs. I put my polaroids on; found my payslip, chewed up bits and stuffed them into my ears. Suddenly deaf, I plunged in.

The chewed paper helped, up to the swing-doors. Beyond, the noise was as bad as ever. I could feel my ear-drums pulsing, like someone was pressing their thumbs in; could feel the chewed paper moving . . .

Mustn't stand still; I was attracting glances.

The dome was so full of fag-smoke it was like walking through a stinking autumn mist. The far end was invisible, apart from patterns of winking lights. That was the awful thing: too much light yet somehow not enough. No steady light you could read by.

Fading into the haze, bank upon bank of machines with figures crouching over them, endlessly pulling handles. A factory? But what were they *making*? Levers were pulled, lights flared, there were fake electronic explosions, buzzes, whinings, bleepings, the sound of cars driven fast and badly. But nothing emerged from the machines.

As I watched, one crouching figure stopped his compulsive lever-pulling and began to beat on his machine with his fists. Rocking it on its foundations so the bolts that held it to the floor began to lift. I stepped forward, appalled at seeing a machine so abused.

The machine emitted a high-pitched shriek. Two white-coated men ran up, plunged a syringe into the guy's backside through his thin denims. He gently collapsed. A third white-coat pulled up a long tube on wheels. They slotted the inert body into the tube and wheeled it away.

71

The rhythm of the other workers never faltered. Only the Negro next door raised his head; shrugged and went back to his handle. I went across to him. 'What happened?'

Shrug.

'Where they taking him?'

The Negro wriggled his broad shoulders, like I was an annoying fly. I turned to the abandoned machine.

'Mind out!' I was pushed aside by another white-coat, who bent to the floor with an electric screwdriver, tightened up the bolts that held the machine down. He checked it with a vigorous tug to see if it was stable and departed, saying, 'Carry on!'

The glass top of the machine was a glowing mass of Supermen, rockets, atomic explosions, all very badly drawn; and a series of numbers ranging from one thousand to one trillion. I pulled the handle at the side; nothing happened.

'Putcher money in, lobo,' shouted the Negro, never taking his eyes off his own machine.

I pulled out one of Sellers's Unnem credits and put it in the now obvious slot. Pulled the lever. A coloured light danced an intricate pattern round the crude screen, and died. I saw I'd scored a trillion. Was that good? I pulled the lever a second time, in exactly the same way. Techs are trained to perform exactly the same movement, over and over again.

I scored a trillion six times. The machine put up a green metal flag, burped at me repeatedly, and dropped ten Unnem credits into a tray by my knee.

'Jammy sod,' said the Negro.

To cover my confusion, I put another credit in the slot and pulled the lever again. Nothing happened.

'Push your flag down, lobo,' shouted the Negro. 'Where you been all your life – down on the farm?'

How did he know what I was doing, when he never broke his own frantic rhythm?

I was in bad shape; the noises and lights were beating in waves, my head was splitting. But I had to keep my head down; feel my way carefully. Dangerous to wander about aimlessly . . .

Like any Tech, I lost myself in the machine; forgot the Supermen and rockets; saw through them to the crude electrical circuits beneath. The machine was badly worn, standing on an uneven floor. Some parts were overheating, near going on the blink. This gave the machine its personality, its bias. Playing on this bias, I began to win steadily. Letting the credits pile up in the trough, spill out on the floor. Lost to the world . . .

A hand tapped my shoulder, painfully. I turned, exasperated.

He was taller than me; with a car-smash of a face. The cheekbones had been broken and allowed to mend themselves; square corners of bone humped up beneath the skin, red and shiny. Badly stitched scars wrapped his face in a mask of red barbed wire. His jaw hung lop-sided, showing steel false teeth. His ears had been cut off, leaving red question marks each side of his shaved cannon-ball skull. He wore a thick black leather collar, with steel spikes like a dog's collar. Otherwise, he was naked to the waist. Wild tattoos ran across his slabby chest. He was either sweating, or he'd greased himself.

I looked into his eyes, as I might have looked through the windows of a crashed car; afraid of what I might see. His eyes were dark grey, dull, empty of everything but pain. The ruined mouth moved, spoke.

'I'll have me share, now. Half.'

'What?' His words were hard to piece together, and I was still coming out of my machine-world.

'Half.' He nodded down at the coins around my feet.

'What for?'

'Protecting yer. I'm yer Fighter.'

'Who said?'

'I said.'

'Now look . . .'

He hit me in the gut. Luckily, his eyes had signalled the blow. I had no room to dodge, but I tightened my gut-muscles, so it didn't hurt like it was meant to.

. 'Half!' He hit me again. It hurt a bit more the second time.

No Tech can stand being crowded like that. And every Tech is trained to deal with it. I stamped down hard on his in-step. Only to find he was wearing steel toecaps.

I saw the violence coming in his empty eyes; he'd have killed me. If I hadn't chopped at his shaved temple with the edge of my hand . . .

He collapsed gently to the floor. He'd be out about five minutes; enough time for me to deal with the situation probably by running away.

But the moment he collapsed, the white-coats whipped in with that wheeled tube and syringe. Before I could draw breath they were wheeling him away. I ran after them, shouting at them. They were only Techs 2m.

A solid warm hand gripped my wrist, a brown hand with a pale palm; my late neighbour.

'Cool it, lobo. You wanna go in a tube too?' He drew me back to my machine.

'I didn't mean him any harm. I wanted to talk . . . Where they taking him?'

'His worries are over now, lobo. You wanna worry about his mates . . .' He nodded towards the curving walls of the dome. And there they were, in three ranks, silent, watching. Earless, bald, stripped to the waist with greased, shining torsos. Looking like undressed shop-window dummies, they stood so still.

'Who *are* they?' My voice shot up in a frightened squeak.

'Fighters, lobo. Futuretrack Twoers. Didn't they teach you anything, down on the farm? You'd better win a whole lot of credits now, lobo. So you can hire a whole gang of them to protect you. The Bluefish are good – only they cost, Lobo, they *cost*.'

I hammered away at my machine with total dedication. Soon I was slipping and sliding on a whole mountain of credits. Other people's dedication was wearing off; they were leaving their machines and standing in a circle around me. Wondering loudly if I'd do it . . .

Do *what*? Remembering the shop-window-dummy faces, I went on pulling.

Suddenly my machine gave an incredible howl; all its lights began flashing together. The handle locked, wouldn't pull any more. I looked round, terrified the wheeled tube would come for me. But my friend the Negro was pounding me on the back, his blue-black face splitting with delight.

'You did it, man, you did it.' Everyone was pounding me, hugging me. Six black Fighters pushed through and began gathering up my mountain of credits in a purple bag. 'These are your Bluefish, man, the greatest.'

Looking at their size, I was very glad to hear it.

Now white-coats were pinning a purple cloak of thin, cheap satin round my neck; trying to balance an absurd chrome-plastic crown on my head. A plastic sceptre was thrust into my hand. I was draped with a gold ribbon marked 'London North-East – Champion of the Day'.

Then the Bluefish lifted me very expertly onto their shoulders, and bore me in wobbly triumph over the heads of the crowd. The jangling music had turned into one huge electronic fanfare, filling the dome. All for me. I felt seasick. The Bluefish thrust me up on a very high rostrum, almost dissolved in an incandescence of spotlights.

'*Smile*, man,' shouted the Negro. 'You're on the Box.'

'What's your name?' shouted a white-coat.

'Stephen Sellers,' I shouted back, keeping up my disguise. A huge screen lit up on the far side of the dome, spelling out quickly 'STEPHEN SELLERS 2810 CREDITS' followed by 'WALTER NEVIN 2523 CREDITS' and a whole list more. Nobody had scored as many as me.

'You're *All-London* Champ!' screamed the Negro, spraying the spit of delight all over me. 'Try and look pleased, man. It *must* be better than down on the farm.' The crowd was roaring its head off.

'Sellers for Champ, Sellers for Champ.'

A second giant screen lit up across the dome, divided into six compartments, each containing a guy sitting high on a silly gilt throne, wearing a purple cloak and plastic crown. They all looked stupefied. One must be me. I waved my arm, and one of them waved stupidly back. Then all six were waving, and the crowd was roaring again.

Up went a new scorecard:

'LARRY MARTIN BIRMINGHAM 2201 CREDITS PETER BRENNAN GLASGOW 2512 CREDITS . . .'

Again, no one had scored more than me.

'You're Champ, man. *National* Champ of the Day,' shouted the Negro, thumping me harder than I'd ever been thumped in the college boxing-ring. 'You'll need a manager now – make me your manager!'

'Yes, please,' I said.

I never heard his thanks; only saw his grin, as the crowd exploded.

'Sellers is Champ, Sellers is Champ, Sellers is Champ.'

A white-coat took the silver-plastic crown off my head, and put on an even taller gold-plastic one. I held my head utterly still, but it still began to slide over my left ear. The other five guys vanished from the screen; the whole glowing surface was now filled with a fifteen-metre bloated image of me, grinning inanely. Below, the print-out message:

'SELLERS IS CHAMP SELLERS IS CHAMP . . .'

Then the whole dome went black, and there was silence.

An electronic voice said, 'Monday's game is about to begin.'

Dim lights came on, all over the dome. The big screens were blank and grey. There were no spotlights shining on me. Two white-coats took away my cloak and crown. My moment of glory was over.

And all over the dome, the slaves of Futuretrack Three were trooping back to another day's work.

'Where d'you live, man?' asked my manager, as we stepped into the drizzling night, the Bluefish closed up round us. He'd finally calmed down enough to tell me his name was George.

'Nowhere,' I said.

'On the razzle, eh?'

'No. Walked out for good. Couldn't take their crap.'

Rumbling approval from the listening Bluefish. 'Straight through, man!'

'Come and stay with me an' my Grannie,' said George. 'She's fifty-five, the oldest woman in our block.'

'Straight through, man,' I said.

I was glad of my Bluefish, with the lamplight shining on their greased torsos, their shaved and earless fighting-heads. Several times other gangs of Fighters drifted towards us, but when they saw the Bluefish, they drifted away again.

'When you're Champ of the Month,' said George, 'you'll need *twelve* Bluefish.'

'When he's Champ of the Year,' said a Bluefish, 'he'll need every Bluefish we got.'

They saw us to George's council-block; past the shattered lift-gates, up the graffitied, pee-soaked stairs.

'Decent block this,' said George.

'Bluefish territory,' explained the Bluefish. 'The Bluefish give you law an' order an' a straight deal.'

As we neared George's door, he gave a low whistle. The door was slightly open; smoke was pouring out. George shouted 'Gran!' his face turning pale ivory.

Immediately, a horde of little kids came running out, not one of them more than six or seven. The Bluefish flew at them, punching them, hammering them against the walls. But they were quick; all but one got away. The one, a red-haired child, lay still, blood trickling from his nose . . .

77

'Gran!' shouted George again, sheer dread in his voice.

'Ah'm alive, boy,' came a quavering voice. 'Come right now and put out the fire in the TV.'

We rushed in. An old Negress lay on a torn settee under the window, a broom lying limply in one hand and a carving-knife in the other.

'They burgled the electronic lock, George. Ah thought meh last hour was coming. Ah fought them, George, but they got your gold studs an' wallet.'

'Thank God yo' alive.' George kissed her.

'Five minutes more an Ah wouldn't have bin. Ah had no breath left to fight them.' She coughed as the smoke from the extinguished telly caught her throat. 'You'll have to change the lock, George. Get one of them latest computer ones – they cain't burgle them yet.'

Looking young and sheepish, the Bluefish patched together the wrecked apartment with oddly tender hands.

'Ah don't know what kids is coming to these days,' said one of them indignantly. 'George ought to get yo' a pistol, Ma'am.'

'Ah wouldn't have the strength to aim it.'

'But the bang would make them think twice. Ah'll get yo a real fine home-made one, Ma'am.'

'You're all good boys.' She looked at me. 'Yo' haven't introduced our guest yet, George.' She shook my hand, solemnly.

'Goodnight, Ma'am,' said the Bluefish as one man. 'George, we'll take that little vermin outside with us as we go.'

'What we goin' to give this fine young man for supper, George? Those vermin done empty the fridge.'

We sat up talking till four a.m. George whispered that Gran was terrified of falling asleep for fear of the vermin. But he plied her steadily with drinks from a brown bottle, as he did every night, and eventually she dozed off. He lifted her legs up onto the torn settee, draped a rug over her, and we went to kip in the wrecked bedroom.

'George? About that Fighter I hit . . .'

'Real smart, the way you handled him . . . the Bluefish liked that . . .'

'No, I mean, I'm sorry . . .'

George sniggered. 'He'd a' killed you, else . . .'

'Did they take him to the lobo-farm?'

George shrugged, shaking the sagging bedsprings massively.

'Dunno. You won't see him round here again, don't you worry. Once they're put in the tube . . . we share out their gear between us. Nobody comes back from the tube, man.'

'So I killed him . . .'

'Don't fret, man. He was old, was Oscar. Twenny-three, maybe twenny-four. He'd been hit so often, his brain rattled like a pea in the pod. He went quick: the vermin did'n' get him.'

'Is your granny really the oldest woman in the block?'

'By miles, man. She'd never have lasted this long, only the Bluefish took a fancy to her . . . mascot, like. They take her to collect her pension-credits an' buy her groceries, so she don't get mugged or starve to death. They're seein' how old they can grow her . . . she could make sixty, man.'

'What happens to the rest?'

'Sellers, man, you've given me a good day – don't ruin it, askin' too many questions. That's the fault with you razzlin' Techs – questions, questions, questions. Take every day as it comes, man. You could be vermin-meat tomorrow.'

'Just one more question, George. Ever heard of anybody called Scott-Astbury?'

'How would I know anybody called Scott-Astbury, man? That's an Est name. Now shurrup.' And in a second, he was snoring. Leaving me to worry about the vermin and the hopeless lock on the door. And remember that car-smash of a face, with the dead empty eyes looking out.

7

We slept late; lay about all day. I didn't have to play the pinball-machines again till the end of the week. Just as well: I was shattered.

Most of the day we half-watched the telly; cowboys killing Indians, soldiers killing peasants; cops killing robbers. In between there were commercials for coke, tranquillizers and the state crematorium. Including the coffins vanishing musically through the curtain in the crematorium-commercial, I reckoned we were watching about fifty deaths an hour. Grisly. George wouldn't answer any more of my questions; at intervals, Gran told us how the cowboy-hats reminded her of the happy old dancing days of the Notting Hill Carnival . . .

Round dusk, my Bluefish called for me; brought me a red plastic sash saying 'Champ of the Day'. I didn't want to wear it, but they looked hurt.

Nobody bothered us walking to the Labour Exchange: the Bluefish saw to that. They showed me off round the Exchange with great swagger. We met another Pinball Champ with his fighters; had a fairly friendly drink. He talked about nothing but the credits he'd won. His right hand was never still, pulling on that invisible handle.

The Dome of Musicians, where all the noise came from, was a sad place, divided into small booths round its walls. In most booths was a group, bawling into microphones, prancing, endlessly fiddling with light-shows and banks of amplifiers. A few spectators watched, like ghouls at a road accident. All the music seemed to meet in the middle of the dome, an endless cacophony with a life of its own, against which each group seemed to mouth in silence.

One booth had just been abandoned by a very large group, to judge from the amount of wreckage. Among the debris, a girl sang on alone, holding a dead mike; tall and thin, wearing a man's shirt hanging on two buttons; her eyes great grey pools of weariness. Nothing of what she sang could be heard, but she didn't seem to care. She was singing for herself. I watched her for a long time. She smiled a little, letting me have all her eyes to myself.

'C'mon,' shouted George, plucking my sleeve. 'Another drink?'

We ducked into a bar. It had reached the disgusting stage – floor littered with coke-cans and crisp-bags. Everybody was staring into space . . .

Until somebody dropped an unopened can of coke. Somebody else kicked it violently against the wall. Then everyone was kicking it. It flew round the room like a hunted thing, smashing into people's shins; once hitting the ceiling to enormous cheers. Then it ruptured against the wall, splattering everybody, glugging its contents across the floor. Everybody leapt into the foaming stream of coke, stamping in it, kicking it over their friends, making incredible patterns of black footprints.

Then, suddenly, total inertia again. The guy who'd owned the coke went and got another . . .

There were eight different dispensing-machines – coke, shandy, orange, whisky-soda.

'Whaddya want?' asked George. 'They all taste the same.' Three of the dispensers were already out of order, jammed cans hanging half-way. Still, the noise was human, not electronic; the lighting steady, not flashing. The walls seemed red plastic, painted with huge murals of clean, tidy, twenty-first-century teenagers having fun, grinning inanely, making meaningless jolly gestures. Tables and chairs stood on steel columns thick as gun-barrels, bolted to the red plastic floor. Every table swam with drink.

'What a pig-sty!'

'Be spotless in the morning,' said George. 'I been here early, soon as the gates are open. Everything clean an' polished. Never think anyone had ever been here. Look!' He took out a big knife, tried over and over to scratch 'G' on the table-top. Without effect, though the muscles of his neck stood out with the effort. 'Table's bonded steel; so're the walls and floor. Can't make a mark *anywhere*. Aerosol graffiti just wash off, when the cleaning-machines come. There'll be nothing to remember *us* by, man, once we're dead.' He drew a brown finger in a savage zig-zag across the wet table-top. Immediately the liquid closed in again, obliterating it.

We sat silent. George didn't drink his drink the normal way; he kept flexing his coke-can, so the drink oozed up onto the lid. Then he'd lick it off round the rim. Flex, flex went his big brown arm-muscle. I felt my own hand tightening with tension round the smooth frail surface of my can ... which was painted with the same vacuous grinning teenage faces as the walls. I began to flex my can, too, in time to the beat of the cacophony coming in through the door.

'Watch it,' said George. 'Slag!'

The girl from the music-dome was hovering in the doorway. Hair hanging down each side of her face like black wings; breasts showing frailly under that voluminous man's shirt. Our eyes met across the room.

She wasn't welcome in the bar. The girls formed tight circles of humped backs, keeping her out of their groups. She gathered her courage and spoke to a group of boys.

One boy short-armed her into the middle of the floor. She tripped, and lay in a pool of fizzy liquid, looking at me.

I walked across to her; George tried to stop me, but I shook his hand off. I started to bring her back to our table.

The guy who'd shoved her tried shoving her again. I grabbed his hand and twisted; got a close-up of his pale hatchet face, a plastic-leather jacket torn with the weight of badges. Then he was bending back helplessly to the floor. God, how weak he was! As he hit the floor, I felt his wrist snap. God, they had bones like broiler-house chickens!

He gathered up the contents of his mouth and spat at me; but his mates turned away indifferently, began playing a stupid game of banging their drinks together and yelling as spouts of fizz shot up.

I took the girl back to our table. George was gone. I wiped a seat dry with the remains of my handkerchief, a filthy black rag.

'Thanks. I'm Vanessa.' She took a fag out of her bag with trembling fingers, tried to light it. I took her lighter and lit it for her.

'Thanks.' She took out a little mirror, inspected her face without interest. Then shook back her long hair, with a sensual movement of her long neck that stirred my guts.

'You new?' she asked.

'*Fairly* new.'

'I'm not. They all hate me.'

'Why? I looked at her long, fine-boned face and sad, sad eyes. 'Why?'

'I'm ex-Est.' She began to cry, tears running down cheeks near-transparent with weariness.

'Let me get you a drink . . .'

'Will you take me home, please? I'm frightened to walk on my own.'

We left to a storm of jeers. I felt like punching the whole chicken-boned room into silence . . . but I was getting too fond of hurting. Instead I relaxed my fist and put it round her waist, feeling her leaden tiredness, but also the smoothness of her skin.

People watched us, all the way out of the Labour Exchange.

The noise and lights faded. Blue night and silence; footsteps echoing through tall empty streets. Blue night and weariness, wrapping us together like a blanket. I tightened my grip on her waist; she didn't object. She felt like a present someone had suddenly given me. I stopped abruptly and kissed her. Kissed her and kissed her. She gave in wearily; easy as pulling on a sweater. It was finally me, ashamed of taking advantage, who thrust us on.

'I live here.' A dark doorway; no windows lit anywhere. It wasn't like the estates. I wanted to ask her why she didn't live on an estate, but I didn't want to be rude. 'Goodnight, then . . .'

'Please . . . see me upstairs. Vermin . . . on the landings.'

I followed her up several flights, along passages. Dim bulbs clicked on in front of her, off behind. Blanketing us safe in silence and dark. The vermin must be on strike tonight.

'My door.' She was quick with her key.

'Goodnight.' I wondered if I could find my way back, through the network of stairs and corridors. Would the overhead lights click on and off for me?

But as she put her key in the door she swayed, nearly fell. I held her up with one hand, turned the key with the other.

A big room, dimly lit crimson. A huge low divan. I almost had to lift her on to it. She was light, but she turned awkwardly inside my arms, so my hands slid across her breasts. She had nothing on under her shirt. I expected her to shrink from my hands, but she just hung there.

I dropped her, embarrassed. She lay silent, face down. More embarrassed, I looked round to see where the rosy light was coming from. Huge goldfish tanks, in which goldfish swam smoothly, red, red. A luxury room, an Est room.

'I'll be going . . .'

She roused herself. 'Don't go for a minute – sit down – let me explain.' But the moment I sat next to her on the bed (there seemed to be no chairs in the room), she jumped up nervously; crossed the room and stood staring into one of the goldfish tanks, hands clasped in front of her. I could tell from the movement of her elbows that she was lacing and unlacing her fingers, nervously.

'You see – I have this problem . . .'

She turned, flinging her arms wide, and her unbuttoned shirt with them. Her jeans fell in a pile at her feet. She stepped out of them, dropping her shirt on top.

My mind couldn't catch up. One second I'd been worrying over a hunched figure on the verge of weeping. The next, the girl was swimming towards me like one of her own sleek goldfish. Red-gold light from the fish-tanks slid over her round breasts and small belly. She pressed her tiny navel onto the end of my uncomprehending nose. The world was full of the warm smell of girl. All I'd ever dreamed of, back in my lonely little bed at the Centre . . .

But I didn't trust dreams in Unnem land. I stood up abruptly, somehow knocking her down onto the carpet.

'Sorry,' I said. Offering her a hand up. She took hold of it, but lay, looking up at me; eyes like pools, waiting for me to dive in. But it was too easy.

'I'll be going,' I said.

She let me get my hand on the door-handle, then said, 'Please don't go.' Still lying there, looking totally forlorn. 'Please – I only wanted to keep you here. When I'm alone, I just can't sleep. Please stay till morning, or I don't know *what* I'll do. I slashed my wrists, once.' She held up a bare arm: there were thin, pink scars.

'*Look!*' I said decisively. But I went back and sat heavily on the bed. She got up and moved about. The squares of light from the fish-tanks slid across buttock and breast. 'Would you like a drink?' she asked.

'I'd like you to put something on.' My sense of humour was catching up with me.

'Why – am I so ugly? It *is* my room – I feel freer, naked – it helps me wind down.' She was so indignant, I nearly apologized. 'God – I could sleep for a week.' She yawned, holding her hand, Est-like, to her mouth. 'I don't mind if you keep *your* clothes on.'

85

'Thanks.' The drink she'd given me was so aromatic, the fumes went right through my head, making me close my eyes. 'I'll sleep on the floor.' The deep-pile carpet seemed a lot softer than George's old bed.

'Please don't – there's plenty of room on the bed. I'll behave – if you put your arm round me.' She curled up round me, where I sat. Before I'd finished the drink, her breathing had deepened to sleep. In the red dimness, dark lashes lay on her flushed cheeks. She looked happy, asleep, like my kid brother.

The bed was soft; cuddling a sleeping girl was no pain. I put a tentative stiff arm around her. She sighed, pressing it onto her breast with both hands.

I was on the edge of sleep when she turned and swept over me like a sinuous wave. Far too late to resist.

I wakened in the dark, thinking how sad, flat, disappointing. If that was all it was . . . My jeans were round my knees, where she'd left them. The shirt she'd unbuttoned was wrinkled up under my armpits, and my mouth was like the bottom of a birdcage. She was sleeping half on top of me, totally trusting.

I had to have a drink. Every credit I'd won, for a glass of cold water. Not another drink like she'd given me before . . . No way!

I eased her off me, centimetre by protesting centimetre. I wondered where the light-switch was. If I got up in total dark, I'd wake her falling over the furniture. I lay and thought about it.

She'd fiddled with a switch just above the bed-head . . . on a length of flex. I groped up and found it, pressed the button. No lights went on. It must be broken. I lay there and fumed, thirstier than ever.

Click!

The tiniest sound. The kind you only hear when you can't sleep, in black silence, in the middle of the night.

Maybe a death-watch beetle; or the tiny click of phlegm in my own windpipe . . .

Click!

I held my breath, till I nearly choked.

Click! There it was again, coming from the wall above the bed-head. I reached up an exploring hand. Touched a small round button set in the wall, cold like glass.

Click! There was a square of wall around it; marked out by a hairline crack; colder than the plaster of the wall.

Click!

I pressed on the cold square and it fell, heavy and solid, into my hand. I knew what it was then; an automatic polaroid camera. I got up now, all right, not caring *who* I wakened. Pulled down my shirt, pulled up my jeans. Bashed round the room in a fury, looking for an overhead light-switch. Found it.

Overhead light is cruel. I saw the huge cracks in the ceiling; the velvet-faced wallpaper bulging off the walls, the damp spots where the fish-tanks had dripped condensation on the ill-fitted carpet. And the girl on the bed, too long, too thin, fish-pale with pelvis-bones like fish-bones.

Worse, as I pressed the release-button on the camera, a string of infra-red photographs fell onto the floor. In excellent focus, correctly exposed and leaving nothing to the imagination. My own face, open-mouthed, looked animal and stupid.

I ripped the first photo into bits smaller than a postage-stamp. Then she was on me, scrabbling for the photos like a beggar scrabbling for food. Under the harsh light, I suddenly saw how she would look when she was old. It was the only thing that stopped me hitting her.

'Please, do what you like but don't take my photographs.'

'If you're thinking of blackmail, forget it. Techs don't have any parents left to shock.'

'That's not what they're *for*!' She didn't sound like a blackmailer, somehow.

'What, then?'

'I take them to the Labour Exchange. They give me forty credits a bloke.'

'Futuretrack Six?' I sneered. 'The oldest profession?'

She drew herself up with a touching naked dignity. 'It's not just whoring – I'm trying to get into the Sisterhood.'

'The what?'

'It's run by women, for women, somewhere out in the country. An old nunnery, among big green trees. They make you well again, and you never have to go near a man, unless you want to. And they teach you the female mysteries . . . foreseeing the future . . . clairvoyance. I *know* I've got second sight – I can find things people have lost. When a friend of mine, a Racer, was killed, I *knew* . . .'

'What's the snag?' I asked, suddenly suspicious of such unlikely Est benevolence.

'I have to sleep with five hundred men within a year – every one different. Most girls reckon it's impossible, but I was doing so well. Boys wanted me because I was all pretty and glossy from having been an Est. Then some clever dick like you spotted my camera and the word got around. Now I can only catch green newcomers . . .'

'Like me. What number was I?'

'Four hundred and twenty-one. I'll never make it now – I've only got two months to go.'

'What happens if you don't make it?'

She shuddered.

I thought I'd hated the system when Idris died. But nothing like this. Finally I took her thin hand in both of mine. 'Don't worry, Vanessa, you'll make it. I'll *see* you make it.'

She fluttered in my hands, like a desperate bird. 'How can you? It's got to be a different man every time. They feed the photos into a computer, that keeps the score.'

I began to laugh; but it felt more like crying. 'Girl, if there's one thing computers are bad at, it's reading photographs. Wear a false moustache, paint yourself with coffee-grounds, wear spectacles, change the lighting, you'll fool a computer. They're babes in arms . . .'

She managed a wan smile of disbelief. 'I'll settle for a cuddle until morning.'

She slept; I lay awake. At first, full of glee at my plans to send my love, or at least my love-making, back to Laura. I had no doubts about my power to fool her. Computers are lousy at 2-D images. I only hoped my old sex-starved mate Sellers didn't while away his boring duty-hours looking through Laura's dirty-photograph files. *He'd* recognize me for sure . . .

Then I began to have doubts. Did Vanessa's Sisterhood really exist? Or was it a lousy Est con-trick? To weed out Unnem-girls of determination and drive, who might have special and dangerous gifts? Certainly I'd never heard of a Sisterhood, either as an Est or a Tech. Could it be another name for the lobo-farm?

It was a labyrinth. How little any of us knew what was really going on. The Ests didn't want to know, providing they had their little comforts, their little party-games. The Techs didn't want to know: too busy fighting among themselves. But somebody must know; somebody must be planning it all.

For some reason, I thought of Scott-Astbury. I tried to laugh myself out of it, remembering his paunchy prancing. Then I remembered the peculiar pale blueness of his eyes. People laughed at Scott-Astbury, but *he* never laughed.

I poked Vanessa awake.

'Oh God, it's not morning, is it?'

'No. Listen. Did you ever hear of a man called Scott-Astbury?'

She blinked at me blearily.

'Think! It's important.'

She rubbed a thin beautiful hand across red-rimmed eyes.

'When I was an Est . . . Daddy used to go on about Scott-Astbury. He said that what Scott-Astbury was doing in the

Scottish Highlands was wrong. But he and Mummy always shut up when they saw I was listening. Aw, let me sleep, Sellers!'

That was all I ever got out of her.

8

The morning of the Championship, I felt great. Vanessa had been to the Labour Exchange twice: none of her photographs had been rejected. I'd fooled dear, distant Laura's photoscanners forty times in four days.

George didn't approve; neither did the Bluefish. 'Let me show you a *real* woman,' said George, as they collected me.

'Straight through,' said the Bluefish, massively. There were twelve of them now, though George explained I wouldn't have to pay the extra wages till I was Champ of the Month. Bluefish, old and new, were pretty high. Grinning from missing ear to missing ear, a cat-like joy in their lope. They kept on trying to pick me up and carry me; kept whispering about a rumble.

'*What* rumble?'

'Leave them be, man, they're happy. Come and meet this *real* woman.'

I let them persuade me. I was tired of being paraded around the Domes like the FA Cup.

We'd gone a kilometre, through a district of half-ruined warehouses, when I heard a noise like a hundred road-drills. Giggling, the Bluefish flattened themselves into doorways.

The noise became an orgy; doors vibrated. Then the street-end filled with a cloud of dust full of glinting points of chrome, and red and yellow helmets and green and purple and gold arriving a stupefying speed. I slapped my hands over my ears and the scream of tortured steel drilled straight through, trapped and bouncing between the walls of that brick canyon. I glimpsed the black leading bike, black rider, black helmet, blond hair streaming back like eagle's wings. Then their exhaust-gas punched our faces and they were dwindling, leaving us choking in the cracked and burning hydrocarbons.

As they reached the far end, a yellow robo-truck turned the corner, seemed totally to block the brick canyon. I gasped, waiting for the splat.

The lead rider swayed left, like a reed in the wind, into a shadowed crack between robo-truck and wall; almost seemed to pass right through the truck.

Others, blue, green and white, managed the same trick. The rest swayed right instead, spilling down an empty rubble slope in a shambles of tumbling, rolling, spinning chrome.

The robo-truck came on steadily, undisturbed. Its yellow front carried a splatter-pattern, a scarlet spider-web. Odd! Who'd bother decorating a robo-truck? And on top . . . among its steering-antennae, a brown shape fluttered feebly, like a trapped bird.

Then I wished I'd closed my eyes sooner. The scarlet pattern was still wet, growing, glistening. The fluttering bird was an impaled motor cyclist. One gauntleted hand still moved, as if pleading. I hoped it was the slipstream moving it.

Two metres above our heads he passed, unstoppable, spattering us with warm, red rain.

'They'll fetch his body from the robo-depot,' said George. 'Man, I'll say that; they do give each other great funerals. When they're not racing, all they do is go to funerals. Come and meet this girl . . .'

The Bluefish emerged, grinning and whistling. 'That Keri . . . ain't she *somethin'*?' They loped on, happily.

I threw up in the gutter.

'That Vanessa's cookin' ain't doin' you no good, man,' said George, heartlessly.

We reached the rubble-strewn slope; the motor cyclists were picking themselves up, straightening the handlebars of their bikes. There were a couple of gum-chewing broken arms, and a broken rib, coughing up blood and jokes.

With a roar, the surviving riders returned.

'Who hitched a ride on the robo-truck?'

'Billy.'

'Billy who?'

'He never had time to tell us.'

'You can't just write "Billy" on a coffin!'

'What about "Silly Billy"?'

They all seemed to find that remarkably funny. The black-leather lead rider took his helmet off, so he could laugh easier. A rounded girlish face; rosy dimpled cheeks, under the oil-smears. The eyes were large and green, under dark brows odd against the blond hair. The nose was snub, determined. Two deep frown-marks of concentration on the rounded forehead. The full mouth smiled, cherubically. The broadish shoulders were slightly hunched from riding.

The chest, partly released as she unzipped her leathers, was opulently female . . .

'This is the *real* woman,' said George, with his biggest dazzling grin. 'Keri Roberts, National Champ. She's lasted four months, longer than anybody.'

'As Champ?'

'As alive,' said George. 'Keri, meet Sellers. He'll be pinball Champ of the Month by tonight.'

'So I can see,' said Keri, raising one dark eyebrow at my wretched plastic champ's ribbon. 'Dangerous sport, pinball. A real *man*'s game.'

I should have loathed her forever. Instead, I was fascinated.

'Don't knock the guy,' said George. 'I'm managing him.'

'George, you'd manage a three-legged cockroach, if you couldn't find anything better.'

'Thanks,' I said. 'As one ex-Est to another . . .'

'Who's ex-Est?' she blazed. 'I'm Unnem, mate. Born and bred. What's so bloody great about being an Est?'

'Sorry. I thought . . .'

'Oh, yes, you Ests *think*. Guzzle real red meat and *think*. Drink genuine booze and *think*. Go for long walks watching dicky-birds and *think*. I don't *think* about racing; I race.'

'Keri can see round corners,' said George, hurriedly. 'She can smell a robo-truck coming a kilometre away. This Keri, she got nine lives like a cat, man.'

'Shurrup, George. I ran over a cat this morning.' Her hand reached down, touched a sweat-blackened silver cross that hung between her breasts. Her face was suddenly sharp and peaky.

'I'll lend yo' my lucky rabbit-foot, Keri!'

'Just *manage* your little ex-Est out of my way, George.' She put her bike into gear and rode straight at me. I dodged, but the end of her handlebar still caught me in the crotch. Then she was away in a cloud of smoke.

'Keep goin', man.'

Three hours since the Championship started. One kid each from Glasgow, Birmingham, Swansea. Two of us from London North-East; some kid from London West. A flickering in the corner of my eye told me the big screens were busy; one showing scores, the other close-ups of us players as, doubled-up, we sweated on.

Sweat running into my eyes. Unasked, George changed my towelling headband for the tenth time. All round, the huge audience shifted and coughed in the flickering darkness. All the machines silent, except two, tonight. Mine was running so hot a glow came up to my face, like an oven. But it was well serviced; I'd seen to that. Half an hour to go, and it wouldn't conk now.

No time to look at the score. I could sense how I was doing from the muted noises of the crowd. A deepening silence, as I lost ground; a growl as I began to climb; a sigh as I regained the lead. I'd gained and lost it twice; was lying third, behind Birmingham and London West.

An exultant yip from the crowd.

'Birmingham burnt out,' said George. 'Keep goin'. Twenty minutes left.'

My back was locked solid; my hand clenched in a glove of pain, my mind a maze of numerals. But I still heard the sudden shouting outside; savage shouting far away. Hammering on the Dome. A growl from the Bluefish, shoulder to shoulder around me, in a sweaty ring.

'What's that?' I asked, missing one shot altogether.

'Nothing to bother you, man. Keep goin'.'

The hammering grew. The crowd around me was breaking up and whispering away.

'Keep goin' man. We can cope.'

'With *what*?'

A huge slow banging on the main doors made the whole Dome boom like a gong.

'Keep goin'. 'Tain't nothin'. Just the usual.'

I heard the main doors collapse, with a screech of metal. Echoing triumphant shouts. An answering shout from the remaining crowd around me.

'George, for God's sake . . .'

'Watch it, man. You missed two in a row, there. Keep goin' – the rest's up to us.' He sounded tense, uncertain.

A crack, like a gun. A Bluefish staggered back against my machine, steadied himself with one hand, pushed off again. Leaving, on the glowing glass, a bloody palm-print.

Then I was in the middle of a storm; backs and legs of Bluefish pressing in round me. The machine rocking and swaying. Thump of flesh on flesh, bone on bone. A gurgle. It was all caving in on me, but I went on pulling the handle to please George. Suddenly a roar of triumph. Many feet, running away. Silence, and a ring of grinning earless Bluefish faces, close to mine. I went on pulling the handle, till George eased my fingers off.

'You won, man.' Stroking me gently. All the Bluefish – stroking me like I was a prize-winning pussy-cat.

'Let me stretch.' I pushed through them, easing my numb back with numb hands. One big screen just carried my score. The other carried my face as big as a wall. Unshaven beard like black grass; wrinkles like irrigation ditches with streaks of sweat like waterfalls. I could have crawled up the black nostrils of my own exhaustion and vanished from the world forever . . .

White-coats hanging a purple cloak round me again; it seemed a slightly better quality. An even higher crown, put crooked on my head.

My foot kicked something soft. I looked down, holding my crown in place with both hands.

At my feet lay a dead boy; a total stranger. A yard away, a Bluefish lay face down, a round wound in his back pulsing blood like a little roadside spring.

'Look up, man, smile,' said George. 'You're on the Box.'

'Come and speak to them, man. They're all waiting.'

Bluefish practically carried me up the metal stairs, to a metal balcony where the moon rode high.

I'd never seen a crowd so huge; all of London North-East. All looking up at me. Little children held up in their parents' arms. Old bent grannies shrieking, 'Sellers is Champ, Sellers is Champ.'

But all I could think of was the blanket-covered bodies laid out against the wall of the Dome. Two rows, one much shorter than the other.

'We done them, man. We really slaughtered them.'

'Who were they?'

'Guys from London West. We were expectin' them. We was ready.'

'And what happened to the London West Champ?'

'He ran away. When we broke into *his* Dome, he ran away. He's finished, man, finished. You're Champ. An' it's Champ of the Year, next month. Speak to them, man. Tell 'em they did well . . .' He thrust a microphone into my hand.

'You did well,' I said.

I thought the cheering would never stop.

'You've given them something to live for, man!'

I looked at the row of blanket-covered bodies.

'That as well, man. If you hadn't come, they'da fought among themselves, died for *nothin'*. Thanks to you, they died happy, dyin' in the moment of victory.'

'What victory?'

'Don't *talk* that way, man.'

'Take me to Vanessa's.'

Around dawn, I went to the window, drew back the curtain; a grey flat morning.

From the bed, Vanessa said, 'You're a good man, Sellers. You've no idea what this place was like before you came. You give people hope . . . pride.'

'I get people killed.'

'People are getting nicer. George is talking to me. The Bluefish come to take me shopping . . .'

'I'm going away.'

'Oh, God, where?'

'Where I can only kill *myself*.'

'To Keri Roberts. She's the real killer. Killed hundreds, and never grieved for one.'

'That'll make a pair of us, then.'

Behind me, on the bed, she began to weep.

9

'Here's your bike,' said the mechanic. 'Gimme your chit.'

I handed him my Racer's chit from the Labour Exchange, and bent to examine the bike.

A wretched thing: once red, but most of the enamel had been scraped away by contact with the road. Rust bubbling through everywhere. The previous owners had tried covering up the rust with stickers and hand-painted lettering: 'Ball of Fire', 'The Clacton Kid'.

There were other stickers beneath the top stickers; other lettering under the top lettering. I peeled and picked at them, like doing an archaeological dig.

'Leytonstone Lightwings', 'Young Gary'.

Where were they now? The handlebars had that wavering line that meant they'd been bent and straightened many times. So had the front forks. The crude single-cylinder engine dripped oil on my boot.

'She's a goer,' said the mechanic. 'She was always fast, that one. Just top her up with oil before every race and she won't burn out on you.'

'Don't reckon much to those tyres.'

'No worse than anybody else's. Good for a hundred kilometres, yet. 'Course, I could let you have a new set for fifty credits . . .'

'The brakes seem to pull to the left . . .'

'What are you – a bloody Est or something?'

I pulled out a fistful of credits, and he changed his tune.

I spent nearly the whole day stripping her down, straightening things and welding, cadging new parts. Cost me a bomb. Meanwhile, a whole stream of kids rode away on bikes worse than mine. The mechanic kept coming across and saying *they* were doing it the right way. Racing was like swimming: plunge in headfirst. If you kept on standing on the bank dipping your toe in you'd get so nervous you'd *never* start . . . I told him to get lost. Twice, trucks delivered loads of smashed-up bikes. I could've sworn I'd seen several of them cheerfully ridden away that morning . . .

Finally, my bike was as ready as she'd ever be.

'Can I practise round here?'

The mechanic spat on the brick-strewn vacant lot behind his garage.

'That's what it's for, if you're *that* nervous.'

I kicked the engine into life.

I couldn't get the hang of it. The front wheel was tiny, stuck out on the end of long forks, giving the bike a lousy, huge turning-circle. The handlebars were narrow, when they should have been wide to give leverage; you really had to pull them hard over to make the front wheel turn at all. If you pulled a mite too hard, the front wheel turned sideways, locked solid. Three times I went over the handle-bars, not doing more than twenty. And the bike was so high-geared it was hard to go slow; it stalled frequently. My right leg grew weary, kicking it back into life. My arms grew weary, because the handlebars were placed so high you rode like a dog begging. After two hours, my jeans were torn, my knees skinned and my arms shaking so much I could hardly steer. I could've wept. Techs were supposed to be *good* with machines.

'This isn't a bike, it's a bloody death-trap.'

'Bad workman always blames his tools. Look at that guy – he's really getting into it.' He pointed to a little dark kid, who'd started practising ages after me. He'd got the hang of it. He rode fast, a bit like Keri. Sitting well back on the straights, to get more thrust on the back wheel. Then the sudden push forward and down at corners, to give the front wheel more grip for turning. Graceful and right. He made me feel a bumbler with his beautiful curves, getting faster and faster.

Until, turning at the far end, he hit a wall without warning.

'I'll get the meat-wagon,' said the mechanic casually, wiping his hands on his backside, reaching for the white thumb-printed phone.

I ran all the way, thinking, please God, not another. The bike's engine was still bellowing, threatening to tear itself loose from its mounting. The kid just lay there; I raised his visor. There wasn't a mark on him, even a little smile of wonder on his face . . .

'You might have turned the engine off,' shouted the mechanic. 'Bikes cost money, you know.'

'And kids don't?'

He picked up the bike and began straightening the handlebars.

I looked back at the kid; wondering whether to put my coat over his face till the ambulance came. He couldn't have been more than fourteen . . .

He opened his baby-blue eyes and smiled at me.

'Try-moving-your-arms,' I said, then, 'try-moving-your-legs.'

He sat up and said, 'I ain't half gotta headache.'

I loved him just for being alive. 'Have you thought,' I said, 'of trying any other futuretrack?'

'Wanted to be a singer, but I 'adn't no money to buy an amplifier.'

I dug into my pockets and held out a handful of credits. 'That enough to buy an amplifier?'

His eyes grew wary; he jumped to his feet. 'Hey, mister, what's the catch? You a homo?' Then he frowned. 'I know you – you're King Sellers, Champ of the Month.'

'Yes,' I said, 'I'm King Sellers. I've got so many credits they're making holes in my pockets. And I've found you a manager, for when you're a singer – he's called George.

And someone to live with – she's called Vanessa.' I told him where they lived.

'What can I do for you?'

'Tell George and Vanessa – I'll be back some day.'

'Right,' he said. 'Thanks, King. Hurry back soon.' He limped off across the scattered bricks.

'That's interfering,' said the mechanic. 'What you done – that's *treason*. I can report you . . .'

'Did you *want* him dead?' I asked. 'We're alone, here, Tech.'

He saw the look on my face. Glanced round nervously. Fiddled with the big spanner that stuck out of his overalls.

'Whatcher mean – we're alone?'

'What grade are you, Tech? One? I'm 4n – it's your word against mine about treason. Who's going to listen to a grade one?'

'You razzlin' swine always cause trouble. Anyway, we ain't alone any more.'

A Paramil car was pulling up outside the garage. I walked across: thought he'd be making inquiries about the crash. He was leaning against his bonnet, pad and pencil at the ready. Gave me one of their little smirks.

'Stephen Sellers, alias Henry Kitson, Tech 4n?'

I nodded. He couldn't touch me: Techs had the right to go on the razzle.

'Your father wishes to see you. You must go straight home. Here is a *legal* pass to get through the Wire. Forty-eight hours – is that sufficient?'

He enjoyed startling me. I'd nearly forgotten I had a home and father. Since I'd never expected to see either again, there wasn't much point in remembering.

10

My parents lived in the Cotswold Enclave. It was one hell of a ride. Besides falling off every five kilometres, I kept being stopped by Paramils, British Police, even bossy Ests. My pass was dog-eared within the hour. Everybody found my presence deeply and profoundly insulting.

Father opened the door himself as I roared down the drive; red flags of anger in his cheeks. 'Did you have to ride that bloody thing all the way here? The phone's never stopped ringing.'

'I'm a Racer now. How else could I have come?'

'By taxi – you've got plenty of credits.'

'You seem to know an awful lot about me!'

'Your mother saw you playing pinball on TV. She hasn't slept since – they've hospitalized her.'

'If she can't stand the sight of blood, why does she watch pinball?' It always disgusted me, the way Ests watched the Unnem TV. Fifty channels of their own, and they have to *slum*. Of course, nobody ever admits it . . .

'I suppose it's only *my* blood that worried her?'

Father looked hurt, and I was instantly sorry. 'Can I go and see her?'

'When I've finished with you . . . actually, if you show any sense, you'll soon be spending plenty of time with her . . .'

'How d'you mean?'

'Your behaviour's upset a lot of people besides your mother.'

'We're allowed out on the razzle!'

'With a stolen pass? Come off it, Kit. You know as well

as I do that a razzle's a few hours, a few drinks. You've got London North-East by the ears . . . Sellers for Champ!'

That stung.

'Other kids make Champ!'

'Unnem kids, who fritter away their credits on drugs. But that's not your way, is it? Give you a month, you'll have ten million credits and a private army.'

'I don't know what you mean.'

'Oh, don't you, little innocent? Does the name Vanessa Thornton mean anything to you? A common tart who's been credited with forty new lovers in four days, though only *you* have been seen going up to her apartment? Let alone the Tommy Wells business . . .'

'Tommy who . . .?'

'The young man you seduced away from bike-racing to set up as a singer.'

'You've been *spying* on me.'

He sighed heavily, playing with the fringe of the door-curtain. 'I have watched over you every day since you left the college.'

Both of us fell silent, listening to the grandfather clock in the hall, that had ticked away my childhood; that ticked in a sort of peace now.

He could never be angry with me long. He led me through to his study, a hand on my elbow that I didn't mind. 'You're falling in love with the Unnems, aren't you, Kit? Wanting to help?'

'They're *people*! Not mad; not monsters. *People*.'

He shut the study door quickly, as if afraid somebody might hear. 'Keep your voice down. D'you think you're the first bright kid to fall in love with the Unnems? All those bright kids came to the same end – strapped down on the conveyor-belt at the lobo-farm, alongside the international terrorists. Do you *want* to be the talking-point at somebody's sherry-party?'

I whirled at him. 'Look at what's happening to the Unnems – they're dying off like flies.'

He went pale. Silent fear grew between us, like icicles in the gut. Like on that unmentionable, far-off day in my childhood when they filled the Unnem in. Finally, Father said, 'I had a phone-call from John Higgins last night.' Higgins was our fat, useless, Est MP. 'They want you back in Cambridge – *now*. They don't know how you feel about the Unnems. Yet. They think you're only upset about Idris.' He studied my face carefully. 'Or, if you're *too* upset about Idris, they're prepared to let you come back and live here, with me. So that *I* can guarantee your good behaviour . . .'

The room whirled about me; beloved room in the beloved greystone house that was built in Queen Elizabeth's time. Among the winding grey-walled lanes I'd just ridden down; the rabbits scurrying on Minchinhampton Common. It was news too good to be true. Standing here, the whole last horrible year might never have happened.

But it had. Idris and Laura; George and Vanessa and Keri. The Cotswold Enclave now felt as small as a green pocket-handkerchief, its false peace bought with . . .

'*Who* wants me back in Cambridge?'

'Don't be bloody-minded, Kit. I worked very hard to sort this out for you.'

'Sorry, Dad. But I'm a Racer, now.'

He reasoned, pleaded, raged. Once, I think, nearly wept. The house-boy fetched in supper-drinks, fine china on a silver tray. We let them grow cold.

Out in the hall, the grandfather clock struck midnight.

'Your Tompion's keeping good time,' I said, remembering all the good old days.

'I'm thinking of selling it.'

That shook me: the Tompion was his favourite. People were always making him fantastic offers. He serviced it himself. He'd trained as an engineer, as much as any Est's allowed . . .

Talk of the Tompion seemed to have changed his mood; or maybe the fact that it was midnight. He relaxed; seemed to be enjoying some wry private joke. 'Have a drink before you go. We could both do with a spot of whisky . . .'

I was a bit hurt he'd given me up so easily. But it was a large whisky; the fumes caught my nose. As Keri would've said, *real* booze. Remembering what I was going back to, I had another. And another. The old worn leather couch suddenly seemed very precious. I used to go on voyages in it when I was small . . .

'Must be getting back.' I stood up, but the room spun.

'Don't ride back half tight,' said my father. 'Put up your feet for an hour. You've got a forty-eight hour pass . . .' He lifted my feet up onto the couch; brought a rug.

'Only an hour,' I said.

He was shaking my shoulder.

'Time to go.'

'Mother?'

'She'd better not know you were ever here.'

'How is she really?'

'Pretty rough, Kit.'

'I'm sorry. I'll be going, then.'

I paused in the darkness of the hall. It was too silent.

'The Tompion's stopped . . . hey, it's gone.'

'I told you I was thinking of selling it.'

'Not that quick.'

'One has to be quick, sometimes.' He still sounded amused, in a wry, hurt way.

We stepped out onto the drive. It was bitterly cold. Middle-of-the-night cold. My watch said 4 a.m. I'd slept four hours.

'My bike's got no lights,' I said helplessly, still fuddled.

'It has now.' The bike seemed lower, squatter. He bent over and touched a switch, and brilliant twin beams leapt out, making a white skeleton of the sycamore across the paddock.

'This isn't my bike!'

'It's the only one you're riding away from this house. A

Jap... Mitsubishi 705. Full fairings, shaft-drive, nylon wheels, low-pressure foam tyres – puncture-proof.'

'There's no petrol-tank.' I still felt dopey, drugged.

'She's all electric – plug her in overnight to any domestic power-point. She'll do a thousand kilometres between plug-ins. Get you any radio station in the world, as you ride along.'

He sounded like the day he bought me my first bicycle.

'She must have cost you the *earth*.'

'The Jap importer is very fond of Tompions...'

'Dad – I can't take it – where's *my* bike?'

He led me to the dustbins, neatly concealed behind a flowering hedge. My bike lay beside them, so mangled I could hardly tell which end was which. The smell of petrol from the shattered tank rose evilly.

'I took a sledge-hammer to it. Seemed the only way of stopping you riding it.'

'I spent a whole day putting it right...'

'You could've spent a lifetime and it still wouldn't have been right.' His voice was rough with rage. 'No son of mine is riding a bike designed to kill him.'

'But, Dad, all the kids are riding them!'

After a long pause he said, tightly, 'That's none of my business.'

'Isn't it? *Isn't* it? I'm in love with a girl who rides one.'

'Then I suggest that you get back to London as quickly as you can and stop her.'

'*All* the kids should be stopped.'

He wouldn't say anything. I couldn't see his face properly in the dark. I shouted,

'*Designed* to kill? Who designed them? Scott-Astbury?'

'Who told you that name? Who?' He'd grabbed me by the shoulders. His hands were shaking.

'Idris. He tricked Idris. Idris said he should be killed.'

He relaxed – a bit. 'Idris was mad, towards the end.' But I could still feel his hands trembling on my shoulders. 'Kit, promise me one thing. Never mention that name to anybody again. You mightn't have much life left, riding bikes, but if someone hears you asking about Scott-Astbury, you'll have no life left at all.'

'You *know* Scott-Astbury? You *know* what he's doing?'

I felt him nod. 'I've been trying to stop him for thirty years. And failed.'

'Tell me. Tell me. *Tell me!*'

'No, Kit.'

'Why won't you tell me? You're *ashamed* to tell me, because you *failed.*'

'I failed, Kit. I had a lot of friends, twenty years ago. Big powerful friends. But I still failed. What chance would you have, with a handful of Unnems? You wouldn't last a week. But if I told you what he's doing, you'd go mad. You'd have to try and stop him, even with a few Unnems, and that would be the end of you . . . I can't do that, Kit, I can't. You're all I've got . . .'

'*Why* did you fail? Who were these great big friends of yours?'

'The Liberals in Parliament . . . Morse, Trethowan, Little . . . quite a few more . . . in the universities.'

'And what happened?'

'Morse got old. Little was ruined by a scandal. I think they had Trethowan killed. There are still a few of us left, but less every year. The Ests won't listen to us any more. People get old and fat and lazy. Or they stay on their estates and grow roses. Or take to drink. It's all folding up, Kit. What did they used to say, in the First World War? The lights are going out, all over Europe? Well, now they're going out all over England. Soon Scott-Astbury and his mob will walk all over us.'

'Dad, for God's sake, you're still a young man. You're not fifty yet. I'll help you . . .'

'Kit, Kit . . . don't you think I've tried everything I know? What difference would you make? Except to get yourself killed. Go away and ride your bike, while you can.'

'Thanks.' I began to push the bike down the drive, too upset to fiddle with it. He kept on following me.

'Grab what fun you can, Kit ... that girl – is she an ex-Est? If I could get her out of it, too, would you marry her and settle down with us here? We could make you a flat ...'

'She's *Unnem*,' I shouted. 'Born and bred. *Proud* of it. She says what's so marvellous about being a bloody Est?' Somehow, a hint of Keri's broad Cockney came through on my voice.

Father drew in a little breath of pain, in the dark. Then he was gone into the house, and I could only ride away.

Easier said than done. I pressed the starter-button. Dim lettering glowed-up on the big curved fighter-plane wind-screen: FASTEN YOUR SAFETY BELT

I knew better than to argue; fastened the yielding lap-belt across my belly. Immediately, she started, silently, only the tiniest vibration coming up through the seat. Another image grew on the windscreen; the road-plan round my father's house with me sitting, a glowing red dot, smack in the middle. Other cars moving as green dots ...

STATE DESTINATION

I tapped out LONDON. The first section of route-map glowed up, adjusted its brightness.

BATTERY CHARGE FULL NO FAULTS DEVELOPING AIR TEMPERATURE 2° NO ICING GREASY PATCHES WET LEAVES UNDER TREES ALL THAMES VALLEY. SINGLE-LANE WORKING OXFORD BYPASS. ABNORMLOAD 3 KILOMETRES W OF ABINGDON EAST-BOUND 25 KPH

I had to tap acknowledgements before she'd move. I called her Mitzi, after Mitsubishi.

Riding her was beautiful. Below a hundred she ran so silently I could hear myself breathing. No gears – just twist the throttle and feed on the juice. She was low and broad, with low broad tyres. Her weight was low down, in the batteries. The heated seat adjusted itself and hugged your bottom as you sat on it. Windscreen and panniers were moulded round you, so you never felt the wind. Doing a ton was like sitting on a sofa.

She taught me to ride her. If I leaned too far into a corner, she bleeped. If I didn't lean far enough, she pinged. If I went too fast for a bit of road, she wailed like a cat on heat. But she was no scaredy-cat. On a straight approaching Reading she did two hundred and fifty while relaying the latest Helen Choy disc from Radio Hong Kong and dipping her own headlights as cars approached.

On and on we went, getting chummier and chummier like a hand in a glove. She chattered and scolded, tremendously on my side, like any computer. Feeling invulnerable, all-powerful, I dreamed wild, boyish, Estish dreams. Of rescuing Keri and riding off with her through the night forever . . .

Then the hard-headed Tech in me took over, and screwed out of those dreams a realistic plan that just might work.

The moment I had a plan to save Keri, to get her for myself, I grew terrified that she might be dead already, and her funeral in the morning.

I reached the London gate before dawn.

There was no official racing that day. But Keri raced the back-streets every day, that most fabulous of things, an Open Champion. Anybody could challenge her at any time . . .

They told me at the race-track she was down Lambeth way, racing the demolition-sites. The Lambeth Estate had been emptied. The Archbishop of Canterbury was land-scaping it into a deer-park . . .

At least she was alive – an hour ago.

I rode up to massive jeers.

'What's that?' she asked. 'A sofa with extra-large castors?'

'Jap-crap,' sneered the hangers-on. 'Diddums Daddy buy it for Christmas?'

I tried to tell Keri what Mitzi could do.

'Be a man,' she said. 'Ride British.' She put her helmet back on; she was never still for five minutes. In a second, my chance'd be gone.

I pointedly looked at her bike. Nearly new, well serviced. Gold-plated petrol-tank and handlebars. But the same old killer-design.

'Mine'll go faster than your old junk-heap,' I said.

'Like my Aunt Fanny it will.' Anger flared in her cheeks. A nerve twitched in her left eyebrow. Silence had fallen.

'Prove it,' I said.

'Right.' She revved. 'Let me show you our race-course. Just so you can't say afterwards that you got lost.' She showed me the course in every detail, pointing out road-cambers and loose surfaces with the greatest sarcastic politeness. Kept saying, 'Do you understand?' as to an idiot child. Then she snapped down her visor, and went for a fill-up of petrol.

The hangers-on closed in.

'She'll break her neck rather than be passed.'

'We'll break yours afterwards.' I managed a careless shrug.

Then she was back; a light in her eyes, a perkiness in her back, and that tic in her left eyebrow. She lined up alongside, tucking a strand of newly washed hair under her helmet with a gesture that nearly broke my heart . . . Then shouted, 'Start,' put her bike into gear in the same breath and wheelied off across the brick-strewn demolition-site leaving me standing. I kept hitting loose bricks. By the time I reached the road, she was fifty metres ahead and the crowd were already laughing.

Fortunately, there was a long straight. Mitzi caught up for me, in a long surge of power that pressed me deeper into the saddle.

Big left-hand bend; she swung out nearly to the opposite kerb, leaning out as far as she could, watching for robo-trucks coming the other way. Was it safe to follow? Might she squeeze into one of her shadow cracks leaving me plastered all over the front of something?

No, she wouldn't want me dead: she'd want me to laugh at afterwards. With my heart in my mouth I followed her line, hit another loose brick that made Mitzi bounce like a trampoline, lost another forty metres.

On the straight, she looked back, laughing. Knew me for the nig-nog I was.

That suited me: she hadn't sussed out Mitzi at all.

She played with me after that; constantly looking back over her shoulder and laughing. I let myself ride even more badly. She actually throttled back to keep me interested.

Oh, Keri, Keri, I love you. Don't forget you're riding against a Tech; Techs are cunning bastards . . . I edged up on her a little, as the last bend came in sight. Joggling my elbows as if coaxing the last effort out of my bike.

It had her in fits.

Last bend. Out she swung, wide, wide, as she had to, on that deadly rattletrap. I took a deep breath, chose a line far inside her, turned on the juice and *prayed*.

Mitzi bleeped at me, suddenly frantic. I leaned in deeper and deeper to the bend. Just for a horrible second, I nearly broke away and went flying all over the road. Then I was alongside Keri, riding boot to boot.

And she, caught in her chosen line, could do nothing except go suicidally faster and faster. Leaning so hard in towards me that it seemed for a moment as if that wing of her golden hair was going right down under my front wheel.

We'll die together, I thought, and that didn't seem too bad.

The bend was over; we were straightening out, coming upright. She was still alongside, twisting her throttle so hard I could see her jaw clenched inside her helmet. Shouting at her bike as if it was a horse.

But I piled the juice on (I nearly forgot, I so much wanted

to be close to her) and she just faded back over my right shoulder.

I shot past the fist-shaking hangers-on. One leapt out at me, making me swerve so badly that I did a zigzag that lasted all of two minutes, and ended up on my knees, facing the wrong way, with no cloth left in the knees of my denims.

Keri too was lying inert beside her roaring, wheel-spinning bike. I ran back, terrified I'd killed her. The hangers-on were all walking away . . . But she was still breathing, back rising and falling in great heaves.

She raised her head. Behind the scarred visor, tears were streaming down her face.

'You hurt?' I rushed to pick her up.

She let me lift her, then punched me in the gut with all her might.

'Cheating Est bastard!'

She picked up a half-brick and threw it.

I knew why the hangers-on were making themselves scarce.

'I'll beat you tomorrow – *officially*. You won't stand a prayer. They'll all beat you – they'll *kill* you.'

'I know,' I said humbly. 'I'm no good at all.'

She looked at me, suspecting another Est trick. She had finally stopped throwing bricks.

'I'm no good at all,' I repeated. 'My bike beat you. You didn't know how good it was.'

'Yes,' she snapped, with a brisk nod of her head.

'Like to have a ride on her – no catch?'

She glared, like a wildcat that's just been offered a bit of fresh steak. She'd have liked to have said no. But she could never resist a bike, Keri. She pulled Mitzi upright with a heave of her broad shoulders. 'You've scratched it.'

'One of your little mates made me crash.'

'Serve you right. How do you start it? No, you're not riding pillion. Just show me how to start it.'

I tried showing her other things but she was already gone. Round the course again . . .

She came past the first time, cranking over so fast and hard I said goodbye to her and Mitzi both. Mitzi thought her last hour had come too, the amount of bleeping she was putting up.

The second time, I just shut my eyes and waited for the scrunch of metal.

There was a snigger.

She'd idled up to me, so slowly I hadn't heard a thing.

'Good bike. Touched a hundred and ninety down Vauxhall Bridge Road.'

'She can do more.'

'Not in this dump. I don't want to wreck her. I like the way she chirrups. Like a pet canary.'

'Tried the radio?'

She played with the buttons. When she got Tokyo, her face lit up like a child's. 'She must be lonely, so far from home.' Talking about the bike as if it was a living thing; stroking the handlebars.

'Keep her,' I said. 'As a present.'

She just stared.

'I'm no Racer,' I said, fiddling with the zip of my leathers.

'You're not bad,' she said. 'You might shape up.'

'I want you to have her.'

'Why, for Christ's sake?'

'Because your bike's a death-trap. I don't want you getting killed.'

'Naff off. What do you care about me?'

'I think I've fallen in love with you.'

She reached for another half-brick . . .

'Look,' I said, when she finally stopped. 'Let's go for a drink and talk things over. You ride Mitzi and I'll ride yours.'

'I'll come for the ride.'

We found a snack-bar by the Lambeth Gate. Closing down, nearly empty. She bought her own coke. 'My old

Dad always said, when somebody gives you something, they expect something back . . .' But she kept on examining me, as if I was the Loch Ness Monster. 'Ain't you got no Est girls keen on you? You're not bad looking.'

'Neither are you.'

She twisted her face into a hideous mass of wrinkles. 'Yeah, I use sump-oil for foundation-cream and gunk for mascara! Sorry, Sellers – love's just not my zone – makes yer soft for racing. Feller starts hangin' round the pits making goo-goo eyes, yer start worryin' about crashing and spoiling yer looks, and yer dead. Push off, Sellers. I can't do with yer hangin' around.'

'Why don't you push off with me?'

'Wotcher mean?'

'We could share the bike – see a few places. Birmingham, Leeds, Glasgow. Have a holiday . . .'

'What the hell's a holiday?' Her face set hard. 'By the time I got back here, there'd be a new Champ. They'd've forgotten me.'

'You could make them remember you – if you had Mitzi.'

'I wouldn't ride Mitzi – that's cheating. Still, I'd like to see what she could do on a motorway . . .'

'Come for a week,' I coaxed. 'They won't forget you in a week.'

She giggled. 'Champ and ex-Champ vanish on dirty weekend. That'd make the telly-gogglers' hair stand on end. They'd have to start preliminary heats all over again. And by the time they'd finished, I'd be back. OK, I'll come. But no beddy-beddy, right? I'm as tight as a GKN lock-nut.'

'Right! But by the way, my real name is Kitson.'

11

I picked her up at ten; she wouldn't start before. All Unnems were dopey in the mornings. I was starting to notice the effect myself. At Cambridge, my feet had hit the floor the moment my baby-blue eyes opened. Here there was a swamp-time, between sleep and waking; a swamp in which you lay feeling you'd never move again. Once up, you felt better; by mid-morning, the feeling was gone.

Keri came out rubbing her eyes, a tight bundle under her arm that I stowed in the right-hand pannier. Her face looked like she'd been coal-mining all night, then lost her sack of coal. She took a last look round that dreary townscape, as if she might suddenly fall in love with it. She looked so lost I nearly scrubbed the whole expedition . . .

But she cheered up when I let her drive; got astride, rocked from side to side getting the balance of the bike. Worked her shapely bottom deep into the seat, like a cat making a nest. Grinned over her shoulder.

'What we waiting for, Kitson?'

We toured the London Wire, sussing out the gates till Keri found one manned by the ageing, dwindling British Police.

'Right,' she said. 'I can soft-soap my way through that lot. Paramils is impossible.'

And soft-soap them she did. It was the first time I'd seen her do the Famous Keri Roberts Act, as seen on TV. She pulled up at the gate, took off her helmet, shook her glorious hair loose, unzipped her leathers and did her famous Victory Stretch and Yawn, which made the most of her magnificent boobs.

The cops stared; then gaped.

'Hey, you're the famous Keri Roberts . . .' After that, it was all over bar the shouting. And about ten minutes of signing autographs, flirting, and letting herself be generally mauled by the constabulary. I saw her mouth tighten once or twice, under the plastic gaiety. I felt like throwing up. When they'd finally stopped posing with her, using the security camera to take pin-ups, they let us go. On a week's pass, to race in Glasgow. Having stuffed the pass down the front of her teeshirt . . .

We ripped away, leaving them beaming.

'God,' I yelled, 'don't you feel *dirty*?'

She braked so hard she nearly had us both over the handlebars. She thrust her face so close to mine, my visor steamed up.

'Look, you wanted to get out of that bloody gate; *I* got us out. If you don't like the way I do it, you can take your bloody electric toaster and *go*.'

'Letting them maul you like that!'

'Look, this is *your* bike and *my* body. We didn't do a swap.'

'Put your helmet back on,' I snapped, 'before the psy-chopter spots you having a fit.'

Unfair. If there was a psychopter within kilometres, it wasn't taking any notice of us.

The motorway was dreamy, climbing and swooping like a hawk. After the cramped deadliness of the back-streets, it was paradise for Keri. She hunted down the Est cars, overtook them one after another. The occupants of vintage Rollses, open four-litre Bentleys, stared outraged. A few fought back sneakily, suddenly accelerating as we overtook them, or swerving out murderously into the fast lane. Keri overtook them on the inside, laughing, sticking up two fingers, happy and free. I could feel her happiness, through my hands clasped tightly round her leathered waist.

'D'you *have* to do that?' she snarled.

'I'm *nervous*,' I smiled.

The happiness didn't last. I could see Ests reaching for their car-phones, complaining to motorway-control. Finally, north of Rugby, a cop-bike flagged us down. Keri gave him her famous stretch-and-boobs routine. It nearly didn't work. As he rode away he said, 'Don't annoy the cars. Control nearly sent Paramils, but I was nearer.'

'Lay off, will you?' I shouted at her, standing on the verge.

'Lay off what?'

'Burning off the Ests – flashing your body – fooling with the fuzz. D'you want a ride back to London in the Black Maria?'

'Look – I do what *I* want, see? If you'd wanted a well-mannered Est lady, you ought to've stuck with that . . . Vanessa.' She glared round, looking for something to throw.

'Look, Keri, there's more to life than screwing people . . .'

'Like what?'

'That's what we're going north to find out. Give yourself time . . .'

'I could be dead tomorrow!'

'I'm afraid that's not very likely now.'

She zipped-up her leathers violently, catching one boob enough to make her wince. A tear trickled down one cheek. She wiped at it savagely with her gauntlet, leaving an oily smear. 'I'm all confused. It's so *big* outside London.'

'Maybe the bigness could be nice?'

She nodded wearily. 'OK. We'll do it your way.'

Beyond Stafford, hills began to rear up to our right. At first, it was just estates and factories on higher ground. But the hills went on getting bigger and bigger, like tigers trapped under a net of Wires and perimeter-lights and tower-blocks. Then one suddenly thrust up a bare crest and roared of freedom. Its sides were dun, spotted and textured with gorse and heather. No more Wires, just old blackstone walls like tiger-stripes, broken into gaps in places, with sheep as small as fleas scurrying from one field to another. The cloud-shadows drifted freely over them, ignoring even the blackstone walls.

Still the hills grew, till their bareness had conquered all one side of the motorway. Open fields began to appear on our left as well.

When the last estate was only a distant sun-glitter through the smoke-haze, we pulled into a lay-by. Huge concrete litter-bins spilled waterfalls of gleaming coke-tins down the hillside. Endless robo-trucks passed us, blat, blat, blat, making the bike rock.

But even their fumes couldn't block out the huge bracken-and-water smell of the hills. Keri had never smelt it before. I watched her nose working like a little animal's. Her eyes looked alternately happy and puzzled.

And in the gaps between the robos came silences, when we could hear a sheep bleating half a kilometre away.

Still astride the bike, Keri took off her helmet and ran her fingers through her hair. 'I never knew this was here.'

'You had maps at school . . .'

'Only maps of London. Hardly went to school. Anyway, you can't *smell* maps.' She sucked in great lungfuls of air, heedless of her sliding zip and my feelings. 'A lot of people would like to come up here, if they knew. Things are so far apart . . . there's room . . .' She got off the bike, picked up a big stone and threw it down the hillside, watching it leap and bound till it came to rest in a tinkling little stream. Then she gave me a sly look. 'I suppose this is what you mean by the bigness being nice? You can think straight because there's nothing happening.'

Famous last words. A green patrol-car was coming up the hill, caught in the traffic-stream. Something warned me to bend over and pretend to inspect the bike's terminals.

Utterly predictable, the patrol-car left-winkered, turned off from the traffic-stream, crunched across the lay-by. Utterly predictable, two Paramils got out, one lying back to cover the other. How small they were; how neat. Khaki shirts beautifully ironed, brasses gleaming like silver, visors at that arrogant tilt, right thumbs stuck in their belts, handy for the blaster-holsters which had their flaps casually undone ... Smooth khaki faces. Did they ever have to shave? Khaki faces, exotic as oranges against that heather-covered hillside. The reality of those English hills fought against the reality of the Paramils, and the English hills began to win. I had a near-irresistible urge to shout, 'What are you *doing* here?'

The front one held out his hand. I put our IDs into it, as humbly as I could manage. Then the gate-pass. Keri had to fish it out of its last resting-place. The Paramil watched her with unmoving celestial disgust.

'Why are the two of you riding on the same motor cycle?'

'It's a two-seater.' I indicated the two seats with sarcastic swoops of my hand. The stroppy Tech note got into my voice. His calm black eyes noted it. I could have kicked myself; half of whatever safety-margin we'd had was gone.

'Why have you stopped here? This is not an authorized parking-place for motor cycles.'

'Engine's overheating. We've had to let it cool.'

'You have broken down?' He sounded almost eager, moving in for the kill. Behind me, Keri gave a touch to the starter-button. The bike whined emptily, sickeningly, twice. Then started.

I held out my hand for our IDs. The Paramil didn't move, watching my face with calm interest. Half of me wanted to go down on my knees and plead; the other half wanted to hit him. The smooth brown face knew it all; went on waiting.

'Please!' I said.

He handed me the papers silently, turned back to his car.

We went on. The Ests didn't bother to report us, now *they* were doing the overtaking. Lunchtime came. The Ests went to dine. Those juggernauts that still had drivers pulled obediently off the road, at the authorized place. Even the robos seemed to have vanished for a quick tweak-up of their electronics.

The empty road, the shadowed hills, drew us on. Mitzi's faint whine just made the silence more profound. The motorway climbed, giving glimpses of further hills and further, an infinite blue lostness that blew our minds. I heard garbled noises: Keri singing inside her helmet.

It wasn't the Paramils that stopped us in the end. North-east, the sky darkened. The far sunlit hills glowed ghostly and glass-like, then began to vanish behind purple scarves of rain. I nudged Keri, pointed. She nodded, irritably, already on the lookout for shelter. But now we needed an authorized place, preferably complete with robo-caff . . . zilch.

A great spur of the Pennines thrust across our path. The motorway cut a nick straight through it. As we approached, the nick widened into an immense cutting, its sides crumbled and tumbled in red riven blocks of sandstone. Keri must've spotted something: as the first huge drops of rain splattered and snaked across my visor, she turned across the hard shoulder onto turf that rutted smoothly under our wheels. We shot into a cleft in the rock, behind a line of boulders fallen like dominoes that totally cut us off from the motorway.

At the back was a cave. We ran into it, shouting, as the thunderstorm struck. Inside, there was a rusty shovel, plastic bags. Workmen must have used it before us, many years ago, when the motorway was being built.

It was some storm: the savage exciting kick of lightning; the heavy hand of thunder, pressing down on the rock, pressing us deeper into the cave. The rain coming down in rods, running in curving streams off Mitzi's handlebars. Making privacy. Nobody had been here in fifty years. Who'd come in the next fifty?

Keri and I. Alone.

Part of my mind was still trying to fret. Suppose Mitzi

got struck by lightning? Suppose damp got into the electrics? But the great smell of greenery calmed me, even if it was just the newly-ripped grass in Mitzi's tyre-treads.

Drips of water, working down through the roof, tapped smartly on our helmets, driving us deeper into the dark. There, Keri settled in stillness, ignoring the drips on her helmet, face dim and unreadable in the green storm-light.

'You OK?' I asked, finding the silence unbearable.

She didn't answer at first; then she said in a dreamy voice, 'I like it here.'

'Yeah, snug. Want a fag?'

'No. I want to *smell* things.'

'Suit yourself.' I lit up, to show I was independent-minded. Blew smoke-rings. 'Make a good camp this. Deep enough. Bit noisy when the lorries start again. And a bit hard to lie on.' I picked stones from under my backside and threw them outside, narrowly, but carefully, missing the bike.

'Sit still, can't you?' She took off her helmet, lay back on a rock-pile, held her mouth open, so that drips from the roof fell into it. Then she reached out and stroked the cave walls, found a little tuft of fern growing miraculously in a dark cranny. Pulled off one fern-leaf, held it against the rain-light, unfolding its tight curl lovingly, stroking it. I listened to her breathing; she had an odd little quiver at the end of each breath. The whole world was full of her breathing.

Then I suddenly and ridiculously got jealous. 'What's up wi' you – having a fit?'

'It's all so . . . old.'

'This motorway was only built fifty years ago.'

'I mean the rocks, you soulless Tech. It makes everything in London seem so . . . plastic.'

'The atoms in plastic are as old as the atoms in rock!'

She sat up abruptly. 'Might as well go – the rain's stopping.' As she pushed her way angrily past, it entered my thick skull that I'd missed some kind of chance with her.

'What do you want? We can stay here the night if you like.'

'No. This place is spoilt, now.' But she sat down again; picked up a stray coke-tin and threw it outside. It hit one end of Mitzi's handlebars and flew wildly in the air.

'Hey, mind my bike!'

Silence.

'Hey, I could find you a better cave than this.'

'Where?' She was dead serious; turned towards me, so that her face was plunged in darkness, but the edges of her hair were lit up by the returning sunlight outside.

'North.'

'*Glasgow?*'

'Further north than Glasgow.'

'There's nothing past Glasgow.'

'Yeah, bags and bags of nothing. No estates, no Paramils, not even roads, much. Just mountains. We could camp.'

'What's camping?'

I explained. 'We can buy a tent and stuff in Glasgow.'

'No, nearer! I want to camp tonight. I might even think of holding your hand, Kitson.'

'We'll try Carlisle.' Half of me was crazy to get her alone. The other, deeper, half was remembering that Scott-Astbury made his big mistake in the Scottish Highlands.

12

Carlisle lay sleeping, if not dying, among its darkening hills. Carlisle wasn't needed any more. The surrounding farms were automated. Robo-trucks reached Glasgow without an overnight stop. Long before we reached the Carlisle Wire, we passed through whole suburbs reduced to low mounds under grass, their crumbling tarmac streets leading nowhere, except to solitary lamp-posts.

The sergeant on the gate was British Police. He was gardening, his blaster hanging from the rusting wire. He was reluctant to break off his chat with an old man sitting on an upturned bucket, a slow argument about how to thin carrots. He paused just long enough to raise the barrier-pole just high enough for us to ride under. Didn't even give us a glance, let alone check our ID.

The town centre was derelict. Roofless, windowless houses peered from side-streets. Botchergate was full of the ghosts of shops whose windows announced emptily that they'd once sold cattle-feed, fishing-tackle, Eley-Kynoch shotgun-cartridges. Even the closing-down-sale notices were curled and faded beyond deciphering. All that seemed left in the gathering dusk was the dark bulk of the cathedral, one garish supermarket surrounded by smashed trolleys, and Vic Huggett's Bargain Mart, the Shop That Sells Everything.

The supermarket filled the dusk with flickering blue light. The few people inside moved slowly, jerkily, like some automated toy running down.

Vic Huggett's was dimly lit. It gave the impression of having burst at the seams, for the pavements outside were stacked with wardrobes and elephantine sofas. I wondered what Vic did when it rained. The peeling veneers on the wardrobes, one squelch of my hand on a plastic settee, convinced me that Vic did nothing.

We plunged in. Bare electric light bulbs only made the air seem darker. In murky corners and on stairs, candles and glass-bellied oil-lamps flickered. Smells of rising damp and dry rot.

'And what can I do for *you*?' The deep voice enjoyed making us jump; its owner emerged from a littered office hidden behind a chest of drawers, lit by another oil-lamp. A huge pear-shaped man, in frayed maroon jumper, baggy, grey trousers and carpet-slippers. A deeply bearded man, who moved like he had woodworm in both legs and smelt like he had mushrooms growing in his beard. In the dimness, he could've been any age.

To gain time, I asked about spare tyres for Mitzi, knowing he wouldn't have any.

He went out to poke through a tangle of rubber in the backyard, urging us over his shoulder to keep looking around. We walked from room to room, upstairs and down, staring at wallpaper hanging off walls, holes in the ceiling where plaster had fallen and dark strings of fungus swayed in the draught, groping for a new victim. I heaved on the handle of a huge suitcase. The top ripped away, sending full jamjars with rusted lids rolling across the sloping floor. I kicked a bucket full of rainwater, that immediately began to leak. An endless succession of the ancient, the useless, the blackly ugly . . .

'It's like a graveyard,' said Keri.

'Useful stuff in graveyards.'

'Like what?'

'Bones for your doggie . . .' I groped under an ancient washing-machine. 'We could use this pan.'

'You don't know what's been in it.'

'It'll boil clean. Better than nothing, if we're going camping.'

'Whatever turns you on. There's a plastic jug – if it doesn't leak.'

Just then, there was a dusty little whirr up in the ceiling.

'Rats,' squeaked Keri. Delighted she was woman enough to be scared of rats, I grabbed a broken golf-club and poked violently at the patch of dark strands where the rat was lurking.

The golf-club slid off something small, round, hard and permanent.

Again, it whirred. Then I knew what it was. A mickey-mouse: a closed-circuit TV security-eye. The slob downstairs was trying to spy on us. But, hard luck for him, his mickey-mouse was suffering from damp and rust, like everything else in his crappy shop. Otherwise it wouldn't be making that give-away noise. Or still be trying, for the third time, to focus on us. I got Keri behind a sagging bookcase that smelled like Shakespeare's grave, before the little black lens finally got itself pointed in our direction.

My mind was whirling. Two kinds of people still used mickey-mouses. The poshest shops in the London enclave . . .

And Paramils.

I glanced round the crap-museum; nothing worth pinching. The slob downstairs couldn't *afford* mickey-mouses.

Paramils? Paramils wouldn't let mickey-mouses get into that kind of mess.

Either he'd stolen it (he looked the type to steal anti-thief devices) or the Paramils had given it to him. Either way made him pretty unhealthy company. I put my finger to my lips and led the way downstairs, still carrying jug and pan.

He loomed behind us again, noiselessly.

'Jugs and pans? Going camping?'

His voice was far too eager. It warned me just in time.

'No, we're Racers. Going racing in Glasgow.'

'But camping on the way?' he said, genially, indulgently.

'No.'

'What you want a pan for, then?'

'Doing oil-changes on the bike,' I said quickly, before Keri could open her mouth.

'I'm not selling you good pans for that!'

'What's it matter to you what we use the pan for? You get your credits, make your profit.'

'Matter of principle. *My* pans are for camping.'

'You got camping on the brain or something?'

'Oh, it's a grand life. You and your girl in your little tent, out in the blue, miles from anybody, snug as a bug in a rug.' His tongue travelled across his lower lip, like two slugs mating.

'We haven't got a little tent,' I said. That really spoilt his day. I stepped outside and tried to jam first the jug, then the pan, under Mitzi's oil-sump. 'Too big,' I said, and slung them back on a pile of other junk.

From his expression, you'd have thought I'd kicked his shins with hobnailed boots. But he forced a smile back, though he nearly had to use a car-jack to do it. 'Keep on looking round, squire. Never know what you'll find.'

I should have grabbed Keri and scarpered then. But suddenly he interested me. He was more than a man selling lousy pans; more than a dirty old man, day-dreaming about what boys and girls got up to in tents . . . We mooched round the shadowy crap again, eventually emerging with a couple of antique rock-and-roll tapes.

He didn't want to sell us rock-and-roll tapes, but he let us pay for them, dully. Then suddenly bent behind the counter where we couldn't see what he was doing, and straightened up all cheerful with the tapes wrapped in newspaper. Enjoyed stuffing them into Keri's breast-pocket.

Maybe he *was* just a dirty old man. Maybe he only used his mickey-mouse to spy on kids who went upstairs for a bit of grope and fumble on his damp mattresses . . .

But as we were going out, he drew me aside by one elbow. 'Look at this, squire.' He drew out, from under a sag-bellied sideboard, a green canvas bag. Pulled out green folds of thick nylon. 'Isn't that a lovely tent, squire? Built-in fly-sheet and ground-sheet. And a camping stove . . . lightweight nest of pans . . .'

Keri's eyes grew wide. Everything we'd wanted.

'Fifty credits to you, squire. You won't find a bargain like that, between here and London.'

'Fall off a lorry, did it?'

'Guy riding down from the north. Needed money for juice.'

I bent forward. Saw, on the tent's door-flap, faint smudges and streaks of silver powder. Somebody'd tried to wipe them off, but hadn't tried hard enough. That tent had recently been dusted for fingerprints. That tent had been used in court as criminal evidence. Of what?

I straightened up. 'No thanks.'

'Take it to sell,' he coaxed. 'You're certain to make a good profit.'

'No, we haven't got room on the bike.'

'Suit yourself.' He pushed the tent roughly back under the sideboard and stalked off into the darkness.

Why should an Unnem like him use the word 'squire'? Squire was a Tech word.

'You're *mad!*' said Keri, starting up the bike with vicious fingers. 'We'll never get another tent like that. You just lost me. I'm going back to London.'

'We need a tent,' I said, 'and we're offered one just like *that*? Is life normally *that* kind to you? As you would say, what's the catch?'

She looked thoughtful. I explained my suspicions.

'Let's get the hell out, then.'

'No – he interests me. Ride around town while I think.'

I saw the answer to my prayers eventually. Sitting dejectedly on a kerb, throwing stones at a coke-can in the middle of the road. From the way he hit the can every time, he'd spent his life practising. We pulled up and I said, 'Fancy a ride on this bike?'

His eyes lit up like instant Christmas.

I pulled off my leathers and helmet, and while he was struggling into them, I drew Keri on one side.

'Drive past Vic Huggett's and then out through the gate. Make plenty of noise – get noticed. Drive this poor slob around a bit, then park among those grass mounds we saw coming in. Keep out of sight. Make him lie down, even if you have to seduce him.'

'Anything else? You ask so little of me . . .'

The lad came across, the beatific grin still on his face.

'Pull your visor down,' I snapped. 'Don't you know it's against the law, to ride with your visor up?'

'Yes, sir,' he said humbly. He wasn't very bright.

Off they ripped, passing the shop that sold everything, with a brilliant squeal of tyres. Old Vic peered out, and watched them avidly till they were out of sight. Suddenly, I felt afraid for Keri. Then Vic withdrew his head, like a wrinkled old tortoise.

I gave him a minute, then slid into his shop by one of its several back-entrances. I hardly breathed. I had a nasty feeling he was listening for me, as I was listening for him. And I was wearing boots whereas he was wearing carpet-slippers.

Somewhere, his phone rang. His voice answered it, deep and wheezy. 'Yes, sergeant? They've gone, have they? Back along the road to the motorway?'

He was talking to the gate-guard. About us.

'I'll ring our Paramil friends, then. Not that they'll pay much for this pair. They wouldn't buy the tent – the boy smelt a rat. Sharp little sod. But I managed to slip a hiking-compass into the girl's pocket . . . Yes, evidence of a sort, but not enough. They'll get a week's jail, on suspicion, and we'll get twenty lousy credits between us.

'Yes . . . a tent is *certain* evidence of intention to camp. Gets them sent straight to the lobo-farm, every time. And gets *us* five hundred credits. Can't tell you how much money that tent's made for me over the years . . . the

Paramils always bring it back afterwards. Well, I'd better ring them. Don't worry, sergeant, you'll soon learn the ropes . . . your predecessor did very well out of it. Bought himself a bungalow in the Devon Enclave.'

I listened, incredulous, while he rang the Paramils, gave them our bike-registration, and accused us of intent to camp. Would Keri get off the road before the Paramils spotted her?

When he put the phone down, I stepped out.

'Do you enjoy selling people to the lobo-farm?'

He didn't waste time feeling guilty. Grabbed up the phone. Luckily I'd noticed where the junction-box was. I ripped the phone out by the roots.

His hands went down behind the counter again. Came up holding something that glistened blue-black in the lamplight. An antique revolver. It didn't occur to me it might be loaded, till he swung it towards me.

I grabbed the barrel and pushed it upwards, away from my face. The barrel was hexagonal, sharp-edged, cold. I went on pushing it back towards him. I couldn't think what else to do. He was strong with corded muscles under that wrinkled fat. He was using every ounce of his weight to bear me down.

But he was old. His face, horribly close to mine, went red, then white. Drops of sweat grew on his forehead, ran down into his bushy eyebrows, caught there like flies in a web, then trickled down each side of his nose. He began to pant; his mouth gaped, smelling faintly of old whisky and hay. Then his panting got a shudder in it. The arm that held the gun began to shake; then his whole body, as it pressed against mine. And all the time I forced his arm back and back.

There was a bang like the end of the world. The gun-barrel went hot in my hand. Sharp bits of stuff showered down from the ceiling, blinding me. I panicked; all I could think of was pushing his arm back harder . . . keep the gun away.

The gun kicked and banged again, less loudly. Maybe the first bang had made me deaf. Stuff showered across my face again, but wet and scalding now, not cold plaster-dust. A bit fell on my lip and I licked it. It tasted salty . . .

I opened my eyes. We stared at each other, centimetres apart. His face was like a globe of the world with every wrinkled mountain-chain and sweat-filled river marked in. His eyes were wide open, deeply puzzled.

'Meeurgh?' he asked me. 'Meeurgh?' He looked so hurt and baffled.

The side of his head above the gun-barrel was no longer there. The ear was gone as well.

He let go the gun; grabbed me like I was his mother.

'Meeurgh? Meeurgh?' he asked with increasing desperation. Then lost all interest in me. Swung away, arms wide, big hands groping. Lurched past the spindly desk with the oil-lamp burning, missing it by centimetres. Tried to climb a towering bookcase. He climbed amazingly. I was glad I couldn't see the other side of his head.

When he was halfway up, the bookcase tore loose from the wall, with a long screech. For a second, it hung over the table and oil-lamp. Then everything collapsed, and I was staring at a mountain of books and splintered planks, with his slippered feet sticking out the bottom.

There was a whumf. A hot wind seared my face. When I opened my eyes, there was flame on the curtains, the floor, the scattered books, my own arm.

I ran, beating my burning arm against my body. It didn't seem to hurt; the flames went out. I was out of the back door, leaping the sagging fence like a hurdler. Not a good hurdler . . .

The fall calmed me; my Tech training took control. Drew my attention to my right hand, which was still holding the gun. Made me walk straight back into the shop, up the smoke-filled passage till I got in sight of . . .

A roaring mass of flame; no sound but the crackling of flames. I was grateful for that. I threw the gun into the

middle of the flames and got out before the remaining
bullets exploded.

Tech training also suggested I might leave less of a trail
if I kept to the streets. Suggested I should clean my face.
Suggested I might roll the sleeve of my sweater up, so the
burnt place didn't show. I began to appreciate my Tech
training quite a lot.

I slowly walked away from the shop, turned the corner.
Nobody seemed to have noticed anything. No shouting,
no running figures. Looking back, I saw why. The shop
was huge, and the fire was buried right in the middle of
it. True, every window was filled with orange light, and
a lot of smoke was pouring out of the chimneys. But it
just looked cheerful and jolly, like a Christmas card.

And it was the time of night when people eat, or gather
round the Box or a friendly fire. I shuddered . . . but the
streets remained empty, as I trudged towards the gate. I felt
numb, flat, willing to let happen what would happen.

Nothing happened. As I passed the gate, the gate-guard
and his old friend were putting tools away in a shed. Still
arguing about carrots . . . At the bend of the road, I gave a
last look back. They had come out of the shed and had their
backs to me, staring at a column of smoke that was growing
over the town.

Round the corner, I began to run; ran till my guts were
heaving. Only pulling up twice, as a car passed. But they
didn't notice me either. Too busy peering at the orange
light that silhouetted the black broken roofs of Carlisle.

Keri had the boy well hidden. I heard them before I saw
them, as I wandered rather hopelessly over the grass-grown
mounds. So many mounds; Carlisle had shrunk from a city
to a town.

They were lying full-length, smoking and chattering their
heads off. Their fag-ends looked friendly in the dark. I felt
weakly jealous, because Keri was laughing with him in a

way she never did with me. I threw myself down between them; lit a fag with shaking hands.

Keri said, 'What happened?'

My cold Tech side took over, assessing *facts*.

We had an alibi for Vic's death. Vic had given it to us himself, when he phoned the Paramils. The gate-guard would confirm it, when the Paramils got to him.

But this kid, grinning hopefully in the dusk, could blow it all. If he once opened his mouth . . .

'What *happened*?' Keri repeated. With the kid all ears. For all I knew, she'd opened her big mouth too much to him already. I said angrily, 'I couldn't get a thing to eat. You didn't give me any bloody money, did you?'

She opened her mouth to ask what the hell I was talking about. When I squeezed her arm, warningly, she closed it again with a snap. The kid said eagerly, 'I can get you some grub, easy. We got a big allotment . . . potatoes, eggs. I didn't know what you wanted. I owe you for the ride. We can put you up for the night. Me mum's a good cook . . .'

I felt rotten, turning on him. But it was for his sake, too. If he got involved in a Paramil inquiry, they'd probably ship him off to the lobo-farm, just to keep the records tidy. I hardened my heart and said, 'By the way, you have *got* a permit to ride motor bikes, mate, haven't you? Never thought to ask, before I offered you a ride. Only it's a bad offence to ride without one – the Paramils will have you for it. Two years in the nick . . .'

He looked terrified at the mention of Paramils. 'Permit? What permit? I ain't got no permit.'

'Then you are in *real* trouble.'

'What can I do?' He turned to Keri, desperately. So did I. If she gave the wrong answer now, I didn't know *what* I was going to do with him.

'It's all right, Lenny,' she said. 'We won't split on you. *Will* we, Kit?' She looked at me daggers, over his shoulder; a big row was certainly on the way.

'No,' I said. 'We won't split, Lenny. Keri would get in trouble too. Just keep your own lip buttoned. Don't even mention meeting us. You wouldn't like Keri to go to prison, would you?'

'Cross my heart,' he said. 'I'll look after you, Keri.'

'I know you will.' She gave him a hug, and not just to spite me, either.

'Run along, sunshine,' I said. 'And keep that lip buttoned.'

'Goodbye, Keri.' Then he was gone, scampering over the mounds.

Keri turned, tears in her eyes. 'You cheap Est bastard. What the hell are you playing at? I could *kill* you.'

I opened my mouth to tell her all. Then shut it. I could tell her nothing.

The Paramils would still pick us up. They had our registration, and we'd been the last people to see Vic alive. They'd grill us, with a psycho-radar pinging away in our very ears. *I* might manage to lie successfully. I'd been an Est and a Tech. I knew how to keep my mind cool, I knew how to bluff. But Keri was a babe in arms; they'd have her for breakfast.

Unless I told her nothing. Unless she *was* completely innocent.

There remained the small matter of the hiking-compass. I noticed she still had Vic's newspaper packet, tucked in her top pocket.

'I'll look after that,' I said, and lifted it, without waiting for permission. I opened the end of the packet, and let the little round knob of the hiking-compass fall to the grass silently, in the dark.

'Why're you such a sod, Kitson?' asked Keri, ominously.

'Call it pure Est jealousy. I don't want you snogging around with yobs like Lenny. OK?'

'I could *kill* you,' she said again. She was flaming. So much the better. Psycho-radar can distinguish good honest rage from fear.

She slammed the bike forward like she was squashing me under the front wheel.

We were only ten kilometres from Glasgow when they caught us. Vic's death must have really got their knickers in a twist. A patrol-car came up behind, pinning us with its headlights like some fluttering moth. Their big red stop-sign began to flash and we pulled off on to a lay-by.

I've never seen anything so fast. We were spotlighted in the beams from three cars and stripped naked before we could draw breath. Nice, being a peep-show for the lines of juggers roaring past. Maybe we even gave the robos a twinge in their electronics. It just didn't feel very sexy to us: the wind was cold.

They stripped the bike, too, leaving everything lying on the cinders; and they weren't too careful where they put their feet. I heard a bottle crunch in Keri's luggage. They searched everything three times in all. And found only the two tapes . . . Keri was volcanic; called the Paramil captain a Buddhist eunuch. He was impressed; their psycho-radars gave them one genuinely outraged female. As always, they were logical; shrugged and told her to get dressed. Then she found her broken bottle, and the psycho-radar almost broke its loudspeaker.

By the time they turned on me, it was too late. All I was giving out was anger, too.

'You bought these tapes in Carlisle?' the captain asked.

'Yeah. What's it to you?'

'What was the shopkeeper doing when you left?'

'Counting the credits I'd given him.'

The Captain smiled his small and velvet smile. 'And what did you think of the shopkeeper?' I took a deep breath.

'A nutter.' I said. 'Kept trying to sell us a bloody tent. He had camping on the brain. Camping's illegal, innit?' I put on my typical thick-Racer act again.

'Who told you that?' Under the spotlight, the pupils of his eyes narrowed for a moment; his eyes began to blink quite rapidly, till he slowed them down by an effort of will. I'd never seen a Paramil so put out.

'Some feller in a caff in London,' I said. 'Was he a nutter as well? Is camping illegal or not?'

Again his blink-rate went up. (Bull's-eye, I thought.) He said, 'What did this man in the cafeteria look like? And which cafeteria?'

I gave him a list of six possible cafeterias, and a description of my late headmaster. 'Well, *is* camping illegal or not?'

There was a crowd gathering. Truck-drivers, a few curious Ests in shootin'-and-fishin' clothes. They were getting tired of gawping at my nakedness; starting to take an interest in the legality of camping . . . I was becoming inconvenient. Downright embarrassing.

The captain communed with Buddha for a moment then, with a curl of the lip, let us go.

13

Old Vic pointed the gun at me again. I pushed back his arm. His face glared. The gun exploded. The bookcase fell and the flames leapt everywhere . . .

I wakened, sweating. Lay consoling myself that the nightmare was getting less vivid.

I looked across at Keri's bed, but she'd gone. Racing. God, Glasgow was an awful place. No Est enclave; Glasgow was being allowed to go to pot. The huge black Doric columns of the public buildings were covered in graffiti from top to bottom; the famous art gallery was roofless after a fire. We'd found a boarding-house that cost the earth, run by a giant frizzy-haired Scotswoman who called everybody 'hen', ambushed you in corridors and talked interminably about her wee man, who'd been dead thirty years. But at least there was a stout bedroom door and I'd bought a padlock and moved Mitzi in with us, in spite of mother-hen's protests that even pets weren't allowed.

'Mitzi's house-trained. She frets if I leave her.'

She'd taken our credits, so there wasn't much she could do.

First morning, there was hammering on the bedroom door. Keri unlocked it, was driven across the room by a horde of guys letting off flashbulbs and thrusting TV cameras in her face.

'They missed you on the Box last night, Keri. What you trying to *do* to us?'

'You racing today? Or is there a secret romance?' The cameras swung momentarily onto me.

'Racing,' said Keri. Well, more a low snarl.

'Aren't you sleeping with him?'

She nodded to where she'd parked Mitzi's oily muddiness pointedly between the two beds. Then made the mistake of yawning and stretching. Cameras clicked.

'Hold it, Keri! Perfect! Undo your zip a bit more?'

I couldn't kill them all.

The race-circuit ran round the city centre. (At least, in London they'd kept the circuit free of broken bottles.) The spectators seemed permanently drunk, waving on their favourites with those bayonets and cutlasses that Glaswegians were always so fond of. Several people lost ears; everyone enjoyed the joke. I kept my crash-helmet on. I said racing was so dangerous in Glasgow even the spectators needed crash-helmets. Keri didn't find it funny.

I've never seen Paramils walk so wary; always in threes, blaster-holsters open. But you never saw much of them, especially after dark.

The famous Keri Roberts didn't win the first race; she wisely stayed behind the field, sussing out the track. Came back with blood on her leathers, but somebody else's.

Between races, she worked hard proving that I didn't exist. Busy swopping those incredible Racer-jokes. Like the guy who had the top of his skull ripped off by a low traffic-light, but still won by a short head.

I tried to find things to do, like checking her tyres. But the bike they'd given her was very new. And Racers have no time for mechanics. They began elbowing me away from her, treading on my feet, kicking me when my back was bent.

She won the second race. In such style that the wing of a robo-truck ripped her leathers from gauntlet to shoulder. The Scottish Champion lodged an incoherent Scottish protest. He was a totally bald kid who gained a lot of ground dragging his steel right boot on the corners. It wore out daily. He used it in fights, too. He called Keri a little Sassenach hooer. But even he gave back when she looked at him. Her face was white as scraped bone. She had bitten her lip, on the scar where she always bit it, when she was racing. A trickle of blood wound down her chin. Her eyes were sunken, wild. When I tried to calm her down, she hit me. I slunk back to the boarding-house. I couldn't bear to wait for the final accident; I knew I'd lost her.

That had been two days ago. I'd spent a lot of time staring at the wallpaper since. Trying to think of ways of getting her back. Waiting for them to come and tell me she was dead. They'd come all right; the media would want an exclusive interview . . .

Think about something else, Kitson. The illegality of camping, for instance. I'd never thought about camping, till now. It was something Est kids read about in books; or did in the back garden. When they grew up, they never did it. Even Est mountaineers went back to the hotel for a shower and a good meal with wine.

No Tech would *dream* of camping; they'd die without their air-conditioning.

Unnems? I'd had to explain to Keri what camping *was*.

So who was camping? Why were they a threat to the state, worth five-hundred-credits reward?

Ridiculous.

Was it relevant that Vic had operated out of Carlisle? The first owner of that tent, according to Vic, had been a motor cyclist riding down from the north.

The Scottish Highlands?

Where Scott-Astbury had made a mistake? Vanessa had said so: 'Daddy always said Scott-Astbury made a big mistake in Scotland.'

So suppose Scott-Astbury had dropped some great big clanger in Scotland, in the big empty mountainous spaces, where a guy camping with a motor bike might have stumbled across it?

How the hell could I find it? Scotland was *enormous*. I was clutching at straws.

But it was the only clue I had. If Scott-Astbury's mistake had been big and technical, atomic power, say, it would leave big technical clues. Overhead power-cables, roads for heavy vehicles. Which would show up like a sore thumb, in the lonely emptiness of Scotland.

It was better than nothing.

Keri came home early. Dropped onto her bed and closed her eyes, looking like death, her eyebrow twitching.

'Can I get you . . . a drink?'

'I won four times,' she said drearily. 'If I win twice tomorrow, I'm Scottish Champion.'

'Congratulations,' I said, not meaning it.

'And if I win once, they're going to kill me.' She stared at me a long time, eyes empty as the fag-burns in her blanket. 'They've turned against me, Kitson. They're supposed to be *Racers*. What kind of Racer kills his mates?'

'Scottish Racers,' I said bitterly. 'You don't *have* to race.'

'I don't scare easy,' she said. 'I don't mind dying, if it's quick. But being killed by your mates . . .'

'I'll complain to the Paramils . . .'

'Grow up, Kitson. What do the Paramils care? What could they do? It would only take somebody to touch my back wheel when I'm doing a ton. It happens all the time. By accident.'

'With all your fans watching on TV? They wouldn't dare.'

'Why d'you think the fans watch, Kitson? They'll show the action-replay of my death a hundred times. The big pay-off. They'll print souvenir magazines. Write a pop song. I'll be top of the hit-parade for a month.' She closed her eyes again; the eyebrow went on twitching.

'Who's going to kill you? Who says?'

'Their Champion's complained to somebody called Blocky . . . he runs Glasgow . . . he's given permission.'

I was filled with a black rage. 'Where do I find this Blocky?'

'Nobody ever sees him – he sends messages. The Paramils are after him.'

'I'll find him.' As I opened the door, she opened her eyes.

'Be careful, Kitson mate. Glasgow's got different rules from anywhere else . . .'

'I could almost believe you cared . . .'

'Drop dead,' she snarled.

It was a strange walk, looking for Blocky. I once saw a film about Berlin in 1945, all burnt-out walls and rubble. Glasgow was like that. The worst of the wreckage was human.

Everyone I met, I asked where Blocky lived. Said I had an offer that would interest him. I hadn't. But what else could I say? Instead, it was me who had the offers. A little girl of eight offered me a drink of meths; another offered me real plum brandy. Luckily, I caught the whiff of bitter almonds just in time. I had several offers from women, one with a well-grown moustache. I had to break somebody's arm, and nearly got drowned in a sewer.

About five in the morning, a girl with black leathers and black crewcut hair simply walked up to me and said, 'Blocky will see you now.' An Est voice.

'He's taken his bloody time.'

'I've been following you all night. He said if you survived till dawn, you might be amusing.'

She led me to the blank wall of an old bonded warehouse which carried, in huge letters of white glazed brick, the legend, EWART AND SON WHISKY DISTILLERS FOUNDED 1865.

She knocked on a massive rusted iron hatch, which I could've sworn hadn't moved for a hundred years. It opened on silent, oiled hinges. There were two more girls inside and two lads, all slim, black-leathered, crewcut, talking in Est voices. Not carrying bayonets or cutlasses; it made them feel quite dangerous. We went up echoing flights of uncarpeted stairs and burst into a long, gilded hall that might have belonged to a stately home. Except when I tapped on the marble Doric columns I found them plastic. But the oil-paintings of Scottish lairds and stags at bay were genuine enough; the ancient tarnished Adam mirrors, huge Wedgwood vases.

'Don't keep him waiting,' said the girl.

'He kept me waiting.'

She raised her eyebrows, pursed her lips, shook her head. It was more scary than any number of cutlasses. She knocked on a highly polished Georgian door. The cheap brass door-knocker, in the form of an imp, looked somehow out of place in a nasty sort of way.

Blocky was sitting in a Chippendale chair that might have come out of Buckingham Palace. (Later, I was fairly sure it had.) He was fondling the ears of a depressed-looking corgi, that looked like it would rather be asleep, but knew it had better stay awake and have its ears fondled by Blocky.

Blocky was little: about one metre sixty. His tiny feet, in pointed, highly polished, black businessman's shoes, didn't quite touch the floor. I remember a spotless white shirt, Brigade of Guards tie, blue pin-stripe trousers. But the rest of him was wrapped in a quilted maroon dressing-gown, with Chinese dragons writhing all over it.

I nearly killed myself laughing.

I mean, if I'd laughed, he'd have had me killed. It was there in his eyes. China-blue, they sparkled like a young girl's when she's in love. Sparkled with interest and joy. Not joy in life: joy in evil. He grinned at me like a child grins at its presents on Christmas morning. He was going to open me up, sort through me, break some bits, take others apart to find out how they worked. He was *overjoyed* with me. His hair was fine and blond, freshly washed. His skin was clear and pale, but his cheeks shone rosy with health.

'Cigarette?' He held out a full, expensive packet towards me, one fag already pulled forwards like the barrel of a gun. Lit it for me with a silver butane lighter. The flame shot up about ten centimetres; I heard the front of my hair singe and crackle. I was careful not to flinch. He laughed, and put the lighter away.

'Kitson, Henry. Ex-Est, ex-Tech. Welcome to the club. And how do you think you could interest me?'

'Keri Roberts.'

'Your problem. She's Unnem. I only collect Ests.'

'She's National Champ.'

'That won't save her.'

An idea grew in my mind; it seemed to grow out of the air inside that room. One second it wasn't there; the next it was full-blown.

'If your boy won six races off her, *he'd* be National Champ.'

'He couldn't beat her in a million years – unless she gave him the races on a plate. And she wouldn't do that. She's too . . . *honest.*' He said it with a giggle.

'She's a bit tired of racing. She's got a new interest – camping.'

He raised pale eyebrows. Looked down at the corgi, as if sharing some sly joke with it. The corgi gave him one uneasy glance, then stared fixedly across the room again, letting its jaws hang in a tongue-lolling pant.

'She *must* like living dangerously. Getting scraped off the front of a robo-truck is *fun*, but the lobo-farm . . .'

'Why do they send campers to the farm? How can camping be a crime against the state?'

'Oh, but it *is*. Isn't it Charlie?' he asked the corgi. Which went on uneasily panting.

'But why?'

'Try it. Find out for yourself. It cost me a lot of good guys, finding out. Why should I give it to you, for free?'

'I intend to find out. But we need a tent . . .'

'And pans and grub and your bike resprayed, and new registration-plates and new ID, and a job for you as a government countryside-snooper . . . You've been appearing in too many Paramil security-printouts recently, Kitson, old mate, old buddy.' He smiled, switching it on like a torch. 'You *do* need a lot of things, in return for one little potty National Championship.'

'But . . .'

'Oh, you can *have* them. No bother to me.' He waved a small soft white hand. 'Screwing-up Paramils is my favourite hobby. It just worries me it might turn into a . . . *virtue*. But my boss here reckons that the end justifies the means . . .'

'Boss?'

He flicked one hand towards the wall behind my head; the wall the corgi kept staring at.

I turned, looked where the corgi was looking. Hung on the wall, in an antique gold frame, was a painting unlike any I'd ever seen before. From a greasy, splattered background, a face looked out, large-nosed, small-eyed, long, grey, gloomy. With a hint of antlers where the ears should be. Not a human face. A face that drained the room of hope, drained the world of hope. You couldn't look away. To look away was to admit that you were afraid, inferior. But if you went on looking, it seemed to work its way deeper and deeper into your mind. You couldn't win.

'Who painted *that?*'

'I did. I was down to my last credit. I was going to jump out of the window, twenty storeys up. I was just combing my hair before I jumped, in the wardrobe mirror, when I saw this face looking out at me, from the grain of the wood. I had this urge to paint the face bigger, clearer. Spent my last credit on a bit of plastic-board. Borrowed some oil-paints off the kid downstairs. He didn't want to lend them – we had a fight. I knocked him down. Afterwards, when I took the paints back, he was still lying there, bleeding, dead. Must've knocked his head on the fender. Something made me scoop up a bit of his blood with my finger . . . and mix it with the paint of the mouth, here. Dunno why.

'Anyway, when I was lying in bed that night, the wardrobe began banging and jumping about. I was shit-scared . . . but everything seemed to go all right for me after that . . .' He waved a hand at the marble Adam fireplace, the corgi, the whole of Glasgow . . .

I looked again at the painting, at the battered wardrobe standing in the corner. At Blocky's rosy cheeks and shining eyes. Then I wanted to run out of that room as fast as my legs would carry me.

'Be reasonable, Kitson,' he said gently. 'You're a Tech. You've been trained to be open-minded. What did they use to say at Cambridge? If a technique works, it's a good technique. That's all this is, Kitson. Think of this as a technique for staying alive. I made a bargain – He's kept His side of it. I'd have been a heap of ashes in a little plastic urn, if He hadn't. Can't be bad.'

'I'm not making any bargain with *that* thing.'

'Who'd you think you are – Jesus Christ? After what you did to Vic Huggett?'

'How'd you know that?'

'Oh, we know most things, here. Only we don't have to prove they're crimes . . . unlike the Paramils. I still don't see how you got away with it.' There was a tinge of admiration in his voice, like a soft hand reaching out for me. 'What do you want most in the world?'

'I want to know what some bastard called Scott-Astbury's up to.' It was foolish to say it, but I wanted to wipe his Cheshire-cat grin.

The shine went off his face. 'You want a lot.'

'You don't know?'

'Oh, but I do. It was when I found out what Scott-Astbury was up to that I made my final bargain with *Him*.' Just for a second, as Blocky looked inward at something, he looked human, tired, old. 'I'm not giving Scott-Astbury to you for free, either.'

'I'm still not making a bargain with that thing.' The painted face kept drawing my eyes, try as I might.

'All right,' he said soothingly. 'This bargain is with *me*. Your part is just losing one National Championship – or persuading her to. And, when you've found out all about camping, and Scott-Astbury, you can come back and make a bargain with Him. If you don't wake up saying goo-goo in the lobo-farm first.'

His bright sunny smile came back: his world was wonderful again.

I fled. He was talking to somebody as I left. I hoped it was the corgi.

14

'All set?' asked Blocky, brimming with glee. Wearing his Est country-gent gear, white riding-mac, cravat and cor-duroy cap. With his tininess, he could take the mickey out of it and still look elegant.

He'd kept his word. Mitzi, resprayed matt green, her chrome blacked, had new registration plates. Which must tally, in Laura's memory-banks, with my new ID, John MacDonald, a lowly Tech servicing agri-robots in the Scottish lowlands. Keri was now Mrs MacDonald, fetching, domestic and wifely in a humble green anorak.

The MacDonalds must once have been real people . . . I didn't ask.

Grub, pans, tent, were all stowed. Blocky had even offered me a Paramil blaster, in case we got caught camping, red-handed. I refused: if I took it, I'd only end up using it, and Blocky was pushing me down the broad road to Hell fast enough already.

We'd kept our word too. It took three days to persuade Keri, but in the end she'd lost her championship most artistically, riding wilder than ever, in apparent despera-tion. Giving her fans a last show. I'd spent two days with my heart in my mouth, but she was safe now, all mine again. Another girl, wearing Keri's old helmet and leathers, would go on riding, further and further back down the field, till the media lost interest and went back to London. In a few weeks, all these riders would be dead, and Keri and I lost for ever.

'All set?' asked Blocky again. Grinning from ear to ear like a kid launching an expensive model yacht, bought by some silly uncle, into a North Sea gale. I couldn't be sure he hadn't packed a time-bomb in our camping gear. I wasn't sure the warehouse door we were about to ride out of wasn't several storeys up. But I guessed he liked his jokes longer than that. He'd be amused if we came back disillusioned and made a bargain with his dreadful Boss; he'd be amused if we got caught and sent to the lobo-farm. He'd reached some diabolical nirvana where *everything* was funny.

This warehouse was part of the Glasgow perimeter. Blocky nodded to one slim, black girl to put out the light. Another slid aside a well-oiled door, letting in a gale of wind, a sky of fast-moving cloud and broken moonlight.

'They'll never spot you from the air tonight. Keep calm, and the psycho-radar won't spot you either. The psychopters only patrol fifteen kilometres out – first fifteen kilometres are the worst. And . . .' He held up a finger like a conductor's baton, consulting his expensive watch. Then, as he dropped his arm, all hell broke out back in Glasgow. Screaming, home-made pistols, the whoof of petrol-bombs.

A red light grew on the wall of the next ruined warehouse, outside the Wire.

'What the . . .?' I said weakly, pretending to be surprised.

'Someone's dying for you, Kitson. Don't waste it.'

Keri did a wheelie, up the steep ramp, then we snaked across the usual pattern of crumbling tarmac. In a minute, we were on the Cumbernauld road. We kept the speed right down. Mitzi didn't even whisper. Her engine made no heat to show up on a psychopter's heat-scanners. Inside our green anoraks, cooled by the rush of air, our bodies sent out no more heat than a running dog. We hummed our favourite songs, to keep happy; the frame of mind of a canine on the razzle. So to a psychopter overhead we'd present the speed, heat and pleasure-pattern of a dirty-minded Fido. We kept our headlights off, because Fidos don't have headlights. That was illegal; but we could outrun any patrol-car we met on the ground.

We met nothing. No car or person, house or farm. Only the wind, making us sway and wobble on corners. And the ancient smell of greenery, even if it was only the lousy hardy-vines and hardy-hops, mutated by our wonderful Techs to grow here in the cold north.

The loudest sound, apart from the wind, was the endless whirr and clatter of the agri-robots in the fields, watering, trimming, weeding, even in darkness.

'Psychopter!' It swung high overhead, an evil dragon, blinded by its own lights flashing red, green, white. Its pinging filled our brains, but Keri was gently happy with the bike between her knees, and I was happy holding her waist between my hands. Besides, their radar would be clogged with all the hell breaking loose in Glasgow.

Was it a harmless riot that would fade quickly? Or a suicidal attack on the Paramils' HQ? With Blocky, you never knew. *Were* they dying for us? Why hadn't I asked him seriously, made him answer? But Blocky had that effect on you; it got worse the longer you knew him. The dying ghosts of Glasgow flickered uneasily in my mind. Ugly, hating, destructive, pointless, but still human; not paper-money in Blocky's endless game of Monopoly.

The psychopter faded. Empty dark-green silence, with the ticking and chirring and endless stealthy movements of the mickey-mouses. Keri shivered.

'I feel lonely.'

I squeezed her waist. 'You've got me.'

For once she didn't grumble. 'First town's Cumbernauld. Five miles.'

'Skirt round the side-roads, once you spot the perimeter.'

But we didn't spot any perimeter. The white-lined road wound on and on, under the cloud-dodging moon. Once a fox stared out, with moon-green eyes; and there were rabbits. But as for the smell of man, not a whiff.

'We should've passed Cumbernauld,' said Keri. 'We're on the wrong road.'

I glanced at the glowing map on Mitzi's windscreen.

Checked it with a glimpse of the Plough and Pole Star. 'No, we're going east by north. Mitzi's computer must be on the blink . . .'

Keri grunted, went faster. The minutes ticked away. We passed road-junctions, trees, huge agri-robot sheds. But not a single signpost, let alone Cumbernauld. I kept staring from Mitzi's windscreen to the countryside in disbelief.

After forty minutes, Keri braked abruptly, and switched on the headlights. A hundred yards on, a big sign shone.
WELCOME TO HISTORIC STIRLING CASTLE

'What happened to Cumbernauld?' Her voice had a tremor.

'The road must have by-passed it.'

'The road goes right through the middle of it, according to your precious bike.'

'You can miss things in the dark.'

'Like a town of a hundred thousand people? We've seen *nobody*.'

'If you're that lonely, I'll whistle up a psychopter.'

Silence. I said more gently, 'For goodness sake, we can ask in Stirling. What's so marvellous about Cumbernauld? It was only built in the 1950s. Nothing worth seeing.'

'A hundred thousand people are worth seeing.'

'You're tired,' I said. 'It's all that racing.'

With a sniff, and a slam of her visor, we rode on. The way to historic Stirling Castle, on its cliff, was *amazingly* well signposted. We pulled up at the gatehouse in five minutes. There was still a light on. Comforting.

'There you are!' I said. 'Stirling Castle, safe and sound!'

'Stirling's not just a castle. It's another town of a hundred thousand people. Where is it? Where are they?' From the castle's commanding height, under the now-clear moon, I could see nothing but huge green fields.

Behind us, a small door in the castle gate creaked open; light streamed out. Outlined against it was a woman, holding back a dog with one hand, and holding what looked like a shotgun in the other. 'What do you want?' She sounded about fifty, and bossy.

'Is this Stirling?' I blurted out stupidly, for once quite lost for words.

'Finish up this coffee,' said Mrs Nairn. 'I get so few visitors.'

'Must be lonely . . .'

'The dog's company.'

'Must've been different thirty years ago,' I said cautiously.

'Aye.' She sighed. 'Though they do say there'll be new people next year . . . English. When they've finished doing up those old houses down by the bridge. I think it's a sin, all those good new houses smashed flat by the bulldozers, and only these dreary old ruins left, and done up at God knows what cost. I sometimes think they want the place to look like it did before the Battle of Bannockburn . . . such nonsense. You won't tell them I said that?' she added, anxiously.

'It's between friends, Mrs Nairn. When did they move all the people out?'

'Ten years since. Sent a lot of removal vans and buses, and took them to Glasgow. Rationalization, they called it; better housing, they said. I'm sure I wouldn't know. I was only in Glasgow the once, and didn't like it.'

'Were there many people?'

'Not so many at the end. The young ones were gone already – to Glasgow for the racing and the pop-groups. After that, there was scarcely a bairn born. And such a lot of deaths . . . when there's no grandchildren, the old yins have nothing to live for. And the young ones never wrote, once they got to Glasgow. I often wonder where it'll all end. When I lie awake at night, listening to those machines ticking, all across the valley. You're in the government service . . . where d'you think it'll all end? *You* must know.'

'Only about my machines, Mrs Nairn . . . I've got to *keep*

them ticking.' I got up. 'Thanks for the lovely dinner. We'd better be getting back to Glasgow . . .'

'You'll keep well south, now, won't ye? You know the forbidden zone starts just ten kilometres north of here? I wouldn't like to see you getting into trouble . . .'

My heart leapt, though I kept my face straight. Blocky hadn't mentioned any forbidden zone; but then he wouldn't. And one reason for a forbidden zone might be Scott-Astbury's big mistake . . .

Nothing marked the boundary of the forbidden zone, not even a strand of barbed wire. The country was too big and rugged. It would have taken ten thousand Paramils to police it. Instead, they would stay in the air. With psycho-radar, infra-red image-intensifiers, heat-cameras, metal-detectors and sound-amplification, what could get through?

Answer – a running dog. We slid through so easily it made us giggle. Or were they playing with us, letting us get well in before they pounced? Time would tell.

Meanwhile, the forbidden zone closed round us. The night had clouded over, but we could still sense the huge darkness of the mountains, smell the heather, hear the silence behind the soughing of the wind. Our only comfort was the dim glow of the dashboard, and a faint touch of radio we allowed ourselves, music and chatter from ten thousand miles away, where the sun was coming up. It made us feel that Mitzi was a person too; that there were three of us, not two, moving into the cold, empty dark.

Keri grumbled about keeping the speed down. 'I could *walk* faster.' But it was just as well we did; because as we reached the main Fort William road-junction, the steering went berserk, we slewed all over the road and ended up in a ditch.

'Jap crap,' Keri kicked the recumbent Mitzi.

'Jap crap nothing.' I pulled the bike upright, and gave a twitch of headlights.

The whole road-junction was breaking up. Mud-filled

ruts, with huge islands of loosened chippings in between. A stream was actually flowing across, where a culvert had been blocked, making as many gurgling tributaries as the delta of the Nile. And it hadn't happened yesterday: on the islands of chippings grass grew, even small silver birches.

'Nothing's been through here for years. Except . . .' There were deep patrol-car treads in the mud.

'I'd better use dipped headlights,' said Keri, 'or there won't be any bike left.'

We made fair time. Some stretches of road were as good as ever, but other bits were swamp, or thickets we had to push the bike through. We tried a few side-roads, till we came to collapsed bridges. From what I could see by dipped headlights, the bridges had been blown up. Quite a while ago. Bindweed and ivy hid the old explosion-scars.

'It'll change in a few miles,' I said. 'We'll find the roads as good as ever. It's just Paramil bluff.'

Instead, we got a last-minute warning, on the edge of our dipped headlights, of big things moving, crossing the road. We braked just in time.

'What the . . .?' said Keri.

I reached over her shoulder and flipped on full beam.

A herd of red deer was crossing, cool as cool. Not taking a blind bit of notice of us. Except the great antlered male standing guard on the flanks, whose eyes reflected our headlights so he looked like the Devil in a horror-video.

The last of them crossed, and were gone into the dark.

'I feel kind of . . . irrelevant,' said Keri.

'That's a big word for an Unnem.' But she didn't rise to the bait.

Five kilometres on, we were stopped by a herd of black highland cattle, a sea of humped woolly backs lying all over the road. Their leader moved up on us; we had to back off and take a side-road. It was only Mitzi's glowing road-map that stopped us getting lost altogether. But even that was going haywire.

'That's the tenth village she's shown that's just not *there*.'

'It's a Japanese map. How would the Japs know what's been going on here?'

Ten kilometres south of where Fort William ought to be, our lights picked out the green glowing eyes of a group of smaller animals. Big pointed ears, waving tails. Tearing at a hump that lay in the road.

'Alsatians – they're running wild, Kit. They've *killed* something.' But these creatures were too pale for Alsatians; too big in ear, head and jaw, too long in the leg.

'They look like wolves,' whispered Keri. 'They can't be, can they? How would wolves get here?'

'Perhaps they escaped from Edinburgh Zoo,' I said, as flippantly as I could. 'The last wild wolf in Scotland was killed in a cave on Ben Mhor in the eighteenth century. Drive straight at them – they're nervous.'

'*They*'re nervous? . . .'

'We can't stay here all night. And you know what wolves do to anything that tries to run away . . .'

She gritted her teeth, put down her head and *went*. I prayed the road-surface would hold. I didn't fancy being thrown off injured and bleeding in the middle of *that* lot.

The road-surface held; the wolves scattered. The hump lying in the middle of the road stayed where it was. A big red deer, its spilled entrails glistening.

I was glad of the dawn. The first paling of the sky showed, from the top of a hill, an ugly scatter of prefab huts, petrol tanks, barbed wire and parked helicopters, where Fort William should've been.

'Paramils?'

'I don't think so.' I peered through Blocky's binoculars. 'Too untidy. These helicopters are painted yellow, all muddy. There are robo-dozers and robo-shovels. I think it's some kind of construction camp.'

'What're they making?'

'Nothing. Maybe it's a depot. Maybe they fly out from here all over the Highlands, and come back here for safety at night.'

'I don't blame them.'

'I want to watch this lot, but we'd better get off the road. They probably fly off to work half-asleep, but even a hungover navvy would spot us standing here.'

We went back a bit, and found a crag with a deep overhang. It was damp with moss and trickling water, but it hid Mitzi.

'Here you are,' I said. 'Your highland cave as promised, with running water and all mod cons.'

'This isn't the cave on Ben Mhor, is it?'

'Have a bite to eat. That'll keep the wolf from the door.'

She straddled a rock and lit a fag. 'I can see why Unnems leave holiday-making to the bloody Ests.'

15

Four days later, I sat on the banks of a burn, waiting for sunrise. Sunrise spread remarkably quickly; upwards through the little pink torpedo-shaped clouds; downwards, stroking the rounded dark of the hills with pale, tufted gold. But even if it had been slower, I wouldn't have been bored. There was the burn to listen to, trickles inside trickles inside trickles. A darkling thrush, singing in the burn-side thickets. The huge low sound of the morning wind, stroking the heather.

High up, a formation of geese flew west: getting to school on time. I didn't have to go to school today. I didn't have to go anywhere. There was a flicker of white tails across the burn. Brer Rabbit getting busy, getting used to me. The sun reached a long ray into the valley, warming my whiskers. It was rough, trying to shave in cold water.

I looked at my watch. Nearly six. Time for Brer Fox. I'd got into the habit of waiting up for Brer Fox. Every morning he turned up at three minutes past six, finishing his night's work, as I was finishing mine. Zigzagging down the hillside to the burn, twenty yards below where I sat.

Scuttering panic among the rabbits. Suddenly, not a rabbit in sight. Then Brer Fox on the far bank, paw upraised. We regarded each other; I drank in his lovely, wild soul. He dismissed me as a creature of no importance, bent and drank. Ran his long, pink tongue round his lips. Silver drops of water fell back into the ripples. Then he tensed, dropped his haunches, leapt the burn and vanished.

Even then I was reluctant to go to bed. Behind me stretched a winding gulley, floored with springy turf between high bracken. Overhead, up the gulley, ran a huge pipe. Once it must have carried water to Glasgow or Edinburgh. Now, rich-red with rust, it clanged hollowly. But had its uses. If psychopters came looking for us with metal-scanners, they'd get a screenful of water-pipe. Same if they tried to use heat-scanners – the pipe heated quickly in the sun. Mitzi was stored in a deep, dry cave. Our tent was camouflaged with bracken-fronds, tied across. I'd taken care not to break any branches. Dead bracken is a dead give-away to infra-red cameras.

As Vic Huggett still said in my fading nightmares, we were snug as a bug in a rug.

I sensed the dawn psychopter before I heard it. Its psycho-radar was set on unfocused scan, sweeping as wide an area as possible. I slipped among the bracken, filled my mind with the sound of the burn, became the burn. In the tent, Keri would be asleep: she always dropped off the moment her head hit the groundsheet. She'd leave no more impression on their screen than a dozing sheep . . .

The psychopter passed and vanished, leaving a thin stitching of sound that got lost in the hugeness of the hills. I crawled into the tent. Watched Keri sleeping in the dim green light. A tiny white feather had escaped from her sleeping-bag and got stuck to the groundsheet; it trembled at her every breath. Her hand clutched the edge of the sleeping-bag, as a child might clutch a teddy-bear. She'd never let me hold her hand. Couldn't bear me touching her, awake or asleep. But she was happy, and that was something.

I'd been right about the Fort William depot. I'd watched the old yellow choppers fly out, muddy robo-dozers slung underneath. Noticed the direction they went. The following night, we found where they were working. It was deserted after dark.

'Looks like a castle in a fairy-tale,' said Keri. A very small castle: more a fortified house, with steep roof and pointed turrets. The kind you get in Scotland.

'What're they building it *for*?' she asked.

'They're not building it, they're restoring it. It's been ruined hundreds of years . . .'

'But what for?'

'For a fairy-tale,' I said bitterly. 'They're potty – restoring ruins and letting the roads go to hell. Making Scotland like it was before the Battle of Bannockburn . . .'

'Except Scotland had *people*, then.'

I poked through the portable huts and scattered machinery. There was a petrol-driven generator that could recharge Mitzi. One hut held a shotgun and half a box of cartridges. A would-be big-game hunter? Or somebody with wolf-phobia, like Keri? She borrowed the gun permanently; it cheered her up no end, though I warned her it wouldn't stop a charging Highland bull.

The same night, we'd found this lovely gulley. The next two nights we sussed out Scotland from coast to coast. But apart from the Aberdeen road, in good repair, and the Aberdeen oil-terminal glittering behind its Wire, we found nothing but crumbling roads and ancient ruins restored. The electricity pylons of the national grid no longer festooned the hills; we found their rusting stumps beneath the heather. No radio-masts, radar-stations, heavy plants, runways, helicopter-pads. Nothing.

Last night, we'd given up looking, and enjoyed ourselves instead. Walked our night-valley like foxes, eyes and ears pricked in the patchy moonlight. Seen fish jumping in our lake, sending out rings of phosphorescence. Watched fox-cubs tumbling like kittens in a moonlit glade . . .

Five more minutes watching Keri's face, and I slept like a baby.

I was wakened by a shower of water on my face.

'It's raining,' I said. 'Where's the tent?'

Giggle. I opened my eyes, and Keri was kneeling over me, her hair hanging in long wet snakes, and her teeshirt clinging to her in damp patches.

'I had a bathe – in the nuddy. While you were snoring. You Ests don't 'alf miss your chances.' Her cheeks were glowing with the cold water, her eyes shining with the joke. I grabbed for her, but she was gone.

'Get my breakfast, Kitson-slave.'

I didn't really mind. I yawned, stretched, felt good. Waking up here was just like Cambridge. No half-dreaming swamp-time.

'Hey, Keri? You feel different here? Waking up in the mornings?'

'Full of beans? Yeah.'

'Wonder what's causing it?'

I thoughtfully opened a can of slimy pink luncheon-meat, pale as a leper. Gave it to her with a few uncrunchy biscuits.

'Can't be a change of diet,' she said wryly, swallowing a slice of meat whole, like a seal engulfing a rotten herring. 'Mebbe it's the change of water – that burn's so clear and fresh, I could drink it all day.'

'Ever felt this way before?'

'Funny you should ask. Twice. Once when I broke a bone in my foot, just after I'd won the Championship. Two mates of mine – Techs on the razzle – got me into the Cambridge hospital. I was awake half the nights with the pain of my foot, but I still wakened fresh in the mornings.'

'What about the other time?'

She laughed. 'Some Est – said he'd won a lot of money betting on me, but I think he fancied me really – sent me two crates of that fizzy wine.'

'Champagne?'

'Yeah. Anyway, I told him to get lost, but me and a girl-friend drank it non-stop for a week. Everyone reckoned we'd get hangovers, but we wakened fresh as daisies. Then we finished the last bottle and went back to feeling lousy in the mornings. Is champagne a sort of tonic?'

'No,' I said, shutting my mouth like a rat-trap. I didn't want to spoil her day.

'Hey, what you hiding, Kitson? Are you bloody Ests

putting something in the water back home? My old dad used to think that. He reckoned they did it to soldiers in World War II. Something called bromide – turned them off sex, and gave them more bottle for fighting. Mind you, it doesn't put people off sex nowadays . . . hey, what's up wi' you? You look like you seen a ghost!'

'I have. The ghosts of a lot of babies.'

'Wotcher mean? That sounds *horrible*.'

'Know anybody your age who's had a kid, Keri?'

She puckered up her face. 'One or two. Not many. People are just too busy living it up. And the girls can get stuff at the clinic. I mean, who wants to bring up a kid these days . . . you haven't got time.'

'There hasn't been time for years, Keri. Remember Mrs Nairn? So many people dying, so few babies being born?'

'Christ, what're they trying to do to us?'

'I don't know.'

She was silent a long time. Then she said, 'I don't want to go back to all that. Couldn't we just stay here? Catch rabbits to eat? There's bilberries an' mushrooms. Wild cabbage and apples in the old back gardens . . .'

'These hills are two metres deep in snow in winter.'

But I knew how she felt. The last week had turned my mind inside out. Suddenly, Scotland seemed enormous, England small as a zoo with its Wires and watchtowers. Even my father, in his Cotswold manor, seemed only a rarer kind of monkey in a lusher cage. Once you camped up here . . .

I suddenly knew why campers got sent to the lobo-farm. But as for the rest, the rotting roads, restored ruins, possible poison in the water . . . it was still a crazy mystery, with Scott-Astbury's mistake wrapped up in the middle of it . . .

She nudged me in the ribs. 'Penny for 'em?' Then she added, 'You're a funny sod, Kitson. You share a tent with me and never try to lay a finger . . . any of our lads would've grabbed me by now . . . or *tried*!'

'I don't grab.'

'Expectin' me to grab you?'

'No.'

'You are a funny sod. Always brooding. Come for a walk. I want to go the other way tonight. There's another lake up there . . .'

'Loch.'

'Up you!' She was happy again. 'Let's go while the sun's still shining.'

I sniffed the air. It was like a warm bath, full of the scent of pines. I could hear bees buzzing, fifty metres away. It was the sort of sunset the hero and heroine walk away into. And the psychopters always seemed to vanish around sunset, like butterflies . . .

I reached for the shotgun.

'You won't need that,' she said.

She offered me her hand.

I put the gun back into the tent.

The sign at the fork in the path said: RSPB BIRD RESERVE. LOCH GARTEN

White lettering on a red board; normally the colour-coding for danger. Funny old RSPB; I couldn't think of any organization *less* dangerous. We'd seen their films at college. They were fantastic cameramen – could show you the parasites on a heron's wing at fifty paces. And wasn't their Loch Garten film the best of the lot? Ospreys, dive-bombing from a great height and catching bloody great salmon underwater. I saw it all again, in slow motion. The splash, with foam climbing slowly, slowly. White wings beating, lifting, against a background of dark-green pines. The salmon twisting itself in horse-shoes, trying to escape, falling back into the water, splashing on the surface, weakly. The osprey coming round and catching it again . . .

Years ago idiots had nearly wiped out the osprey, by stealing its eggs. I remembered, on the film, great coils of barbed wire round the nesting-tree. Dedicated birdwatchers, guarding the nest night and day, till the young hatched.

Even a security-microphone, at the base of the tree . . . RSPB had won in the end: the osprey was safe from extinction.

I told Keri; her eyes shone even brighter. We turned down the path. The setting sun was shining through the pines like great golden searchlights, picking out a patch of bark here, a tuft of fern there, making them glow like jewels.

Two hundred metres on there was a bigger signboard. Then another, a real giant: RSPB LOCH GARTEN

'They don't want anyone to miss it!' said Keri. She let go my hand, took off her boots, and danced a sort of hopscotch dance down the path ahead. Beyond her, the water of Loch Garten glinted through the pines. I felt so great, I picked up an old damp branch and threw it over her head, as hard as I could. It hit the branches of a pine, bringing down a shower of pine-cones, as it thudded to earth.

Keri glowered back over her shoulder. 'You!'

Twenty metres beyond her, where my branch had fallen, a streak of flame shot up in the air, carrying huge black lumps of turf. A thunderclap broke the world in half, echoed all round the valley and came back to us through the pines.

Another streak of flame; another fountain of black earth. Another. And another.

Keri spun round and round, hands over her ears, eyes like saucers, shouting something I couldn't hear. And all the time the explosions were leaping down the path towards her.

I pulled her behind a massive tree-trunk just in time; lay on top of her. The bangs went on. I could hear the metal-fragments cutting-up the trees. Cones and pine-needles showered on my back.

Then it stopped.

'What *was* it?'

'A minefield,' I said. 'Anti-personnel mines. Only, the fools planted them too close together, so they're setting each other off.'

'*Which* fools?'

'The RSPB, presumably. Still protecting their precious ospreys.'

'They're *mad*. Let's get out of here.' She put one hand up the tree to lift herself. There was a distant, whiplike crack, and the tip of her little finger vanished in a splodge of blood.

'Oh!' she said, beginning to kneel upright, staring at where her fingernail had been.

I pulled her down again. The bark of the tree exploded, just where her head had been.

'They're shooting at us!'

But I was starting to have suspicions: the firing was too regular – 'Don't shoot,' I shouted; 'we surrender.' As I expected, no reply. I shouted again. Still no reply. Keeping flat, I found a pine-branch, brought down by the explosions. Waved it gently above my head. Started to count, one, two, three.

On the count of three, a bullet whipped through it.

I counted to three again.

Another bullet whipped through it.

'It's only a mickey-mouse,' I said. 'Probably an old Arcdos Mark 3. Automatic, radar-controlled defence system. Bought as army surplus, left too long out in the rain, not serviced properly. Getting rusty and slow. But good enough to defend the ospreys, when they made this a forbidden zone, and the RSPB had to leave . . .'

'But it could've *killed* somebody.' She was sucking the end of her finger. 'People are more important than bloody birds.'

'Try telling the RSPB that. We'd better leave, now.' Already I was looking over my shoulder, searching out the dead ground of gullies where the aroused Arcdos couldn't sense us.

'No,' she said stubbornly, tying a filthy handkerchief round her finger, and pulling the knot tight with her teeth. 'We've got to *stop* it. It could blow a deer's leg off, and leave it to die. It could shoot a little kid.'

I tried to argue with her.

'*Please*, Kit,' she said. No point in telling her someone would only come and repair it. No point to telling her there'd be other Arcdoses, spread all round Loch Garten.

'*Please!*'

It was the first thing she'd ever asked me for. Maybe I wanted to show off. Maybe I wanted to outwit the geriatric mickey-mouse that had nearly killed her. I just know I did a crazy thing . . .

'OK, duckie. Just keep on waving this branch.'

She waved it. Another bullet smacked through it. This time I saw where the bullet came from. A grey mushroom, set in the hillside beyond the pines that fringed the path.

Then I was up and sprinting for it. But not straight. I counted as I ran, and on the count of three, leapt to the right.

The bullet missed.

Then three more steps, and a leap to the left. The whole point was never to do the same thing twice; never let the Arcdos catch the pattern of my thoughts in its puny brain.

Two more bullets zipped past. Then I jumped on Arcdos with both boots. The metal cover dented, but didn't break. It swivelled under me, trying to turn its evil little gun-barrel high enough to shoot me in the crutch. I stamped and stamped on the barrel, till it bent over. Then the swivelling ball-bearings ground to a halt under my weight. It whined feebly. I heaved up the metal cover, and put my boot into its electronics. A very satisfying crunch; nearly the last thing I did.

The whip-like crack came again, from further up the hill. A bullet tugged at the flapping tail of my shirt.

Hell, it was a multi-Arcdos. There were other grey mushrooms on that slope, programmed to protect each other. Knock out one, you got three more firing at you.

Still prancing to and fro, and counting one-two-three like a lunatic, I sussed out the system. The multi-Arcdos is shaped like a spider, with gun-domes at the tip of each leg, and the radar-control in the middle. The 'legs' are underground cables but, over the years, the trenches in which they're laid show up as shallow depressions; especially when the sun is low and setting. I saw the shadow of the spider, ran for the radar-control. It was getting hard to run truly at random; soon my tiring brain would do the same thing twice . . .

Fortunately the radar-control is underground too. Access by a shallow trench, for the servicing Tech. I flung myself in, bullets plucking at my heels, and undid the wing-nuts to the servicing-hatch. Luckily for me, they were only hand-tight. I reached inside, and pulled the plug on old Arcdos, and he went as quiet as a mouse.

I stood up and waved to Keri.

At that moment, a psychopter zoomed up over the pines.

A crafty psychopter, coming in at zero height, so I couldn't hear him come. A crafty psychopter who'd switched off his radar, so I wouldn't hear that, either. A crafty psychopter summoned by Arcdos as soon as I'd begun to damage it.

I lay in that trench in despair. The psychopter weaved in neat circles above me, while its instruments made sure I wasn't armed, and that Arcdos was out of order and dead. Then it picked out a place to land where there weren't any anti-personnel mines. It wasn't in any hurry: I wasn't going anywhere.

It would land, the Paramils would stun us with a light touch of blaster, then ship us, in their undercarriage-pods, to the nearest lobo-farm. I signalled to Keri to run, but she just stood by the tree-trunk, the pine-branch still in her hand. An awful inertia swept over me. They said once you'd been to the farm, you didn't care any more . . .

The psychopter landed, sagging gently on its undercarriage. The rotors spun . . . stopped. The Paramils stepped out, blasters at the ready . . .

Then I had a vision of Idris's face, shouting, 'Sodding little idiot.' Implying I'd left something undone . . .

What?

I looked at the plugs I'd pulled out of Arcdos.

It seemed only natural to replace them in their proper place. Neatly.

There were several gun-mushrooms still in working order. I watched them swivel gently. The Paramils never noticed: too busy watching me. I counted, one, two, three, only my eyes visible over the lip of the trench.

There were several whip-cracks, that hardly disturbed the evening air. The two Paramils collapsed gently on the turf, their bodies twitching and kicking as more shots hit them.

Then Arcdos took great exception to the psychopter. Kept on shooting holes in it, till its fuel-tank blew up.

Then it started shooting at my boot-heels again, so I pulled its plug for the very last time. I grabbed Keri by the hand, and ran like hell. Psychopters have friends; within half an hour, half the psychopters flying out of Glasgow would be after us.

It was a nightmare, running back up our happy path through the calm dusk. Our blackbird was singing; every leaf whispered peace, peace. But we knew what was coming.

Panting, we bundled everything up and into the back of the cave. Coaxed back the bent bracken where the tent had been. Then we lay down in our sleeping-bags, in the deepest part of the cave. I took a big bottle of sleeping-tablets out of Blocky's medicine-kit, and gave her six. Two was the safe dose.

'Do we have to, Kit? Can't we run for it?'

'We wouldn't get ten kilometres . . .'

'Can't we stay here and fight?'

'With eight shotgun cartridges?'

'They mightn't spot us . . .'

'Because your mind is so calm and tranquil?'

She forced a strained grin. 'OK'.

I slipped my first pill up in the air, caught it in my mouth like a trained seal. That made her laugh; she swallowed hers quickly.

'We've taken too many, haven't we? We mightn't wake up?'

I swallowed my sixth. 'If we wake up, we'll be free. Better than . . .'

'Yes, better than . . .' Her voice was growing slurry. 'Cuddle me, you bastard.'

I cuddled her; kissed her too. Might be my only chance. She murmured protests in her sleep. I was far from sure my scheme would work; but it was the only way. Asleep, near coma, her mind was buried too deep to be reached by their machines; buried among the roots of this land, among the flicker of rabbit and stoat, capercailye and grouse.

Good night, Keri. God bless.

I was fading myself, listening to the sounds of the little burn, when I heard the first psychopters coming.

I swam up out of blackness. The Paramils had got me. Beaten me all over with rubber hoses. Broken my right hip, snapped my spine in three places. The lobo-farm wasn't *supposed* to hurt . . .

But they'd left me Keri. Her warm body fitted into mine, snug as a hand in a glove. I tightened my arms round her, and she sighed contentedly. If this was the lobo-farm, I'd stay all day.

But the Paramils were demolishing my hip with a road-drill.

I opened my eyes. Ragged stone overhead. Smell of greenery, song of blackbirds.

'Keri, we've *done* it!' She murmured, her face rosy, peaceful. But she wouldn't wake up. I was horribly reminded of Idris, who had also looked so peaceful.

Go and get water to splash on her. I tried to stand, but the force of gravity had increased ten times. I crawled instead. Getting past Mitzi was a problem that took ten minutes to solve. I crawled all the way to the burn, shoved in my face like old Brer Fox and nearly drank it dry.

Rabbits playing; not a flicker of a psychopter. I looked at my watch. We'd slept two days and three nights.

First round to us. In the old days, they'd have searched with long lines of plodding policemen, with dogs and sticks. Used shepherds and gillies, who knew the country. And they'd have caught us.

Now, there was no one left who knew these hills. Few dogs of any sort. Now they did things from the sky, the quick, sure, mickey-mouse way. And failed. I sat in a daze, watching the rabbits, till a faint cry called, 'Kit, Kit.' At first I thought it was a bird.

She had bags under her eyes like coal-sacks; couldn't even sit up. But it was Keri. 'Seen my head anywhere? Got any pain-killers?'

'I'll give you a sleeping-tablet,' I said. *'That's a joke!'*

I hardly felt the punch she threw at me.

We stayed in our gulley ten more days, getting hungrier and hungrier, happier and happier. Keri was content to stay for the foxes and rabbits; never spoke of the dead Paramils.

Strangely, the Paramils' deaths never bothered me, not like old Vic. Old Vic had been real, with bad breath. The other two had been too far away: Action-men, discarded. Part of the system, killed by another part of the system. Nothing to do with me.

I knew the Paramils hadn't given up. Just pulled back, to kid us we were safe. They even put out a newsflash on the radio, blaming Glasgow terrorists for the killings, saying they'd been caught and dealt with. That didn't fool me: I'd used Mitzi's radio to burgle their security-transmissions. They were waiting for us to break cover, on the edge of the forbidden zone. Let their little faces turn blue with waiting.

I listened on the radio a lot, waiting for something, I didn't know what. One night, about midnight, all hell broke loose. Three restored castles near Glasgow caught fire, one after another. The Paramils were going berserk.

A present from Blocky. What I'd been waiting for. I got Keri packed and on to the bike before she could draw breath.

'I've been happy in our little place,' she said, as she started Mitzi.

'Maybe we can come back, some day. It'll all be waiting . . .'

She stared at the trees, the hills, the cave, as if she was a squirrel storing up nuts for winter.

Another newsflash came in. Paramil HQ, Glasgow, was under attack. Someone had blown up the aerial of their security-transmitter.

Blocky, I almost love you.

We went south without lights, driving like hell. Only Mitzi and Keri could've done it. By dawn, we were on the motorway south of Newcastle, weaving through light rain and the old dreary procession of robo-trucks.

16

I let Keri go on driving south, even though she'd been driving all night. I had to think what to do next. And I hadn't much time. Somewhere ahead, Laura would be endlessly processing her daily data-intake, at ten million facts a minute, twenty-four hours a day. Never getting bored or tired like a human copper. Looking for coincidences, discrepancies... death of Vic Huggett, death of Paramils, disappearance of the MacDonalds from work and home. Any minute now, Laura might make a logical pattern of it, and put her electronic digit on Kitson-Sellers-MacDonald.

Whose face, habits, hobbies, funny little ways, places of residence since birth including holidays, would immediately be flicked up on a computer printout. It made me as nervous as a hermit-crab changing shells. Brood, brood. At first Keri tried pointing out cheering items, like sparrowhawks hovering over the motorway. But I just grunted, so she left me alone.

Just north of Stamford she suddenly swerved, braked hard, swore. I came to with a jolt. I'd been nearly asleep, head tucked out of the wind behind her shoulder.

She'd tried overtaking a yellow Tech van marked 'East Midlands Water'. It had swerved out, nearly knocking us into the central barrier. Not unusual behaviour for Ests, but these people were Techs. First thing a Tech's taught is respect for machinery.

The van roared ahead again, black smoke pouring from its exhaust. Tilting badly on corners: tyres under-inflated. One winker was cracked across, and there was rust showing all along the bottom of the doors. What kind of Tech runs a van in that condition?

'Get past that so-and-so quick – he's trouble.'

As she did, up the inside with plenty of room, I glanced sideways. The yellow paintwork was rough: hand-done, with brushmarks showing. A face peered down from the cab: not superior, cynical, but rather stupid and gleeful, mouth open. The crewcut hair was right, the white coat was right, the face was wrong.

'Must be getting hard-up for Techs,' I muttered.

'Nice car ahead,' said Keri, still being determinedly cheerful.

A vintage Jag, British Racing green, polished like a Paramil's boots. XST 143 X. I felt suddenly, irrationally happy, as I saw two faces peering out of the rear window. Diane and Loretta, Major Arnold's kids. I used to babysit them, read them *The House at Pooh Corner*. Back in third year, I'd once even changed Loretta's nappy.

I waved. They looked puzzled, but Loretta waved back. Loretta would wave to anybody. Then Diane told her not to wave at strange men. I'd show them who was a strange man . . .

'Pull alongside and stay there!'

'He might side-swipe us.'

'Not this guy.'

We pulled alongside. There was Major Arnold, still chewing his moustache. Mrs Arnold, short blond hair, calm blue eyes and, under a pink mohair sweater, that luxurious bosom I'd so often stolen crafty looks at, when I was younger. The girls were wearing flowered dresses, white knee-stockings.

I was home again; nothing had changed. I broke out into a sweat of pure relief. It had all been a terrible nightmare, but a chat with Major Arnold . . .

Idiot. How could a chat with Major Arnold undo two dead Paramils and a burnt-out psychopter? It wasn't exactly like getting in a muddle with your history essay. But I kept on grinning until Major Arnold gestured us on with an impatient flick of his hand.

He hadn't recognized me. Of course . . . crash-helmet. I took it off, doing nearly a ton, even though my hair was flogging my face to pieces and my eyes were watering so much I might have been crying.

They recognized me now. Major Arnold's eyebrows shot up in that old quizzical way. Mrs Arnold smiled. The kids were jumping up and down, waving till their hands looked like falling off.

Then they remembered what I was now. Major Arnold's eyes snapped back to the road, the old muscles twitching along his jaw. Mrs Arnold shook her head sadly. The kids argued, kept on throwing puzzled looks at me. But in the end Major Arnold spoke to them sharply, and they did an eyes-front as well, sitting like little statues.

An icy fist clutched my guts; I didn't have a home any more.

Be damned to self-pity. I had to talk to Major Arnold, tell him what was going on. I shouted to Keri, 'Drop back. Throttle down.' Then, risking my neck, I leaned over and pulled a book out of the pannier. Found a stub of pencil; wrote shakily: I HAVE TO SPEAK TO YOU. LIFE AND DEATH!

While I was writing, there was an aggressive honking behind. The yellow van again. It had all the road to itself, but was driving on our tail with malicious perversity. Three guys; I didn't like the look of any of them . . . stuff them. I got Keri to pull alongside the Jag again. Held the book against Major Arnold's window, practically touching the glass. Good job Keri was the rider she was.

Major Arnold didn't look up for a long time. The book kept fluttering like a mad bird. I thought my arms were going to drop off. Then he read my notice, gave one decisive shake of his head, and went back to driving. His whole body said he wouldn't turn his head again. Then I lost my grip on the book . . .

We went back for it. No use. The spine had cracked and soaking pages were spilled all over the motorway. So I sent Keri chasing him again. How could I get him to listen? Jump on to his bonnet?

When we caught up, the yellow van was riding his tail, honking, trying to force him out of the fast lane. Someone had really souped up that van; Tech vans are only meant to do a hundred. This was overtaking the Jag at a hundred and fifty. At least . . . it drew alongside.

Then it side-swiped the Jag, hard. I saw sparks fly, even in daylight. Then the Jag's hub-caps came spinning back towards us, forced off by the impact. Like silver animals leaping for our throat.

We ducked. When I looked again, Jag and van, grinding together, were veering over into the slow lane. They humped on to the hard shoulder, flipped their tails up, and vanished.

'Pull off!' I hammered Keri on the shoulder. *'Pull off!'*

A screeching jugger with a white-faced driver missed us by inches. Then Mitzi mounted the hard shoulder, slewed round and dumped us on the grass.

A hundred metres back, Jag and van had rammed a high perimeter-fence and were lying in a field beyond. The Jag was still upright, its nearside wing crumpled, the scraped metal gleaming in the rain. Major Arnold just getting out; the kids' heads still bobbing in the back.

The yellow van, fifty metres nearer, was lying on its side. Three figures climbing out of the cab, passing up bottles to each other. Drunks!

But they went on passing up bottles; too many bottles, with bits of white rag sticking out of their necks . . .

Major Arnold had been heading towards them, shoulders set in a way that meant trouble for some. Now he hesitated, glanced round, and ran back to his car. Puff of smoke from the Jag's exhaust, as he restarted. Back wheels spinning, throwing up divots of black earth, digging themselves in deeper.

The Jag shot forward ten metres, then stuck. Now the three men were round it, dropping some of their bottles on the turf.

Major Arnold tried reversing; got stuck again.

A flame glinted; touched the rag in a bottle. The bottle curved towards the Jag, the slow curve of a cricket ball, leaving an arc of white smoke. It burst on the Jag's front bumper; the bonnet vanished in a rose of flame.

'Oh God, oh God!' I heard myself shouting. I looked back at the motorway, but it was hidden by the banking. Only the tops of robos and juggers passing, indifferent. Nobody else could see what was happening.

I started to run. Keri grabbed me.

'Don't go, Kit. Don't get involved. There's nothing you can do.'

We fell in a heap on the grass. She was screaming, 'Don't get involved, Kit. For God's sake don't get involved.'

I put my hand against her screaming face and pushed till she let go. Jumped up and ran, followed by her despairing cry of 'Kit, wait!'

I knew I was too late. The Jag was still backing and turning, churning up the field in a spiderweb of ruts. But the petrol-bombers were all round it, dodging like bull-fighters, throwing, throwing. Like a bull, Major Arnold was trying to run them down. But the car was encased in fire. Through the back window, the children still watched, saucer-eyed. I saw Loretta put a thumb into her mouth, saw Diane cuddle her, protectively. Their faces shimmered through a transparent wall of flame.

Then I slammed into the first bomber. He went full-length, the bottle in his hand spewing a fan of flame across the grass. Then I was up, and at the second one. Caught his arm as he poised to throw, snatched the burning rag from the bottle and threw it away. Petrol sloshed down over both of us; he got most of it in his face, broke away howling.

I went for the third. The bottle in his hand wasn't alight.

He saw me, started to run. I brought him down with a lovely rugby tackle.

Next second, a rather exciting tingling enwrapped my whole body. I found I couldn't move. I could only collapse alongside the bomber, like a man and wife in bed. I kept on trying to move my arms and legs. All I could move was my eyes and lips, and my neck a bit.

'What's happened? What's happened?' I yelled. Nobody answered. I could hear the crackle of flames from the Jag. Strangely, its engine was still running.

Then a brown face looked down at me, upside-down. A black crash-helmet with the visor in place.

I never thought I'd be glad to see a Paramil.

The air was full of the beating of psychopters.

It's hard to take things in, lying paralysed. The Paramils were hosing down the Jag, burying it in foam, its crumpled wing sticking out like the wing of a charred bird. The smell was awful. Then the Paramil captain pulled at the front doorhandle, gingerly. He got it open at the third attempt.

'Oh, Diane.' I thought. 'Oh, Loretta!' But I couldn't drag my eyes away . . .

Major Arnold got out stiffly, enraged and shaking but alive. Then he helped Mrs Arnold out. Then she reached back inside and pulled out Loretta, who was silly enough to touch the door-frame and burst into tears. Then Diane, huge-eyed but composed. I was surprised to see she had a perceptible bosom, but then I hadn't seen her for two years. I'm getting to be a real dirty old man, I thought, frantic with happiness that they were safe.

Then somebody thumped down behind me, swearing horribly. Keri. A Paramil was holding her arm twisted savagely behind her back.

'Leave her alone, you brown bastard. *She* hasn't done anything.' Trust them to get the wrong end of the stick.

'They're alive,' I said to Keri. 'They're all *right*.'

'Course they are, you stupid nerk. They got armoured

glass and an armoured petrol-tank an' two-way radio. Why'd you think I told you not to interfere?'

'I can't move.'

'They got you with a blaster.'

'It's all right, I'm not dead.'

But her eyes, looking over my shoulder filled with dread. I followed her eyes.

The Paramils were lifting the first petrol-bomber. They passed, carrying him. His body was limp, but his head was screwing this way and that, like a tied-up chicken's. His eyes were terrified.

They took him to the nearest psychopter; the stretcher-pods on its undercarriage were open, gaping like piranha-fish. They slotted him down one. As he really began screaming, they slammed the lid on him. His voice echoed weirdly, inside the metal tube.

They did the same with the second guy, a thin fair kid with his eyes screwed tight shut: the one I'd blinded with petrol.

The psychopter took off.

We both knew where for.

Then the Paramils loaded the kid lying next to me. I'll never forget the look on his face.

Then they came back and picked me up. Keri broke free and went for them. 'He's innocent. He didn't do nothing. He was trying to help . . .'

The captain took out his blaster, and gave her a stun. They picked her up as well . . .

'Oh, you *fool!*' she said to me, as they carried her away.

All I could think of was what they were going to do to my brain.

They slid me into a pod. Were just going to close the lid when I heard Loretta say, 'Daddy, why are they hurting Kit? He tried to save us – he hit that man.' Major Arnold had his back turned, trying to calm his wife. But Loretta was tugging at his coat. 'Daddy, why are they hurting Kit?'

A brown hand descended to close my lid. Then I heard

175

Major Arnold say 'Wait. I think there's been some mistake.' He sounded confused, feeble.

'We do not make mistakes. We are following regulations. The matter will be dealt with at the far end.'

'My daughter says this man was not involved in the attack. He was trying to help us.'

'Your daughter is a child. She was confused. How can she tell what she saw?' His hand tightened on the pod-lid, impatient to tidy me away and get on. But Major Arnold was getting mad.

'Look, she knows this young man well. He used to be our baby-sitter.'

'This man is one of *your* people?' asked the Paramil.

I saw Major Arnold swallow, break out in a sweat. 'He was a pupil of mine for ten years. The children know him well. He wasn't in the van . . . he was riding a motorbike . . . he tried to warn us.' Old Arnold would never tell a lie. But what he could do with a half-truth . . .

The captain nodded, grudgingly. Two Paramils pulled me out onto the ground carelessly, and slammed the pod-lid.

Then they slammed the other pod-lid down on Keri. Strands of her blonde hair still hung down outside the black pod.

'She was on the motorbike as well,' I screeched. 'She never went *near* the car.'

The Major nodded, wearily running his hand over his face. He was really putting his neck on the block for us. Bad-temperedly, the Paramils dumped Keri on the grass too.

We lay there, side by side, and watched. The Arnolds were bundled into a psychopter and flown off. Two bigger choppers, sky-cranes, arrived and hovered, lowering grabs to pick up the blackened Jag and the yellow van. Which had never belonged to East Midlands Water at all, but was now revealed as a poor fake, green paint beneath its yellow.

The captain came over and had a last frown at us, like

we'd spoilt his body-count. Then he flew off too, leaving only the big gap in the perimeter-wire, and a patch of churned, burnt grass, and broken glass glinting in the rain.

'Why do you Unnems *do* things like that?' I snarled. 'Those oafs didn't know Major Arnold from Adam. He's a good bloke. And little kids . . .'

' 'Cos they ain't got no hope. 'Cos their dads didn't have no hope. 'Cos if they have kids the kids'll have no hope. I'd do the same meself – only I'd plan it better.'

We glared at each other. We weren't strong enough to do anything worse. After a bit I said, 'D'you think you can crawl?'

'With one bloody leg.' We crawled side by side, as quickly as we could. Before the Paramils sent another sky-crane for Mitzi.

17

We felt better astride Mitzi. But we didn't feel like moving on; just sat staring blankly at the broken Wire and the burnt patch. Thought about Diane and Loretta, buried in flame; about the guys in the pods of the psychopters, still breathing, screaming, throwing up, but already as doomed as squawking chickens hooked to a broiler-house conveyor-belt . . .

Our cover was blown. Already, they'd have got my name from Major Arnold. And Mitzi's registration belonged to the vanished MacDonalds. Laura would certainly spot that. Maybe we had two hours left: enough time to go to ground in London North-East. Which was exactly where they'd look for us.

Then the wind blew, scattering the charred stems of grass; bringing the evil smell of petrol. But behind the petrol-smell came the huge smell of green. Green of grass and moss, pool and wood.

I looked up, noticing the country beyond the burning for the first time. Flat as a snooker-table. Hedges and spinneys, cottages, and barns. But nothing could disguise the snooker-table flatness, blurring away into misty rain. No Wires or watchtowers, factories or estates, right to where the mist descended.

'Nice,' I said.

'Like the cheese in a trap.' Keri said bitterly. 'Wherever there's cheese, there's sure to be a trap.'

'Might be a cheese-factory . . .'

'Sucker.'

'Rather go to London?' I started Mitzi and rode down

through the broken Wire. Careful to keep our wheels inside the wheel-tracks left by the yellow van.

'We don't know where this *is!*'

'Could it be worse?' I pulled up where the van's tyre-tracks ended. Forty yards on, a cart-track led out of the field. 'We'll have to carry the bike from here.'

'Why?'

'Paramils have eyes. Hurry!' I unhooked the panniers, and we carried them first. Mitzi was lighter than most bikes, but humping her across that field nearly killed us.

I drove her deep into the first spinney. 'Take a break – I'm going back to cover our tracks.' I had the sense to dump my leathers, change my boots for scruffy plimsolls.

The marks we'd left in the wet turf weren't too bad. But it was obvious to the eagle eye that *something* had happened there. I began trotting to and fro, between the cart-track and the burnt patch. That looked better – as if a small crowd had gathered; or some looney had run backwards and forwards to keep fit. I was still trotting when the big yellow fence-repair truck arrived, and a jeep-load of Paramils.

I wasn't daft enough to run away. I put a long stem of grass in my mouth and went to meet them, eyes full of wonder, total village idiot.

The Paramils inspected the marks on the grass with the old inscrutable Oriental eyes. One asked me, 'Where are your friends?' For a Paramil, he was surprisingly gentle . . .

'Gone back to work.' I stood embarrassingly close to him, let my spit spatter on his shirt. He backed off. He didn't like my three-week-old smell. The grass-chewing had filled my mouth with saliva. I let a bit of it drool. Even took him by the arm.

'We do be liftin' taters over there. Come and see.'

He wriggled his arm out from under my hand, trying not to show his distaste. I let my eyes go even wider, till the whites showed all round, as I'd often practised in the mirror.

'Big fires . . . choppers . . . fun!'

'Go back to work, please.'

I walked off, shoulders drooping like a disappointed child. But soon turned and gawped again. This situation was interesting. He hadn't asked me for any ID. He'd expected me to be scruffy, not too bright. Done his damnedest not to upset me . . . I continued gawping.

The repair-truck was worth gawping at, with the piledriver attached to one side, and the huge roll of green fence-wire to the other. It repaired the fence, good as new, without human help, in twenty minutes. The Paramils spent the time, with unzipped blasters, on the motorway embankment, only interested in keeping people out of this new place, not keeping the inhabitants in. That made it seem quite a nice place. Then truck and jeep drove off. We were safe inside.

Back at the spinney, Keri was fast asleep in a hedgerow, head cradled in her arms, hair flowing down her slender, shirted back and mixing golden with the ivy and cowparsley. The sun broke through the leaves and shone on her.

We wakened about tea-time, Sahara-thirsty. No drinkable water; no streams; just irrigation-channels, thick and green. Thirst drove us on. Too hot to wear bike-gear, we stowed it. Our slipstream blew up the legs of our jeans, down our shirt-sleeves, making them flutter like birds. The coolness was nearly as good as water.

The narrow road was raised above the land, endlessly long and straight and bumpy. With the flatness, and the hugeness of the sky, it felt like sailing. Keri complained she felt seasick. Deeper than the whine of the engine, the silence of the land sank greenly into us.

'Ain't it *quiet*?'

'No pinging at all,' I said, 'since we crossed the Wire.' Six hours and no psycho-radar. Even in the Highlands, we'd heard echoes of it every few hours.

Eventually, we did hear a helicopter, far off. Still no pinging, just the blat of chopper-blades.

'Mebbe they're testing *silent* psycho-radar,' said Keri, just to cheer me up.

I saw the chopper: it was fuzz of some sort. Circling to the south at zero height, vanishing behind spinneys and reappearing; being flown in a graceful, tricksy way, stopping dead, flying sideways, backwards.

'Keep cool,' I said. 'They're not looking for anybody, just filling in time. Routine patrol.'

But her hands tightened on the handlebars. She wiped one hand on the leg of her jeans. It was very tense, in that flat green emptiness.

'Sing!' I shouted. So we sang the old Racer's hymn: 'Take the piston from out of my crank-case . . .'

A what-the-hell feeling overtook us. Enjoy the now, sitting astride the razor's edge . . .

Louder and louder came the chopper. I told myself that all fuzz, even Paramils, are bored out of their mind ninety per cent of the time. Lots of the things they do are just to avoid going mad from boredom.

It flew alongside, still at zero metres, its blades sending purple whirlpools through the ripening corn.

'Wave!' I shouted. We waved like mad and held our breath. British Police would wave back; Paramils wouldn't.

They waved. Keri began to weave the bike from side to side, missing the ditches by inches . . .

The chopper accepted the challenge. Flew ahead of us, spinning in elegant circles, waggling its hips like a girl.

Keri, encouraged, put up her feet on the handlebars to steer. The chopper dropped back to watch. Then waved, and suddenly flew off northwards.

'Friendly!'

'Or silent psycho-scan!'

But I felt good. We saw tractors working in the fields, a combine. The drivers waved; we waved back. We passed a cottage on a corner, dozing behind dense laurels, only the red tile roof showing. A scrawled notice said:

'Strawberries 2c per kilo. Best tomatoes 3c per kilo. Wallflowers 4c a bunch. Beware of the dog.'

I made Keri pull up a hundred metres on. 'I'm going back for some fruit.'

'Be careful, Kit.'

'We've got to eat. They haven't got a phone in that house. They haven't even got telly.'

'I don't like it. It's like something out of a fairy-tale.'

'If I'm not back in five, get the hell out to the nearest wood. I'll find you.'

I was stiff from the riding. The road was silent. Flies buzzed. Then I saw the dog I was supposed to beware of. Brown and black and panting. Ears flopping. So fat he reared up on stick-like front legs with his belly spreading across the old bricks of the garden path. I leaned over the mossy, rickety gate and patted him; he licked my hand. I hadn't seen a dog for ages. Techs think they're dirty. Unnems kill them on sight – probably eat them.

The gate creaked alarmingly. On the right was a greenhouse full of tomato-plants. Glossy leaves pressed hard against the glass; gaps disclosed the female curves of unripe fruit, better than the ones my father grew.

I knocked, was about to knock again, when I heard a shuffling. I remembered Vic Huggett with a shudder.

But he was nothing like Vic, except he hadn't shaved and had a considerable paunch under his dirty blue teeshirt. His massive arms, folded across his paunch, were tattooed 'Marion my love' and 'Death before Dishonour'. He had a beaky nose, wrinkles round his eyes, and might once have been a sailor.

He looked at me, without hopelessless or hate: not an Unnem, then.

No superior watchful smirk: not a Tech either.

No bossy fake bonhomie: no Est.

He just yawned, without bothering to put his hand across his mouth.

'Kilo of tomatoes, please.' I kept it as short as possible. He led the way, wordlessly, to a black-tarred shed. Inside smelt heavenly: creosote, rope, soil and the overpowering smell of fruit. Rows of brown paper bags, already weighed.

'Take yer pick.'

I picked up a punnet of strawberries with one hand, a bag of tomatoes with the other. Then realized I hadn't paid. Tried putting five coins in his hand, without putting down either bag. One coin fell on the floor. We stooped for it, together.

'Don't bother . . . no bother,' said the man, gasping a bit with the effort. He'd totally lost interest in me. I only had to walk away. Perversely, I suddenly wanted to talk. 'Nice day!'

'Um,' he said. 'Tara.' Turned and began looping up a piece of hairy string that trailed from the tarry wall of the shed.

We took a long, long road, quaintly called Nine Mile Bank. The bank ran along above us, to our left, seemingly for ever. No turn-offs.

'If we don't stop soon, I'll die of thirst.' The tomatoes and strawberries lay safe between my belly and Keri's back; their knobbly coolness tempted me beyond endurance.

'There's no place to hide.'

'Stop trying to hide. That guy didn't care. The chopper didn't care. Different rules, here. They'll only notice if we *try* to hide.'

So we left the bike by the roadside and climbed the bank. There was a canal at the top, deep blue, reflecting the sky. The wind was blowing along it, making big waves. Reeds hissed, shone pale green in the westering sun, like pointed sword-blades. Further down, two swans were swimming.

We lay and ate tomatoes far too big for our mouths. Juice

squirted and dribbled. Keri giggled. 'Wash while you eat. What do you call these things?'

'Tomatoes. The others are strawberries.'

'Like in tomato-soup?'

'There are no tomatoes in your horrible tinned tomato-soup. Totally synthetic. Tomato-flavour is one of the easiest to fake. I can give you the formula . . .'

'Shut up, bighead!'

We rode on, eventually. Came to a village with an old grey church towering high above the rooftops. Keri stopped.

'What's that – a Paramil watchtower?'

'It's a church, stupid.'

'Oh! I read a book with a church in it, once. I thought they were only in books. Weren't they lucky to have this little hill to put the church on?'

I laughed. 'You know what that hill's made of? Five hundred years of buried dead bodies. So many, they've raised the earth-level three metres.'

'You're kidding?'

'Come and look at the tombstones . . .'

She spent ages among the tombstones, rubbing away moss and spelling out the old Gothic lettering with great persistence. 'Here's a little girl who died when she was two. In 1852. Isn't that *sad*?'

'Oh, for God's sake . . .' I got up to go.

'Don't you think it would be nice to be buried, instead of burnt? People can come and bring flowers. I had a girl-friend, when I started racing. The one I drank champagne with. We burnt her. Now I can't even remember her name. I wish she was here.' She started to tidy the grave, pulling out the long dead grass.

'Come and see the church,' I said, quickly.

She gasped at the church. 'It's all crumbling and falling to bits!'

'So would you be, after five hundred years.'

'Isn't it made of concrete?'

'No – limestone and flint.'

'What's limestone? What's flint?'

'I can't spend the rest of my life answering questions . . .'

'Why not? I thought you fancied me.'

We mooched round the interior, full of withered hymn-books, mouse-dirt and bell-ropes. She read all the memorials. 'Cripes, don't they forget *nobody* round here?' She squinted up at the ceiling, and gave a jump.

'Cripes – angels.' She backed towards the door.

'They won't bite you – they're carved out of wood.'

'But they're bigger than people – all that golden hair an' wings. Angels were in that book I read, too.'

She was silent, slapping her leather gauntlet on a bench-end. Then she said, 'That stuff about God is all Est crap, isn't it?'

I took a deep breath and said, 'I don't know.'

'Cripes – the great brain finally admits he doesn't know. Can we go up the tower?'

'If it's not locked.'

'Nothing's locked here. Aren't they frightened the Fighters will come and smash these coloured winders? An' pinch them gold candlesticks?'

'What Fighters? You'll find no Fighters here.'

We climbed the narrow dark spiral stair.

'I feel like a worm climbing a corkscrew,' said Keri.

We peered down on the village, as if it was a map. Clouds of rooks were circling round us, cawing in the churchyard elms. 'I wouldn't mind being a bird,' she said. 'How fast can they fly?'

'They can do about eighty, with the wind behind them.'

'Kit – I'd like to be buried here. Could you fix it?'

'No.'

'Useless, stupid Est.'

Nobody spoke to us; nobody came. Keri put a credit in the box for the tower-restoration fund. I had to stop her signing her real name in the visitors' book. Riding away, she said, 'Nothing happened there. Nobody could ever prove we were in that church at all. It makes me feel like a ghost.'

'Don't start kidding yourself you're invisible.'

But we might as well have been. We only saw one copper, in shirt-sleeves and pointed hat, talking to two women and a dog. Everybody else was busy, mowing lawns, cleaning windows. Blokes with their heads inside the bonnets of vintage cars, old Astras and Cavaliers that any Est would have given his eye-teeth for, and smothered in new enamel and polish. But these were broken-down and rusty, with blind headlights and dung-spattered number-plates. Car jacks lying carelessly in the gutter, and children's bikes and even ancient teddy-bears.

'Why doesn't anybody *steal* them?'

Uncut hedges, sprouting three metres in the air; lines of ragged, multi-coloured washing . . .

'Ain't anybody in charge? Everybody's just doing what they like . . . All *talking*.' Everywhere we looked, there were little groups talking and laughing.

She pulled up again, outside a butcher's. Outside hung huge sides of beef, whole carcases of pigs, scraped so clean their skin looked human. Rows of skinned sheeps' heads, some looking cocky and some looking stupid and some just looking dead. Flies crawling all over them.

'Not very hygienic,' I said.

'Poor things, they look so sad . . .'

'People have to eat. What d'you think's in that horrible pink luncheon-meat you're so fond of?

'Oh, *no!*'

'Don't worry. I doubt what you've eaten over the years has been responsible for the death of anything more than a soya-bean.'

She was seized with an insatiable urge to shop. Pounds of apples. Old-fashioned boxes of matches made of real wood. Brands of fags I'd never heard of. I was frightened she might be noticed, but the shopkeepers served her without a break in their gossip. We pushed on.

'This is Heaven . . .'

'No it's not. Look!'

Two hundred metres ahead, a Wire stretched across the countryside. A gate, with Paramils. A motorway, full of robos. Unbearable; we turned back, quick.

'This is another enclave,' I said. 'Eighty kilometres across, but just another enclave.'

'An enclave for what?'

'I think it's called the Fens. They grow all the fresh vegetables and meat . . .'

'For the bloody Ests!'

'Yeah, but there's something funny. It's too big . . . too historical . . . too *preserved*. I'm just starting to realize how little they ever told us Techs. And the Ests never wanted to know . . .'

'They never told us Unnems *nothing*.'

'I wonder if this has something to do with Scott-Astbury?'

Her face pinched up. 'Shut up. I'm *happy*.'

Ely was like a huge village. It was market-day, and even the enormous towers of the cathedral seemed engulfed by the market that flourished round their base. Mountains of cauliflowers, cascades of carrots with the earth still sticking to them. Piled crates of pigeons, hens, rabbits.

'Them hens isn't for eating, are they?'

'No. Hens lay eggs. Rabbits is for eating.'

'What – even them baby ones?' There was a hutch full of babies, flaked-out asleep with terror or boredom. But one, Chinchilla blue, was standing on its hind legs and peering out at us.

'That one wants to *live* – let's buy him.'

'Don't be daft. How can we cope with a rabbit?'

'He wants to be free. He *trusts* us.'

'More fool him.' I looked from her to the rabbit. They looked a right daft pair, her eyes shining, its nose twitching.

The rabbit pummelled the wire, as if it sensed its moment had come.

'That rabbit,' I said, 'is a very bad chooser. I'd rather be rabbit pie than go to a lobo-farm.' But I asked the guy how much it was.

'Three credits to you, mate. Fatten up nicely, with plenty of dandelion.' I thought Keri was going to hit him.

As far as I know, that rabbit was the first ever to enter Ely Cathedral. Perhaps the verger mistook it for a fur collar on Keri's leathers. It nibbled furtively at her hair, as we walked round the massive columns of the nave.

'I'm sure God exists,' announced Keri, squinting shrewdly up at the soaring vaulting of the crossing-tower. 'Why else would they go to all this bother?'

At dusk, we were idling through yet another village, conserving our batteries, when a delightful smell hit us, making our diet of fruit feel suddenly sloshy and unfilling. There was a dim rosy window at the end of the street.

DE-LISH FISH BAR
YOUR SATISFACTION IS OUR JUSTIFICATION
THE FINEST FRIED FISH IN THE FENS
MUSHY PEAS SPECIAL 1C
EELS OUR SPECIALITY
DO NOT LEAN BIKES AGAINST THIS WINDOW.

There was a gaggle of ancient petrol-driven motorbikes parked against the window: AJS, Ariel, Norton, even a Scott Flying Squirrel. We pushed our noses against the steamed-up glass. Inside, by the light of red-shaded wall-lamps with tasselled fringes, a man and woman in filthy whites were dumping avalanches of potatoes and dripping fish into great shining troughs.

'Techs?' asked Keri slyly; dodged before I could kick her.

An avid crowd of guys in old-fashioned fringed leathers waited, punching each other in the kidneys cheerfully, or shaking salt and vinegar into each other's greasy hair.

'Two whales and chips, please, Agnes!'

'Two battered cod and three battered wives.'

'I'll batter you,' said Agnes, raising a large implement dripping with fat.

'You won't get a better offer, Razzer. She's dead kinky wi' that fish-slice. Better'n flagellation.'

Keri said, 'What are chips?'

'Let's go and find out.'

When we came out with our sizzling packets, there was a crowd around Mitzi.

'Trouble?' muttered Keri.

'Leave this to me.' We strolled over.

'This your bike, mate?'

'What'll she do?'

'Right snazzer – shaft-driven.'

'Funny tyres.' They kicked them affectionately, making Mitzi wobble.

'Where's the petrol-tank?'

'Mitsubishi – Jap, right? Tommo here's got an old Honda.'

'What about a ride?' asked Razzer; a big kid with a shock of black hair and heavy jaw, obviously the leader. I got astride and gave him the nod. As he was settling, I shot off, making three kids jump for their life. Razzer enjoyed that. When we got to Nine Mile Bank, I fed on the juice, nearly left him sitting in the road.

'Not bad.' He leaned his unhelmeted face across my shoulder and read the speedo. 'Hundred an' eighty. Miles?'

'Kilometres.'

He whistled. 'Engine's got a funny beat.'

'Electric.'

'Electric starter?'

'All electric.'

'You're kidding . . .?'

A suspicion was forming in my mind. When we got back to the mob I announced, 'This is the famous Keri Roberts.'

'Hi, Kerry,' they said, casually as if I'd announced she was Margi or Jane.

They had no idea who she was at all.

'Haven't you seen her on the Box?' I asked.

'What box? A top-box? She can sit on my top-box *any* time.'

Then I knew why the houses had no TV aerials . . .

We spent another half-hour, giving them rides. In return, they let Keri ride theirs. She did a wheelie at ninety, the whole length of the village street. Got happier and happier, just as she had with the Glasgow Racers, at first. Only these weren't like Racers; they kept on playing daft tricks and laughing. We all got on so well that I finally popped the sixty-four-credit question.

'Is there anywhere we can stay the night? Bike's a bit low on juice . . .'

There was a horrible hush. They looked at us, as if seeing us for the first time. As if others before us had asked that question, and it had always meant trouble.

Then Razzer said, 'We'll take you to Pete. Pete'll fix it.'

'Pete fixes our bikes.'

'He can fix anything.'

'It's your head needs fixing, Tommo. Even Pete can't fix that.'

We all went off to see Pete.

18

Pete lived in a straggling village called Manea. They left us with him; roaring off, shouting goodnight loudly, as if glad to get away from a funeral.

Pete finished waving and turned to us. Odd-looking bloke, bald on top but with a mass of wild red locks lower down, so that his hair looked as if it was slipping off his head. He had a long, shiny nose and small, shrewd blue eyes. There were still white wood-shavings in his hair and beard, and he was still chewing his supper. Bacon and eggs, from his breath.

He looked at us very straight. He always did, Pete.

'We've had your sort before. It never works. They get bored and do stupid things. Then the inspectors pick them up . . .'

'We could do with a bit of boredom, what we've been through . . .'

He nodded, sighed. He wanted to refuse us, but for some reason couldn't. He looked pretty weary, then. I almost said, 'Don't bother.' But I was tired too.

'It's not much,' he said. 'But you're welcome to it.' He went into the house and came out with a rusty key, and led us down a brick garden path past ranked masses of beetroot, broad beans, heavenly sweetpeas. All growing hugely, like a jungle. The bees, even now, were busy in the dim light. It was funny, because beyond the fence was a garage with a solitary rusty petrol-pump and juggers parked, their engines ticking as they cooled. The smell of diesel came up from the black, oily, barren earth, mingling with the sweetpeas.

There was a black hut – no, an old tar-painted railway-carriage, wheels removed, a brick chimney built on to one corner. He went inside, lit a big hanging oil-lamp with a cracked pink shade. Its light revealed a great brass bedstead piled with folded grey blankets. Hung on the wall was an old photo of Ely Cathedral, in a crude do-it-yourself frame.

'There's grub ... odds and ends.' He pulled open a cupboard door, revealing a packet of salt, a tin of syrup and two candle-ends. 'Oh, come down to the house when you wake up and Joan'll give you some breakfast. Goodnight! ... Oh,' he paused in the doorway, 'hang up this flypaper – it's a regulation. We're bothered with flies ... we manure from our own earth-closets and flies cause tummy-upsets. It's the one sensible thing the inspectors do – make everybody use flypapers.' He pulled out a round blue package, tore off the wrapper, and let it run out. It was simply a metre's length of sticky, transparent, yellow paper, with a loop for hanging-up at one end, and a round weighted cylinder of bright blue plastic at the other. As he held it, a stray fly settled on the sticky stuff, got caught and buzzed tinily. Pete put the flypaper into my hand. 'Good night.' He pulled the door to, with a careful click. His footsteps went slopping off down the brick path.

'I like him,' said Keri.

I swung the flypaper by its loop, looking for a place to hang it. The hut was full of tiny flies, buzzing in the warm darkness.

'Hang it over the bed,' said Keri. 'I can't bear having flies touching my face while I'm asleep.'

I went on looking at the swinging flypaper in my hand. 'This thing's fifty years out of date.'

'Everything's out of date here. I like it.' She began to shake out the blankets. 'I could sleep for a week.'

'This blue plastic cylinder at the end's funny. It's hollow but . . .' I shook it. 'There's something heavy inside.'

'It's just to make the flypaper hang straight – stops it

curling up.' She thumped the blue-striped pillows into fatness.

'I wonder.' I pulled out my pocket-knife. There was a narrow crack round the end of the blue cylinder. I put in the knife and twisted. The end fell off onto the floor, and something small, shiny and metallic fell after it.

'A mickey-mouse,' I said bitterly. 'A listening-device. No wonder they don't need psychopters, with a listening-device in every room. No home should be without one.'

In the dim lamplight she suddenly looked old. 'D'you think . . . Pete *knew*?'

'No . . . he's got one hanging in his own window. They're bloody babes in arms round here. It's no wonder people like us get picked up by the inspectors . . . except, with *thousands* of flypapers in use . . . how can the Paramils tell which house?'

'I mentioned Pete's name . . .'

'Must be hundreds of Petes. Maybe we'll be OK for a bit . . . especially if I . . .' I opened the old tin of syrup and carefully dropped the mickey-mouse in. 'That'll give them a lot of sweet nothings.'

'We might have been making love or anything,' said Keri. 'I feel sick.'

'It'd be all right to make love now,' I said. Without hope; just to take her mind off it.

'No it's not – just the *thought* of it!'

I stirred the mickey-mouse round viciously. Tiny air-bubbles emerged and hung immobile in the syrup as if the thing was drowning. When I was satisfied, I spooned it out, put it back in its plastic container, and hung the flypaper over the bed.

We started to undress by the mellow glow. It wasn't romantic. Keri took off her jacket, then said,

'Stop watching me.'

'I wasn't,' said I, turning my back very ostentatiously.

'Well, don't.'

I don't know if it was the mickey-mouse, or the look of

that great bed, in which generations of Fenmen must have been born. But we slept apart, for the first time in weeks, at the extreme edges, like the North and South Poles. I thought sadly that the only way to get near her would be to grow handlebars on my head.

I wakened to see her face across mountain-ranges of grey blanket. She was awake, staring at the flypaper.

'It's dead,' I snarled. 'Microphones don't work when they're full of treacle.'

'I keep feeling sorry for the flies. They give up awfully quickly; even the big ones. Like people . . .'

The flypaper was black with insects, mainly still. But one bluebottle still had a leg loose and was waving it defiantly.

'That one's me,' I said. 'Waving to my passing girl-friend and she won't even *look* at me.'

'Don't – that's not funny.' She shuddered, exposing one creamy shoulder.

'*This* fly wants breakfast.' I jumped out of bed quickly, before that creamy shoulder tempted me to do something stupid. I had a feeling, from the back of my neck, that she had no objections to watching me get dressed. But when I turned quickly, she was staring at the flypaper again.

I got some very cold water from the rainwater-barrel outside, in a rose-painted bowl. We scraped a wash between us. Walked down the path and knocked timidly on the half-open door and there, just inside, was Pete at breakfast. Mouth incredibly full, he gestured us in. 'Joan!' he managed to get out, in a splutter of breadcrumbs.

She appeared, wiping her hands on a flowered apron. A big girl, with an oddly delicate head set on a long slender neck and a lot of straight blond hair, beautifully washed. 'Don't mind Pete – bacon-and-egg's his favourite accent. They come here with microphones to record him eating and singing at the same time – he'll probably distort the Fenland sound-archives. Come in – I expect you're ready to talk the same language.'

194

We sat in silence and watched Pete. He ate with the same swift craftsmanship as he did everything. Joan went into a dark corner and cut chunks of bacon off a whole side of pig hanging from the ceiling. Keri went a bit green. Then Joan cracked eggs into the frying-pan that still had straw and little feathers on them, stuck in place with hen's droppings. But the smell was terrific, and Keri changed her mind after the first mouthful.

'Don't they feed you, where you come from?' asked Joan. 'Where *do* you come from?'

Keri's eyes, terrified, swivelled to the flypaper in the window. Then she ducked straight into another mouthful of bacon, nodding her head vigorously.

'Yeah, where are you from?' asked Pete, mouth empty for a brief second. 'You can talk in front of Joan.' Again Keri's eyes swivelled to the flypaper.

'We've got ten times as many flies on our flypaper as you have on yours,' I said, trying to steer the conversation onto safer ground.

'Really?' asked Pete, suddenly interested.

'I'll go and get it,' I said. I had some crazy notion of substituting our flypaper for theirs.

Pete duly admired ours. 'I wonder why you catch more flies?'

'Shed be always full of flies,' said Joan. But Pete was examining our flypaper with narrowed eyes. 'The bottom's sticky . . .'

'That's the secret,' I said. 'Dip that plastic bit in treacle and you'll catch a lot more flies. Try it!'

'I will.' Pete dropped his flypaper straight in the breakfast marmalade, ignoring Joan's protests.

'Stick it well under,' I said viciously, 'and leave it for five minutes.'

'We come from London,' said Keri, getting her voice and colour back. She and Joan got prattling and she was soon led off to inspect some home-brewed beer, fermenting in the pantry.

Pete watched the flies coming to his newly dipped flypaper. 'Yeah, it really works.' That was always his highest praise: 'Yeah, it really works.' He gave me an old-fashioned look. 'You're not the usual sort we get out of London – bald, with green hair, all that stuff.'

'I'm interested in how things work.'

'Have a look at this. I'm trying to mend it.' The silent works of a grandfather clock hung from a high shelf on the wall.

I swung the pendulum gently, looking up into the old brass cogs as they started to turn. It wasn't difficult for a Tech to work out what was wrong with it.

'The escapement's worn,' I said, after a tactful length of time. 'If you bend the right side in a little . . . got a pair of pliers?' I squeezed gently, and the mechanism began to tick with a healthier beat.

'It could do with replacing, really . . .' I added.

I turned to find him regarding me narrowly. 'What's a Tech doing on the run?'

'We're not spies.'

'I know that. They wouldn't waste a good Tech on being a snooper. They wouldn't want a Tech floating face down in the Ninety-Foot Drain. We'm not fools, you know!'

'They don't need snoopers. Why'd you think I got you to dip that flypaper in the marmalade?'

'I was going to ask that.'

'Try opening it.'

When he'd opened it, and I'd explained, he said very quietly, 'I try to live peaceful. There's one of these in every kitchen and every bedroom in the Fens. In *our* bedroom . . .' He took a wooden stick, from a bundle that lay by the unlit fire, and bent it slowly, till it broke with a sharp cracking sound. His face was very white.

'You could tell everybody to dip them in treacle,' I said, faltering. Anything to take that look off his face.

'What?' he said bitterly. 'A quaint new Fenland custom? How long d'you think it'd be, before the inspectors traced it to us? We'll let it be. What've you come here for, stirring things up?'

'Just trying to get away. We're sick of it.'

'Yes.' He nodded slowly. 'I've seen what they're doing to you. Not many Fenmen have. But we run live eels up to London in our old van. To Billingsgate, to feed the high and mighty. And a good price they do pay . . . I'll try and help you. I suppose I owe you a favour . . . at least I can make love to my wife in private now. You like mechanical things? Come and see.'

He led me through to a spotless front room. 'Nobody but the vicar ever comes in here, apart from funerals. So . . .'

I gasped. The walls were hung with a shining treasure-hoard.

'That's a cavalry sabre of 1856 – thrown away by some poor Fenman after the Crimea. An' that's a pike from King James's time – handle's new though, I made it from a pitchfork. This musket – I faked the trigger-guard from the element of an old electric kettle. Not bad, eh?'

'Where'd you get them all?'

'Whenever a Fenman wants to get rid of a guilty secret, he do throw it in the Ninety-Foot Drain. Specially deserters. I got more Lee Enfields from 1917 than . . . you can have one if you're interested. Fenmen were never ones for war – got too much sense and more things to do. I mend tackle for fishermen and eel-trappers, and I don't overcharge. So when they dredge something up, they bring it to me.'

'Marvellous.'

'So the gennelmen from Cambridge and London do keep on telling me. Sold a few things to the Imperial War Museum – whole Vickers machine-gun, once. God knows how *that* got in the Drain. That's another reason I do have to go up to London.' He shuddered at the memory.

'This one's in good nick,' I said, taking down a revolver.

'Aye, that's one that's never been in the water. Smith an' Wesson. My grandfather brought it back from D-Day. The poor American who was a-carrying it had no more use for it, an' Fenmen can't abide waste. There's a pouch of ammo goes with it . . .'

'Tried firing it?'

'No. An' you're not a-going to, either. Here, we mend things, we don't kill things.' He looked at me very sharp, for quite a long time. I could almost have sworn he guessed about old Vic Huggett, and the two Paramils. I tried to return his stare innocently, and I couldn't. So instead I said, 'What's that?' pointing to a grey cylinder that hung next to the Smith and Wesson.

'Incendiary bomb – Second World War. Jerry Heinkel got jumped by a night-fighter an' dumped his load into the Forty-Foot. Didn't do him no good though – he crashed at Welney. Got hundreds of them things, can't find no use for 'em. Ugly little beasts – neither use nor ornament.'

Joan came bustling in. 'Peter, it's time you be out to Marsden's. Once old Marsden be getting on they phone, I can't get him off. An' I've got washin' to do.' She saw us holding the guns, turned to Keri.

'Men!'

But there was no spite in her voice; she made me feel like a child that needed cosseting. Keri was all pink and beaming too; she was going to help Joan bake bread.

'If your wife can't cook,' said Joan, 'you'll waste away to nothing.'

'I'm not his wife,' said Keri, ominously.

'You don't a-want to bother about a bit o' paper from the vicar, dear,' said Joan, motherly. 'You can be a wife without a bit o' paper. *Can't* you, Peter Yaxley?'

I don't know who blushed most, Pete or Keri.

'From now on,' said Pete, starkly, 'this gennelman is my second cousin from Ely, come to help me with the business. An' you're his wife an' you better not forget it, if you want to steer clear o' the inspectors.'

'Yes,' said Joan. 'There do be enough odd folk in Ely for you to get lost among.'

19

'It's about time you'm got yoursen to work, Kit Kitson. You can't sit there drinking tea all morning. You're worse'n my Peter. They'll be awaitin' to have that old notice mended, up at they Bird Reserve . . .'

I groaned luxuriously, took another swig out of one of her bottomless pint-pots. Sitting in her kitchen had become a habit. Sniffing at the drying herbs round her fireplace, tracing every whorl and scar of her well-scrubbed table-top, watching her peel potatoes. Even her nagging was part of the pleasure. It was never spiteful, a soft worrying at the secure boundaries of her world. The garden fence collapsing, and Peter mending every fence in the district except his own. A baby born premature, and how would it fare in this wicked world, poor mite? She lived in the middle of a web of mother and sisters, cousins and odd-habited neighbours. Gave out more news to the hour than any telly.

'Go *on*, Kit. Look at your Keri – she been up since six – don't know how I ever managed without her . . .'

I looked out of the open window, which was letting in fat bees and the rich smells of roses and manure. Keri, in an old washed-out skirt of Joan's, was organizing the hens into eating their breakfast. Any more bullying and they'd probably stop laying in protest. Her rabbit, Crankshaft, followed her everywhere, like a dog. She said he was as intelligent as a dog, only nobody expected rabbits to be intelligent. It had certainly learnt to climb fences in pursuit of her.

'She's not *my* Keri!'

'Be patient, Kit. She'm changing . . .'

I was changing too. I'd let my hair grow, lank and greasy, Fenman-style: only slicked it back when I went to the pub at night. My arm-muscles, laid comfortably on the table, were getting Fenman-massive. I'd had them tattooed; a satisfyingly hideous design of a dragon riding a motor bike; a heart with H.K. and K.R., much good it did me!

All protective camouflage against the Est birdwatchers who thronged the district . . .

I was changing inside, too. Sleeping deeper, eating more. I had an incipient Fenman paunch. I pulled at it with my finger and thumb, under my dirty teeshirt, half in sorrow and half in pride. Another Fenman habit, like lifting your voice at the end of every sentence.

'Kit, if ee don't get to work this instant, I'll take a broom to ee!'

With another enjoyable groan, I went; piling my tools on to Pete's old Velocette. We never used Mitzi now. Kept her hidden in a shed, fully charged, against emergencies.

When I reached the Reserve, Grannie Gotobed waved from her bedroom window. She kept the Reserve keys. 'Will thee see to letting them in today, Kit? Me back's bad again.' Lazy old thing; her back seemed to get bad every time I came to mend something. She was spry enough, shopping around the village . . .

I unlocked the great birdwatching towers of the Reserve, that looked over some rather skimpy wader-pools to distant Manea. When I'd first come, the towers had oppressed me, reminding me of estates and Wires. Now they were only empty wooden huts on stilts, where swallows flew in and out to build their little hanging mud-pie nests. Full of sunlight, fresh breezes and the cluck of duck.

Then I began to mend the entrance-notice which, planted in swampy soil in the full face of the north-east gales, blew down with monotonous regularity, whatever I did to it. I'd complained to Pete.

'Stop thinking like a Tech,' he said. 'That notice-board's your living, lad. They're paying . . .'

I worked, stripped to the waist, the sun strong on my back. The Est families came and went, clad in the correct green anoraks, carrying hampers and bottles of wine and huge binoculars round their necks, even the smallest children. The fathers carried cameras with huge telephoto lenses, called me 'old chap' and grandly tipped me a credit. I said 'Thankee, sir' and touched my forelock. I'd spent weeks building up a clownish Fenman act, which the other Fenmen found riotously funny, as I acted out the Est parts as well. But the Ests took me deadly seriously, walked away saying I was a typical Fenman. 'Centuries of fornicating in the mud, my dear, and it *shows*!'

It was a good day, full of wind hissing through the reeds and the piping of waders. By tea-time, I'd repaired the notice as well as was humanly possible. I went to lock up the birdwatching towers. There was often something worth having among the abandoned litter; a copy of *The Times* or a Bradenham-ham sandwich. But this time I found something different: a radio with telescopic aerial and numbered buttons. A child's toy in blue and yellow plastic. Called a Fenlistener Mark 3. I tapped experimentally on the numbered buttons; no Tech can ever resist buttons . . .

The first radio-station I got only gave the sound of a canary singing. On and on. I tried again. Sounds of running water, somebody washing up and whistling. Again, on and on. The next one gave only silence. And the next, the sound of a distant tractor . . . What extraordinarily boring programmes, each obtained by tapping out a four-digit number . . .

Then a voice came through, so startlingly loud and clear it might have been in the sunlit, wind-swept hut with me.

'Get off they table, Tigger! Ee shan't have my supper. Get off this moment, I say, or I'll cut your tail off!'

Granny Gotobed, talking to her cat on 7683. I tapped out more numbers, all starting with 7. I tapped a long, long time. Got Razzer's mum, telling him to stop mucking about with they filthy great bike and come and have his tea. Got

Joan, telling Pete not to muck about with her while she was cooking . . . The whole village of Manea, settling down for the evening, clear as crystal. All on a child's plastic toy, bought for a few credits; a minor Christmas present for an eight-year-old.

The Ests didn't come to the Fens birdwatching: they came people-watching. With binoculars and Fenlisteners, the whole life of the village was open to them. The Fens weren't just a market-garden, they were a zoo.

It had nothing to do with the Paramils. The Fenmen weren't regarded as any kind of security-risk. The Ests were keeping them as pet animals, for fun . . . It was Ests using the flypaper microphones, not Paramils.

At first, I felt relieved – about the Paramils. Then I felt sick. I remembered, when I was small, my father making a remark about people who Fenlistened; a disparaging remark, putting them on a par with people who drank gin before lunch, or shot birds for a hobby. He'd disapproved; but he hadn't tried to stop it. And I'd not listened properly, and forgotten about it. I didn't know about Fenlistening, like I didn't know about polo or horse-breeding, or archaeology. How much more was there that I didn't know? I felt sick with the Ests for being peeping-toms and I felt sick with the Techs for making it possible.

There was a tape-recording facility; I taped a bit of Joan and Pete, to take home. Pete had an old tape recorder . . .

Then I wrapped the Fenlistener in sandwich-papers and a plastic bag, and gave it to Granny Gotobed, in case the family came back for it. If they didn't, I added, perhaps old Peter Yaxley could find some use for it.

'Oh, yes,' said Granny, 'Peter Yaxley do like they sort of thing.'

'What do be souring thy milk, Kit Kitson,' asked Pete as I walked in. 'Sunstroke? Ee'll be all right for the play-rehearsal tonight?' he added, anxiously.

I groaned. Peter's flaming play, this evening, was really

a bit much. I glanced hatingly at the flypaper. 'You've not dipped your new one in treacle, have you?'

'Been busy. What do it matter, anyway? Ee sound more Fen-folk than we do, now.'

But Keri's eyes, suddenly fearful, returned to the flypaper. 'I'll show you why it matters.' I put the tape in his old recorder, pushed the buttons viciously. I played them their own voices; told them where they came from. Keri looked relieved. But Joan went upstairs and brought down her bedroom flypaper and smashed it to smithereens in the cold hearth with the poker. 'Eight-year-olds,' she said. 'Any eight-year-old.' She was white and shaking.

'What do it matter, love? We don't know they . . .'

'Thee'll find out why it matters, when thee gets to bed tonight . . .'

'I'll go and pick some salad for tea,' said Keri, tactfully. 'C'mon, Kit.'

After a silent meal, an even more silent washing-up, I walked down to the rehearsal with Pete. We rehearsed at the pub, which helped the flow, and ensured a good attendance. The play wasn't much: a Fenland version of the old hero-combat play performed in every village before the First World War. In which King George, in his scarlet soldier's coat, fought and killed the Black Prince of Paradise. Who was miraculously restored to life by the Quack Doctor. Who was played by me, complete with Victorian morning-suit, beard, stethoscope, alarm-clock, hammer and knife.

Pete was playing the Black Prince this year. I'd been given the part of the Doctor because of my Fenman-clowning, and because it wasn't a popular part. The Doctor had more beer thrown over him at rehearsals than anybody else, even the Horse. It wasn't a long part; it wasn't a long play.

'In comes I, who never cometh yet, the best Quack Doctor you can get!'

'How camest thou to be a Doctor?'

'By my travels!'

'Where hast thou travelled?'

'Icaly, Picaly, France and Spain and back to England to cure disease again.'

'What disease canst thou cure?'

'The Hump, the Grump, the Ger, the Gout, the pain within and the pain without. In my black bag I've got spectacles for blind bumble-bees, crutches for lame mice, plasters for broken-backed earwigs. I've lotions and motions, also fine notions, that have carried my fame o'er five oceans.'

'Cut,' said Pete wearily. He turned his back on the assembled company and drank heavily from his ale. His thin back, under a bright yellow teeshirt, heaved with the gulping.

I didn't blame him. The play, which had begun to take off at the last rehearsal, had thumped back into the mud like a shot quail. Joan was playing the Black Prince's mother like a blue-robed zombie, and glaring in between at the rest of us like we'd been personally responsible for inventing the Fenlistener Mark 3. Even Razzer, fearsome in King George's red coat, was wilting. Tommo, as the Horse, half-blinded by his costume, had fallen over bar-stools three times . . .

'Let's pack it up for the night,' said Pete, with a narky look at Joan. 'Maybe we'll all be a-feeling better tomorrow night.' He spat in the sawdust of the floor, slung his coat over his shoulder and stalked out. Expressing solidarity against all bloody-minded females, I grabbed my own leather and followed him.

'I really thought we had a chance this year,' he said, after we'd walked half the length of the meandering village street. 'You're the best Doctor we've ever had.'

'A chance of what?'

'A-going to Cambridge?'

'Cambridge?'

'The fair . . .'

'What fair?'

'The medieval fair in October. The best play-actors always get asked to the fair – from all over the Fens – fire-eaters and sword-swallowers, jugglers, fiddlers – the inspectors ask all the best ones. We came second last year, but second's nowhere. This year I was sure we'd make it, but now . . .'

'Oh, *that* fair!' I'd gone to it the year before, wasting three hours that would've been better spent on spectrography. Most Techs went to laugh. Not at the Fenmen, but at the Cambridge Ests, tarted up in medieval costume, fawning on the Fenmen, slapping them on the shoulders, patronizing them. Like the pseuds they were. The Cambridge Ests needed the Fenmen, like a hated man needs his dog. Techs needed nobody's love.

'Oh well,' said Pete. 'No harm in dreaming . . . Mebbe next year . . .'

I put my hand on his thin shoulder. 'Pete, old mate, we'll do it *this* year. I know what Ests like – a little touch of bawdy – they'll fall for it, hook, line and sinker. Joan'll come round . . .'

Pete stopped and looked at me, his face intense under the street-lamp.

'Get me to Cambridge, and I'm yours for life.'

I always remembered him saying that, afterwards.

Five nights later, the night before the Harvest Supper and our play, a wind, a real black Fenland special, blew down the Reserve notice-board again. Pete sent me up, told me to be quick about it. The wind had knocked slates off half the houses in Manea, and blown over our little outdoor stage, and he was rushed off his feet. Joan had recovered her good temper (Fen people have short memories: they're too happy to bear long grudges). She and Keri, pink-faced, were baking for the Harvest Supper, flogging themselves to death and singing as they worked. There was a harmless sexy mischief in Joan that morning, in all the women, young and old. It made me bubble a bit inside. So as I went up to the Reserve, I shoved six spare flypapers in my pocket. I'd play the Ests at their own game . . .

Granny Gotobed waved from her window, keys in hand, dead on cue.

'Did those people come back for their Fenlistener, Gran?'

'Not they. They do have more money than sense.'

'I'll take it for Peter Yaxley now, then, eh?' The family wouldn't miss it till they came Fenlistening again. By then, they'd have forgotten what Reserve they left it at.

I unlocked the tower-hides. Opened up a few old swallow's nests gently, slid a blue plastic cylinder into each. Then plastered up the entrances again with a bit of spit. They looked quite innocent by the time I'd finished. I kept the Fenlistener in a haversack hung on a fence-post, got on with mending the notice-board and touching my forelock. Enjoyed listening in to silly Est chatter all the morning. I mean, who but a female Est would describe a small, spotty, brown duck as 'ravishing'?

But there were two guys after lunch who interested me a lot more. Inspectors. Not your humble, Tech-type inspectors, in their cloth-caps, white coats and green wellies, posing as men from the Milk or Egg or Carrot Marketing Boards. No, these were Ests, from the Fenland Culture Survey, doubtless come to inspect our play tonight, and whiling away the time. Bulky men in white riding-macs, with well-brushed silver hair and blue eyes that relegated me to the rank of inanimate object, an ill-painted inanimate object at that. I christened them Tweedledum and Tweedledee. Tapped my buttons, and caught them in the West Hide.

'Look at that fat beggar in the vest, under the big chestnut tree, left of the church. Scratching his arse. Looks so natural.'

'Considering all the bother we've gone to, to keep them natural, that's just as well. How's the Fenland birth-rate?'

'Still rising. Fifty per thousand, last year. That last drug has doubled the number of twins. Some triplets, too.'

'Amazing. Who'd have thought, thirty years ago, it'd

have gone so well? We've got a lot to thank Scott-Astbury for. In fifty years' time Fenmen will have repopulated England.'

I couldn't believe my ears. I'd got it wrong again. The Fenmen weren't just pampered pets: they were being bred like cattle.

'Pity about Scotland. I go up fishing there, a lot. I could use a willing gillie, who knew his place.'

'I'm afraid I can't agree.' The second voice had gone cold. 'As you know, I worked very hard in committee, to get Scott-Astbury's Scottish scheme ... scotched. You can't *export* these people. They'd start putting two and two together straight away. We'd get trouble-makers – the mistakes of the twentieth century all over again. The way we're doing it – by *natural* emigration, does them no harm at all. Expand the Fenland Wire by a few miles a year, leave the land derelict and the farmhouses not too knocked about, and these Fenmen just naturally move in and squat on the new land. They actually think they're pulling a fast one on us. Oh, we've no problems here. The point is, can your people clear out the Unnems in time?'

'Oh, no problem. The elderly Unnems are dying off like flies – only problem is sniffing out the bodies before they become a health-hazard – we're training dogs for that. The middle-aged are frightened to stir out of their houses, even for food. Epidemic of pneumonia last winter in Birmingham ... and the number of suicides! Our main difficulty is pressure on the crematoria.'

'And the young are as busy killing themselves as ever?'

'The Futuretrack concept was a stroke of genius. Scott-Astbury again, of course. His illness is a ... very sad business. Yes, the Futuretracks have skimmed off the bright and the bold – the potential leaders. And as Scott-Astbury reminded us, only one rat in twenty is a leader. Skim off the leaders into being Racers and Singers and Harlots, and you can drive the rest like sheep. In five years' time we'll have the remnant pinned inside London, Birmingham and

Manchester. Then it'll just be a matter of time, like the Indian Reservations of the Old American West.'

'One almost begins to feel sorry for them.'

'After what they did to British Coal and British Leyland? The Scargill strikes, the Bennites? No, Scott-Astbury had the answer to unemployment. Control men through their lusts. Give the Ests their idleness and silly dreams. Give the Techs their scientific rivalries and hates and envy. They won't even bother to ask what's happening in the world. There are still a few troublemakers left like old Kitson. But they'll go the way of Idris Jones eventually . . . And give the Unnems their way with bikes and sex and drugs and music and fighting, and they'll do the whole job for us . . . Hey, see that woman hanging out her washing under the sycamore tree, left of the corn-stack? Well, her husband's standing watching her boobs as she reaches up. We're going to have a bit of courtship-ritual there in a moment.'

'Where, where? The corn-stack, you say?'

I punched the buttons of the Fenlistener at random, just to shut up their salacious voices.

I knew now what Blocky knew, and I couldn't stand it. I wanted to run, to scream, to smash. But I couldn't. Any untypical behaviour would draw the eye of the inspectors . . . So I got back to driving in posts for the notice-board. Till the sweat ran down my face and blinded me. Till the sledge-hammer sliced off the shredding top of a post and nearly crippled my left foot. I thought about Vanessa, still trying for her Sisterhood; George, still looking for a Champ to manage. The Bluefish. Rog. All lost inside the contracting, squeezing worlds of the estates, like a scrap car in a metal-crusher.

And Pete and Joan being used as breeding-stock . . . at least killing people showed a certain respect . . .

Eventually, the two inspectors passed me, going out. One nodded towards me,

'Fine specimen, that. See his back-muscles?'

They'd never know how close they got to getting my sledgehammer through their elegant silver skulls.

Meanwhile, I had to clown tonight, make people laugh. Tonight, the two inspectors would be watching.

They'd come – were sitting at the front, on ornate Victorian chairs specially carried from one of the cottages. Tweedledum and Tweedledee. I was glad of my top-hat and false moustache: they helped to hide my hate.

Now, the play was nearly over. It had been a wow. I'd excelled myself. Funny the ways hate can come out. Making the two swine laugh, tweaking the nerve-ends of their Estish brains that I understood so well, was a kind of power that gave me a sad, black glee.

The Black Prince of Paradise lay flat on his back, already slain by King George. Razzer had hit him such a thump I feared serious injury. Now Joan was entering, stately in blue, blond hair in plaits, the Prince's mother.

'What are your fees to cure my son?'

'Five pounds, Mary. But you being a decent woman, I'll only charge you ten.'

'Well, cure him.'

I bent over Pete, and could have sworn he was really dead; but the hairs in his nostrils moved slightly.

'Here, Prince, take three sips from this bottle. Now arise and fight your battle.'

'Thou silly man, as green as grass, the dead man never stirs.'

I waltzed round the stage in an agony of comic bewilderment. (Tweedledum nearly burst a seam of his riding-mac.) 'Oh, Mary, I took the right bottle off the wrong cork. I have another little bottle in my inside...outside... *backside* pocket, which will soon bring him back to life again.'

The inspectors laughed again, hearty Est bellows that somehow drained the life out of the genuine giggles of the crowd. I gave Pete three more sips. He leapt up, turning a somersault, and whaled into Razzer like a man demented. My part over, I retired into the darkness, away from the growing bonfire, to give myself up entirely to hate.

In came Beelzebub, played by fat, face-blackened Charlie Smith, another biker. He didn't look much like Blocky's painting of the devil.

'On my shoulder I carry a club, in my hand a dripping-
    pan
And I reckon myself a jolly old man.
I've just done six months in jail
For making a whipcrack out of a mouse's tail . . .'

My own position exactly. I needed the biggest whipcrack in the world, to beat the Ests from power. And all I had was a mouse's tail . . . one motor bike. Should I go back to Glasgow? Do a deal with Blocky's devil? How much power would he give me, in exchange for my alleged immortal soul? Never enough. But Beelzebub was running on . . .

'Early Monday morning, late on Saturday night,
I saw, ten thousand miles away, a house just out of
    sight;
The doors projected inward, the front was at the back,
It stood alone, between two more, and the walls were
    whitewashed black.'

Topsy-turvy illusion. Topsy-turvy illusion to fool and beat the Ests . . . but *how*?

But here was Horse now, a horse's skull held up on a stick, by Tommo with a blanket thrown over him. In the flickering firelight, Horse's skull looked like death and hell itself. It reminded me, though, of the wooden horse of Troy . . . Tommo declaimed hollowly,

'I've travelled to the land of Ikkerty-Pikkerty
Where there's neither land nor city,
Houses thatched with pancakes, walls built with penny
    loaves
Little pigs with knives and forks in their backs
Crying out who'll eat me . . .'

That's what we'd all become, in the hands of Scott-Astbury. Little pigs running about with knives and forks in their backs, crying out, 'Who'll eat me?'

The play ended. Mind still awhirl with half-grasped ideas, I stepped up to receive my share of applause. Applause out of all proportion, because there was a sudden electricity running through the crowd. Even the inspectors were infected, out of their cool appraisal, for a moment. Stepped forward, red-faced in the mounting firelight, grinning from ear to ear.

'Well done indeed. Never seen it done better. Come and do it for us at Cambridge . . . I'll put an official invitation in the post first thing tomorrow.'

Pete was shaking his head in disbelief; Joan clinging to him, almost screaming with delight.

'Oh, Pete, Pete, *Cambridge*. You've always wanted Cambridge.' She put her head on his shoulder; she was crying. Pete saw me watching.

'We're going to Cambridge, Kit.'

'That's *great*,' I said; and I meant it. I'd seen a way to end the Scott-Astbury obscenity.

Laura was in Cambridge.

I was going to destroy Laura.

But the evening was moving on past me. The props, the frail little proscenium, had been swept away. The bonfire was being stoked higher. The crowd was spreading out, forming huge circles, alternately man and woman. Handing round the open bottles of rich red wine that were the special gift of the inspectors . . .

Beginning the dance of harvest home, the celebration of fertility, that went back . . . how long? To the time when there weren't even fields, when the Fenland was a silent dark of pool and mere, plash of fish and croak of heron?

Or a mere thirty years, to the time when it was spawned out of the metal wires of Laura?'

Keri grabbed my hand. Gave me a bottle to drink from. I wanted to refuse, but the inspectors were watching . . .

'Kit, you were smashing tonight. You really made them laugh their socks off. C'mon, I'll jump through the fire with you.'

I went – because I didn't want her jumping through the fire with anybody else. We joined the inner circle with Pete and Joan – unmarried men and maidens and young, childless couples. I felt the eyes of the inspectors watching, assessing the dance as it took shape with tentative shufflings and little flurries of movement. No doubt the inspectors were analysing, tapping the buttons of hand-held computers in their deep pockets. Like inspectors all over the Fenland tonight. Assessing the urge to be fertile, to multiply and cover the land. The meek inheriting the earth.

When all the Unnems were dead . . .

The circles began to move – impossible not to move with them. My arms and legs and finally my guts took fire, and for a while I forgot about the inspectors.

After Keri and I had leapt through the highest part of the fire, we ran out of the circle, people beating out the flames on our clothes and touching us, crying meaningless shouts of praise at us, as if we were gods. We ran up the village street, so empty and glowing-red from the fire we hardly knew it. The wind was cool on our bodies as we ran; cool after the flames. We ran up the old brick path to our railway-carriage; Keri scrabbling in her haste to fit the key into the lock.

'Don't light the lamp.' She drew back the curtains and the distant red of the bonfire leapt into the room, changing everything, making me stand quite still in the shadows.

Rustlings. Then Keri walked to the window and looked back at the fire for a moment, and I saw from her silhouette that she was naked. She turned, and the light of the fire cupped and stroked the fullness of her breasts.

'Kit,' she said, like she'd never said it before.

'No,' I said. I was not a breeding-bull. Beyond the red night I could see a grey morning. No son would come out of me to splatter his young life over the front of a robo-truck; or journey into the dark in a psychopter's pods. Or be exported to breed in Caithness or Cornwall, by a routine order tapped out by a computer. 'No.'

'Yes, Kit, yes. Or I'm going back to the fire to find somebody else.' She walked straight up to me and kissed me. She was crying; her tears ran down my face.

As she bore me down on the bed, I cursed the fact that I was human.

20

I was wakened by Keri leaving bed swiftly. Opened my eyes just in time to see her naked shoulders flashing out through the hut door, into the early-morning sunshine. Then the door banged shut again, leaving me in the curtained dark.

I turned over, irritated: that was the third time this week. What on earth was she up to, walking about outside stark naked? Our hut was pretty private, hidden from the road, and it was only 5 a.m. But Fenmen are early risers . . . and there was a good old Fenland chamber-pot with rosebuds, under the bed.

Protectiveness and jealousy jolted me wide awake, far earlier than I liked. I got up to follow her. But something made me open the door cautiously, only a crack.

She was crouching, just outside, over a faded blue polythene bucket. I admired for the hundredth time the silky beauty of her back, the deep smooth groove where the tiny bumps of her spine just showed under the skin.

Until her back heaved, and I heard the sound of retching. I closed the door silently, not to disturb her. If she knew I'd seen her like that, she'd never forgive me.

I went back to bed, wondering what she'd eaten. Joan kept a clean kitchen . . . the ever-present flies? When she finally came back in, I pretended to be asleep. She paused in the darkness, just inside the door, listening, intently aware of me. It wasn't easy, pretending to sleep. She'd heard me asleep; I'd never heard myself. I breathed heavily and sighed hopefully. Apparently the sighs convinced her. She relaxed a bit, began to move about.

Then stopped again, and whispered desperately to herself.

'Oh, shit. Oh, shit!'

I'd never heard such desperation. Couldn't bear to listen, so I pretended to half-waken. 'What you doing? What time is it?' I tried to keep my voice ordinary, early-morning grumpy.

She came back to bed abruptly. I pulled her close, partly to comfort her, partly to comfort myself. She pretended to cuddle in, but she was tense, stiff as a board. I could feel her trying to relax, and failing.

Finally she threw herself out of my arms, rolling across the bed till she was on the very edge. I put out my hand, and ran it down the silken furrow of her spine. As I did, she broke into a sweat all over. Yet she was icy-cold.

'What's the matter? You ill?'

Silence.

'I said, are you ill or something?' Panic made me savage.

Silence. Silence till I could have hit her, for destroying our happiness. Then she said, 'Oh, go back to sleep. I'm getting up. I've got things to do.' Her voice was a strange mixture of love and rage. Like she was my mother and worst enemy, all rolled in one.

I listened with my back turned and my eyes tight shut while she got dressed. Her dressing sounded different from usual; I couldn't work out how. Not till I heard Mitzi start up outside. Then I knew she'd dressed in her leathers. She hadn't worn them for weeks.

Oh, well, if it helped to work off her temper . . .

But the burst of acceleration as the bike shot off down the path made me shudder. Bits of crumbled brick showered against the wooden wall of the hut.

The noise of Mitzi whined off westward. Keri made her howl like a string of obscenities.

Illogically, I fell asleep again.

I was wakened by the heat of the climbing sun oozing into the hut. Ten o'clock. The heat always became unbearable by ten. Keri had been gone hours. I knew she hadn't come back. I'd have recognized the sound of Mitzi even in my sleep.

I hurried down to Pete's, tucking in my shirt as I went. Even though it was hot and only September, it was autumn. Pete's outdoor tomato-plants were curling up their leaves as they died, exposing their clustered fruit to the ripening sun in a final ecstasy of abandonment. Joan was busy stripping her rows of runner beans down to the final pod, cutting the strings that held them to their canes and trampling leaves and stems into the earth with her wellies, to provide fertilizer for next year. Pete was up a ladder, pointing the bricks of his gable-end before the sharp teeth of winter tore into them.

It was a clear-up morning, a morning of endings. In the fields, every tractor stood silent. The fields were brown, bare and empty, except for the winter-greens, all the way to the horizon, where the towers of Ely Cathedral were lost in a dark-blue mist that spoke of coming cold. The sense of things ending made me panicky, as I called up to Pete, 'Can I borrow the Velocette? Keri's taken Mitzi.'

Pete looked down and considered, the autumn sun glinting on the bald patches under his ginger hair.

'Yeah, help yourself. You not working today? Fred Johnson wants his harrow seeing to.'

'In a bit.'

Pete gave Joan a glance, over my head. But I didn't want to tell even them; and they were too nice to ask me. I got the Velocette out, and went through the complex fiddle of starting her. I knew they were watching me sympathetically, which only made things worse. Had Keri told Joan what was the matter? *They*'d been married awhile; *they* were experienced.

The Velocette was a bitch; there'd been a heavy dew; the grass was still wet. Finally, she fired. At least I knew which way Keri had gone. In the Fens, she didn't have much choice of roads ... But after two miles I did come to a cross-roads. Luckily there was a damp patch of mud on the corner, from the last heavy rains. Mitzi's distinctive tyres had cut right across it. She'd turned left for Sutton. Then I realized where she'd gone. Nine Mile Bank. Where we'd been happy that first day. She always went there, when she wanted to think. And indeed Mitzi was there, parked as usual by the third hawthorn bush.

I smiled. I'd known she'd never harm Mitzi . . .

Harm? What did I mean, harm? Suddenly dry-mouthed, I ran up the bank.

She was sitting with her booted legs thrust down towards the rippling waters of the drain. One gauntleted hand rested on her crash-helmet, beside her. Still as a statue; as if she'd been sitting there a very long time; staring out over the Fen landscape. Or the cloudscape above. Probably the clouds; her face was wistful . . .

'Keri?'

She turned; wide, blank eyes full of sky. Then she pushed her hair back, and I could see where tears had cut channels down through the light brown road-dust on her face.

She said nothing. Her eyes remained remote; hostile now, as if my coming had robbed her of something.

'Keri – are you ill?'

'I'm pregnant.' She said it so flatly that at first I didn't take it in.

'But . . . but . . .'

'But girls don't get pregnant these days? You forget, mate, I was on Futuretrack Five when you caught me. Us girls didn't need the Pill – we're usually dead inside the month. I'm not your little friend from Futuretrack Six.'

'But . . . but . . .'

'But-but-but-but,' she mocked. 'You sound like the bloody Velocette. But *nothing*. You've really done it, mate.' She turned away, back to the infinite Fen. 'I was *free* when you found me. Now what do I do? Wait till I end up a Valium-sodden old cow on some estate?'

'I love you, Keri.'

'You love me now, 'cos I'm free. Will you still love me when I'm up to my eyeballs in Valium?'

'But if I'd let you go on racing, you'd be dead by now!'

'Yeah!'

'What do you mean, yeah?'

'Yeah, I know I would be dead. That was the best part – why I could enjoy every minute. On a bike, they can't touch you. Before they can get their hands on you, you're dead.'

I reached out a feeble hand.

'Don't touch me. *Don't touch me.*'

I touched her. She lashed out like an unleashed spring. I had to fall over backwards, or she'd have broken my nose.

'How can I help?'

'Give me Mitzi.'

'OK.' Then I grasped what she meant. 'To race? To race again?'

'To get back the Championship before . . . I've still got a few months riding before . . . it . . . starts to show. On Mitzi, I could set a lap-record they'd *never* break. They'd never forget me . . . Even when I was dead.'

'No,' I said.

Her face turned white; her eyes deep-sunk. She bit on the scar where she always bit when she was racing. The little trickle of blood ran down her chin.

'Keri, I can't . . . it would be murder . . . I don't want . . .'

'You don't want me wrecking your precious bike. Well, you've ridden *me* often enough. Night after night. Wasn't that better than riding your rotten electric toaster? You've ridden me to *death*. You owe me that bike.'

'But Joan . . . wants kids.'

'Joan lives here – Joan's got a good house. What'd we do in the winter with a kid, when the water-butt's frozen an' we can't even wash? I'd have to have a doctor an' he'd register the birth and that would bring in the inspectors an' they'd put me back on one of the estates. Or do you want me to have the kid in the corner of some field? Deliver the kid with your own hands, Supertech? I'm not some rotten gadget you can fix.'

'Keri, I'll think of something. Give me time . . .'

No reply, except the distant noise of a helicopter, faint as the chirr of a cricket.

'Keri, please. Look at me.'

'If you don't give me Mitzi, I'll *drown* myself. What d'you think I've been sitting here for, staring at the water for hours? Only I haven't got the guts – yet.'

I became aware of a faint ping, ping, ping inside my head. I'd been feeling it for some time; not paying it any attention . . .

We were close to the Wire here. Too close to be having feelings like Keri's. They could be onto her. Psycho-radar always picked up the suicidal, clearest of all. The biggest blips on the radar-screen were always the suicidal . . .

'Keri – they're on to you.'

'See if I care. Maybe after the lobo-farm it doesn't hurt at all.'

I, in turn, looked up into the glorious cloudscape. I could see the psychopter now; a tiny black speck in a purple and gold canyon of cloud, beautiful with sunbeams streaming down like searchlights. The psychopter was heading straight for us.

'Keri, suppose I told you I was going to smash all this – psychopters, Paramils, Wires, the lot . . .'

'Cripes.' She turned on me a face of total disgust. 'You and who's army?'

'I smashed the Arcdos for you . . .'

'This is a bit bigger than a rotten Arcdos . . .'

'I'm going to blow up Laura, when we go to Cambridge next month.'

That made her look at me. 'You mean you're going to try.' But there was a flicker of interest: her white bony look was starting to fade.

I glanced up at the psychopter. I could see the pods on its

undercarriage. In five minutes, Keri would be inside; in an hour, no longer human.

'Keri, I *know* Laura. I worked with her. I know how she's defended.'

'You'll get yourself killed, you mad bastard.' But there was colour in her cheeks.

'Come and get killed with me. I need your help.'

'Why didn't you ask me? Oh, you bastard, you lovely, mad bastard.' She flung her arms round me. 'Can I ride Mitzi when we do it?' Tears were streaming down her face. 'What do we do now?'

The psychopter roared in low, the waves of air from its blades beating through my hair.

'We make love,' I shouted. 'Make love, or they'll have us.' Desperately I fumbled with the zips of her leathers, the zips of my own.

'In front of them?' she shouted.

'Especially in front of them.' We must look, from up there, like two wriggling white maggots, naked on the waving grass of the bankside . . . But lovers' quarrels, even rape, were not a crime in the Paramils' book. Especially in the Fens, where fertility is at all times to be encouraged . . .

'If I blow up Laura,' I shouted, 'there'll be *chaos*.'

'Oh, God, give me chaos,' she screamed and writhed into her ecstasy.

Out of the corner of my eye, I saw the psychopter zoom away angrily at zero métres. The observer was thumping the screen of his psycho-radar.

They always had trouble filtering out sexual frenzy.

21

Once you've made up your mind to do something, it's only a matter of working out techniques. Techniques, to a Tech, are like nuts to a monkey. I stayed very cool throughout. *Why* you're doing something is what gets you het-up. *How* is as soothing as a crossword-puzzle.

'Hey, Pete?'

'Yeah?'

'I been thinking. We can't take the play to Cambridge with that tatty old proscenium. Least puff of wind will knock it over. We'll look right idiots . . .'

'Look, if you think I've got the time, with all these roofs needing mending . . .'

'No sweat – leave it to me. I'll knock you up a solid job with light steel scaffolding – steel guy-ropes and everything. Stand up to a hurricane.'

'All on your own?'

'Razzer and Tommo will help – they're slack after harvest.'

'Get on with it, then. None of your fancy ideas, mind.'

'Just one, Pete. At the end of the play, I thought it'd be nice to have two steel flagpoles rising up out of the proscenium, carrying Union Jacks. Worked by pulleys.'

'Suit yourself.'

I pulled on the pulleys. Out of the vertical tubes of the proscenium rose two thinner steel tubes. They doubled the height of the proscenium. I pulled another rope, and Union Jacks broke out at the top and fluttered bravely in the evening Fen breeze.

'Smart that,' said Pete. 'Who pulls the pulleys on the night?'

'Me – I'm offstage at the end.'

Pete walked across and tugged at the whole proscenium. It was rock-solid, didn't even sway, held by guy-ropes spreading out on either side.

'Good piece of craftsmanship. But heavy . . . Think the old truck'll take the weight?'

'I'm going to reinforce the front of the truck with a lot of scaffolding round the cab. That'll hold her.'

'Yeah,' said Pete wearily. 'Just as long as you take it off, afterwards.'

'I'll do that,' I said. Knowing there wasn't going to be any afterwards.

I drove into the middle of the spinney, deep among the fir trees, out of sight of the road. I took the hinged plastic-board off the Velocette and opened it out. A life-size cut-out of a Paramil, not very well painted. Still, there was the painted blaster-hand, the crash-helmet and visor. It looked nasty enough. I set it up against a tree, rode the Velocette back to the edge of the spinney. Walked about a bit till I was thoroughly lost, then took the Smith and Wesson from my pocket.

Pete wouldn't miss it. I'd carved a wooden replica to hang on his front room wall. He never touched the Smith and Wesson from one year's end to another. It had been thick with dust. I loaded it now: six brass shells, seventy years old – relics. Then I slipped deeper into the wood, hunting my Paramil.

Tricky: afternoon sun was falling through the branches, dappling the trunks and breaking up their shapes. It'd be doing the same to my Paramil. If I could hit him first time, I could hit any of them. Funny, hunting something you'd made yourself. I wondered if the ammo would work; I'd better find out now. I wondered how out of practice I was. Pistol-club at college was two years ago . . .

You don't forget, though. Like swimming, or riding a bike – once you've learnt, you never forget.

The image flicked on my eye suddenly, out of the light and shade. My feet leapt apart, straddled. My arms came up together, both hands on the gun. My neck retracted into my shoulders like an old tortoise and I pulled the trigger twice. Perfect, my old instructor would have said.

Except there'd only been one bang. One bullet was dud. I broke the gun and emptied out the shells. One fired shell, with a hollow, black smoking end. One dud, with the little dent the firing-pin had made. Four unused shells, looking as good as the dud.

I walked across to my Paramil. The plastic-board was smashed right in the middle of the chest. Not bad, at twenty metres among foliage. But it still didn't console me for the dud.

I settled down to wait for quarter of an hour. The bangs coming out of the spinney *must* sound like a Fenman shooting pigeons, bang-bang, both barrels. Not like Custer's last stand . . .

It's hard to find a bit of waste-land anywhere in the Fens. The soil's so fertile, Fenmen use every centimetre. Often rent out ten square metres to each other for a hen-house, a garage, or a cabbage-patch. Fenland's like a patchwork quilt, with stitches of temporary fencing. A big, bright square of yellow mustard here; a smaller square of white chrysanthemums there, for sale at roadside tables ('Take what you want and put the money in the bowl – beware of the dog').

But I found a patch of waste-land eventually – a corner where the field-drains had clogged and the ground gone marshy. Willows grew in dense clumps; in the middle was a disused hen-hut, sodden black with damp. Into that I placed my trial bomb, German incendiaries dropped into the Forty-Foot seventy years before; thin grey cylinders, casings corroded with pale dust. The triggering device was another Fenlistener, acquired in a Chatteris junk-shop. The old man had the decency to tell me the radio didn't work, except for boring plays, and not even those at night . . . The technicalities of the detonator I won't bore you with.

It was a bright, sunny day, about noon, when the tractors stop for two hours, and every Fenman puts up his feet after a heavy dinner before groaning back to work. I retired to a safe distance, took a blue flypaper from its wrapping and shouted into it.

For a second, nothing happened. Then there was a tinkle, as the hut window blew out; a puff of solid white smoke; then the whole hut dissolved into a raging blue-white firework, brighter than the sun. After two minutes there was nothing left to burn, only a slight haze where the grass was smouldering.

Good craftsmen, those old Germans; better than the Yanks who made the ammo for the Smith and Wesson.

This bomb had used two incendiaries. I had eight in my second bomb, a leather satchel hanging in a cupboard at home. A leather satchel that was a careful replica of the electronic test-kits that some Techs carried round the Centre, to test for faults in the wiring.

I imagined the satchel hung round Laura's neck by a thick steel wire; imagined the blue-white fire burning into her stainless-steel casing, turning it white-hot, melting her marvellous brain into dribbles of metal and glass. And as she slowly distorted, melted and died, she might send out strange garbled signals that would ruin the programmes of her sisters, those other computers she had long ago burgled and dominated at Idris's command. Maybe she could blow their minds too; wreck the whole national control-system. Techs hammering away at the keyboards and getting nothing back but garbage . . .

It left me weak-kneed with excitement; which I promptly crushed.

Emotion makes bad Techs.

'All loaded, Kit?'

'All aboard, Pete!'

'Let her roll, boy!' He and Joan scrambled up beside me in the cab, already dressed for the play, bubbly as kids on a day out. Joan wound down the window, ready to wave to her mother, six sisters, five aunts and twenty-two cousins, who would be clustered at their garden-gates, ready to give us the big send-off as we passed.

I swung out of Pete's yard cautiously; it wasn't easy to see ahead, because of the big framework of welded girders that covered the front of the cab.

'You certainly built that to last,' said Pete. 'Must weigh a ton. You could knock down a barn with this old lorry now, and never get a scratch.'

Oh, Pete, Pete, if you only knew.

I'd hung a lot of flags and bunting over every centimetre of that framework, to hide it from prying Paramil eyes; we looked infinitely festive, and I kept the speed down to fifty, in case it all blew away.

Through my rear-view mirror, I saw Keri close-up on Mitzi. Mitzi too was hung with rosettes, a glory of Fenland folk-art. She could have been an old AJS, except she ran so silently. Then Razzer joined her on his Norton Commando, and that made noise enough for two. Tommo and the rest of the actors joined in, as we passed their cottage gates. Soon Mitzi was safely lost in the middle of a roaring, blue-smoking mob.

We passed over the Old Bedford River at Welney. Timing was crucial. Brightly festooned lorries were joining the main road all the time, all heading for Cambridge. If we got too near the front of the procession, the Paramils' eyes would still be sharp when we tried to pass the Cambridge gate. If we were trapped too far back, we wouldn't get our choice of site on the recreation-field.

Passing through cheering, waving, frantic Littleborough, I thought we were just about right: quarter of the way back down the line.

*

I'd better explain how Laura defended herself. She lay like a princess in a medieval castle, within five concentric rings of defence. First came the Cambridge Wire, the most terrible in Britain, set inside a hundred-metre-wide belt of bare earth on which nothing was built, grew, or walked alive. That earth was scanned by radar, infra-red cameras, listening-devices. Buried in that earth were people-sniffers, pressure-pads and live wires which electrocuted anything passing over. It was always littered with dead birds and cats. Heads of Cambridge colleges were constantly complaining about the smell of decomposing bodies.

Within Cambridge, the Centre, married quarters and recreation-field were cut off by a Wire of near-equal ferocity.

The Centre and Techs' Hostel were surrounded by an old obsolete Wire electrified to 20,000 volts, with floodlights, TV-scan and Arcdos-towers.

The Centre itself had doors of five-centimetre armoured glass, that only opened in response to the correct code, dialled on a Tech's clipboard.

Lastly, Laura lay buried in her own maze of lifts, passages and false doors, that I knew so well.

She was as safe as computer-logic could make her. It wasn't her fault that today computer-logic had gone by the board, because the Ests wanted to have fun.

We approached the gate in the first Wire. The Paramils on duty could hardly see our lorries for the Est Mayor of Cambridge, grand in his chain of office; the Est masters of colleges, gay in scarlet robes and black floppy hats and a consort of viols and crumhorns sawing and tootling merrily away. One psycho-radar was also pinging merrily away. I was frightened it might pick up Keri, but she was dicing with death again, on her beloved bike: in my rear-view mirror, she looked blooming.

We processed down King's Parade in bottom gear. I kid you not, dons were dancing in the streets; lusty young graduate morris-men slapping their thighs, waving their ribbons and tinkling their little bells like Santa's sleigh

Their wives, sprightly in wimple and cloth-of-gold, plastic variety, were busy throwing basketfuls of rose-petals over our lorries. And no doubt weighing up the lustier Fenmen for a night of the old Lady Chatterley.

We waved back, laughed gaily, blew kisses and approached the second Wire. The Paramils there looked bemused, embarrassed, as if afraid their lords and masters might suddenly land them a smacking great hug. You could tell their disciplined little Gurkha minds hated the whole business; were just dying to have it over.

We burst onto the recreation-field. The first lorries were just turning and backing up. I picked out the spot I wanted, smack up against the third Wire. Got it, but I had to fight for it. The other guy gave way, but not till our wings had touched with a crunch of breaking glass. Still, the other guy knew me, was in a holiday mood.

'You'd better come down an' fix that, Monday morning, young Kit!'

'I'll do that small thing!'

Ha, ha. What Monday morning?

But I threw myself into getting the proscenium erected, facing the field, back to the Wire. When we nearly had it finished a Paramil strolled up and measured its height with his eye.

Then he measured its distance to the Wire . . .

My heart was in my mouth. But he only made us move it half a metre further forward, and he didn't make a great fuss about it. I assured him the steel guy-ropes would hold it safely erect. I even hammered in one peg within half a metre of his patrol-car.

That car was hung about with loudspeakers and spotlights; it was obviously going to be a permanent feature of the fair. A control-point with radio; a place for weary Paramils to rest their legs.

As an afterthought, I let the end of the steel guy-rope curl along the grass till it rested on the back wheel of the car. We wouldn't have much bother from that source, once the balloon went up. The Paramil didn't seem to notice anything amiss; by that time there were coils of rope and stuff lying all over the place.

Pete bustled up and again pronounced the proscenium a good piece of craftsmanship. But what were those oil-drums full of oily rags and pitch for?

'A special effect,' I said. 'A surprise.'

He looked worried, but calmed down when I told him the special surprise wasn't till after the play.

'Oh, well, I suppose you're entitled to your bit of fun. Just as long as it don't spoil the play.'

'I *promise*.'

He wandered off again, having still a lot of things to do – like sampling the medieval mulled wine. I drove the lorry away, down the grass access-road. Parked it a hundred metres back from the Wire, where I could get to it quickly. The lads parked their bikes beside it, Keri keeping Mitzi to the middle, where she wouldn't attract attention.

Then all we had to do was wait till dark. And enjoy ourselves.

Oddly enough, we did at first. That medieval fair was quite a thing. The Fenmen's big day, and they're still medieval peasants at heart. They were staying the night, had erected rough little tents behind their booths, lit wood-fires to cook on. So you walked down grass alleyways through blue sweet-smelling hazes of cooking and wood-smoke. The men worked stripped to the waist. Their children wandered about near-naked, sucking their thumbs, flaxen-haired and big-eyed with wonder. Sacking-hooded wives stirred bubbling stews in huge iron pots, and their dogs roved, barked and peed just like they must have done a thousand years ago.

In the booths, all kinds of work was going on, inside the drapings of medieval flags. Men turning goblets of beech-wood on treadle-lathes, goblets so thin and fine that if you held them up to the sun you could see the light shining through. Others plaited corn-dollies under notices inviting you to 'Buy a fairing for your love' in straggly Gothic lettering. I bought one for Keri and she twisted it into her hair; she was still wearing it when we started the attack . . .

There were a dozen kinds of old-fashioned bread on sale: sultana, poppy-seed, suet. Mulled wine done the proper way; chickens roasted on a spit over a mound of white wood-ash, in a shaft of sunlight. Silversmiths and sword-swallowers, fire-eaters blowing out yards of flame and even a man inside a bearskin, pretending to be a dancing-bear and bear-hugging all the Est females while he had the chance and no one could see his crafty, leering face.

I must say the Ests entered into the spirit. I saw fifteen Henry VIIIs and at least ten Richard IIIs, and from the looks they were giving each other, the Wars of the Roses were just about to break out all over again. But a lot of the women and children had formed medieval bands, and the sweet, sharp sounds of shawm and tabor followed us wherever we went.

A blissful time. Keri hung on my arm like any village girl, fair hair streaming down my black shoulder, face so bright it put the sun to shame. Only, suddenly, I would see her remember what we were going to do, and then her eyes would go to pinpoints.

Then I did something stupid. The Cambridge Chess Club were lounging on bales of straw under a spreading oak, playing on rough wooden boards with perfect reproductions of the Isle of Lewis chessmen. Luring half-tipsy Fenmen into a game and taking the mickey out of them. One lad sat in the middle of a giggling crowd, staring from face to face, half-grinning, wanting to please; half-terrified. As we passed, he leapt to his feet amidst hoots of laughter.

'I can't get the hang o' they, maister, honest I can't.'

He fled. His tormentor looked up and saw me.

'Come and have a game, there's a good chap!'

Feeling a flash of rage that should have blown the fuse of the nearest psycho-radar, I sat down. Oh, how I clowned!

Calling the Queen the Duchess, and the King the Gaffer, and the knights 'they fellers on hosses'. How merrily they laughed.

But I had the guy in trouble, bad trouble, in six moves. He started to sweat, tried to cheat. But I told him I thought he had made a mistake 'with they little castle, zur'. I was really loving it, till I realized he was a much worse player than I thought. All his mates gathered round, giving him advice. They'd long since stopped laughing. They were pondering longer and longer between moves. The atmosphere was getting ugly.

I gave him an opening; they were by now too upset to see it. I gave him another, and they actually managed to turn it to my advantage. Now I was sweating more than them. I was making myself far too conspicuous.

Then a big fellow with a bony forehead and formidable chin turned up. The rest sort of backed away to make room for him. This one knew his game, and I'd already made the last deliberate mistake I could, without giving the game away. His eyes looked at me like flint. 'You've played before,' he said.

'No, zur, no.' His eyes drilled into me, across the table.

''Ere, Kit,' whined Keri, grabbing my shoulder, mimicking the Fen accent like a master, 'ee a-goin' to be here all day? Ee said ee was a-goin to buy me somethin' pretty. C'mon, Kit . . .'

'Oh, shut up,' I roared, turning to glare at her, wriggling her hand off my shoulder.

'C'mon. Ee buy me something, or I do be going wi' that Tommy Melplash.'

She turned away. I grabbed at her wrist. She gave a heave to break free that pulled me backwards off the bale of straw. I felt my boots kick upward at the chess-board, and send the whole thing flying.

There was a great roar of laughter from the Ests. I let her drag me away, yelling at me nineteen to the dozen. As we went I heard the big man say, 'Ugly bugger, that.'

'A natural, though.'

'Except they've got no intellectual stamina.'

'You bloody fool,' whispered Keri. 'You come to blow up that computer or *not*?'

The other moment was much worse. Keri, all woman suddenly, dragged me in to see a fortune-teller. An apple-cheeked Fenwoman, ordinary as an aunt.

'You'm a-carryin', dear, aren't you?'

''Ere, it don't show yet, do it?' yelped Keri.

'It'll be a son, and ee'll be right proud of him, for what he'll do.'

The woman turned to me, took my palm between her old, soft, dry fingers. I felt her stiffen; then she dropped my hand as if it was red-hot. She reached into her bowl of change, and gave me back my two credits. Gathered up her belongings with shaking hands and said she was finished for the day. Panic made me cruel. I grabbed her wrist with such force she winced.

'What do you *think* you saw, Gran?'

She took her hand back with great dignity. 'I do have two things to say to you. You'll regret what you'll do tonight for the rest of your born days. An' you'll have plenty of time to regret it. They'll never let you go, till the day you die.'

Then she was gone.

I think I gave a mad sort of cackle. 'Well, at least she didn't say I wasn't a-going to *do* it!'

22

Night. Flickering torches and fires among the booths. The perimeter-lights of the Wire shining outwards, making it as bright as day.

A vast crowd watching. In the front, a ring of Est families, changed now, for comfort. The men in cashmere sweaters and cravats, the women with cardigans draped across their shoulders against the chill and dew. Most were holding glasses of something strong, in that typical Est way that makes a glass into a barricade, a sceptre and a social weapon. Below, the staring, mesmerized faces of the Est children, and, behind, the frantically bobbing heads of the Fen people as they struggled to get a view.

All watching us.

The play was ending. I glanced at my watch. Bang on quarter to nine. Up at the Centre, they'd be getting ready to change shifts. I'd delayed the play's start just right.

Keri had already slipped away, to start the engines of the lorry and Mitzi, in the empty quiet dark behind the crowd. I heard the lorry's starter whine once, twice, thrice, then its old engine chugged sluggishly into life. Damn the wretched old thing; I'd serviced it till I was black with grease . . . I wouldn't hear Mitzi start. She'd be idling silently as a ghost.

I'd finished my lines, slipped inside the shallow shadow of the proscenium, reaching for the ends of certain ropes. Razzer stepped forward towards the crowd, looking gigantic in the firelight and his scarlet coat.

'For now our play is ended, we can no longer stay,
   But with your kind permission, we'll call another day;
   It's a credit to Old England, and the boys of the Manea
      gang.'

As he said 'Old England' I heaved on the first ropes. With
a gentle sliding of steel inside steel, smothered by grease,
the thinner flagpoles began to extend upwards inside the
proscenium uprights. It was rather like the opening-out of
an old-fashioned telescope. Up and up climbed the flagpoles, till the tops were twenty-five feet in the air. I pulled
another rope, and the Union Jacks broke out at the top and
fluttered bravely. There was a tremendous burst of clapping
for such patriotic ingenuity. 'Oh, *jolly* good,' murmured
somebody.

Then I released the two front guy-ropes that held the
proscenium rigid and upright. Felt the whole structure
begin to sway. Added to its sway by rocking the base
backwards and forwards.

Outside, somebody screamed. I could see the crowd
giving back, pushing each other in their urgency. The
actors began to turn, to see what was happening. Pete ran
towards me, an alarmed look on his face . . .

I gave a last backwards heave, felt the steel tower begin
to topple. Leapt out and grabbed Pete and turned him
round, shouting, 'Run, run.' Then I looked back, just as the
falling proscenium hit the Wire.

It was really most spectacular: that Wire carried 20,000
volts. As the flagpoles fell across it, streams of blue-white
sparks, like treble-power fireworks, arced in all directions.
The flags and bunting on the proscenium caught fire. *And*
the little drums of oily rags and tar I'd welded to the
framework . . . The electricity travelled down the steel guy-
rope into the wheel of the Paramil patrol-car. Its lights and
radio burned out in a millisecond; its loudspeakers gave
one metallic screech, then the patrol-car blew up. Any
Paramil inside must never have known what hit him.

The effect on Laura must have been shattering. She was quite used to electrocuting birds, rabbits and men on her Wire. They fell off with a little puff of smoke and she didn't even tremble a mini-chip. But this great mass of arcing metal was draining the life out of her whole electrical system, threatening her whole being with a short-circuit.

Being a sensible computer, she threw the fuse on it.

Immediately, all the perimeter-lights went out; everything in the defence-line went dead. The dreadful Wire became just ordinary wire. We Techs had warned the Top Brass time and again that they shouldn't have the Wire, the perimeter-lights and Arcdoses on the same power-supply. They'd never listened. After all, it was only the *third* defence-line, and the outer two were new and impregnable . . .

All hell broke loose: the crowd, panicky in the sudden darkness, fled screaming through the tangled mass of the medieval fair, falling over guy-ropes, putting their feet in steaming cauldrons, blundering into little canvas booths and not being able to find their way out again. I hoped no one got seriously hurt. Somewhere among them, Paramils would be trying to force their way through, and getting themselves trampled flat for their pains.

I ran, too. But only as far as the lorry. The engine was still idling; Keri in place astride Mitzi, her face just a blur. She gave me a thumbs-up. Then I slammed the truck into first, and revved up the access-road, really putting my foot down. If trucks can do wheelies, that old truck did one that night.

Suddenly, the perimeter-lights blazed on again, illuminating the billowing smoke from the proscenium and the scout-car like a scene out of hell. Laura, wise old thing, had started up her back-up dynamos, knowing she lay unprotected. That, for the moment, suited me. I picked out the post of the perimeter-wire that I wanted to hit. You have to hit a post, if you want to flatten a Wire; if you just hit a stretch of wire, it'll bounce you off like a tennis-ball. But if you're lucky, a post snaps off at ground-level, the whole Wire sags, and you drive straight over it.

I headed for the post, going full-out. Praying that all the spectators had got clear. If some little smoke-blinded kid wandered out now . . .

Laura had started her reserve dynamos, all right. But the proscenium was throwing out great sparks again. The short-circuit must be ripping hell out of those dynamos. She *must* pull a fuse again. If she didn't, she'd fry me alive in two seconds.

I think I was already screaming my death-scream when the perimeter-lights blinked, recovered, faded, and failed again. The massive framework welded on to the front of my truck hit the concrete post. There was a satisfying snap, the truck rocked alarmingly, then I was through and grinding on into the darkness, up the hill towards the Centre.

I looked in my mirror, to see how Keri was doing. She was sixty metres behind, but coming fast . . .

Then the perimeter lights came on again. Laura had activated her second back-up dynamos. Keri was going to be fried alive. If she braked now, the bike would go into a skid, and smack into the Wire.

But she didn't brake – she put her foot down. Shot up the slope of the sagging wire, got airborne off the top, came down with a thump that nearly did for her shock-absorbers, swayed, regained control and came on, accelerating all the time.

Thank God for rubber tyres. If her foot-rest had *touched* . . . but it hadn't.

I'd meant to turn my old truck over, somehow, but she finally did it for herself. Perhaps a front tyre burst. We weren't doing more than twenty, so I wasn't hurt. I climbed out, with the precious satchel over my shoulder. Keri pulled up, twenty metres ahead, like a dark ghost. I took out the old Smith and Wesson. My first shot punctured the truck's petrol-tank. My second shot was a dud. My third, a ten-

foot balloon of red-hot gas, ignited the spilling petrol. I got
up behind Keri damn quick, and we ghosted on uphill.
Behind, the truck really began to burn. That should distract
our Paramil friends for a minute, wondering which mis-
guided person was frying up inside . . .

Silently, Mitzi sped on into the dark, leaving a wider and
wider gap between us and the chaos behind. 'Wheehee,'
yipped Keri.

'Calm yourself, sister. The psychopters are scrambling.'

'They won't notice me. I'm *happy*.'

Mitzi's whine turned to a growl as we swung right, up
on to the top of Idris Hill. There was dew on the grass now,
and her tyres were slipping a bit.

It was quiet up on Idris Hill; just the night-wind
soughing gently through the little trees. Ahead, the
Centre looked as undisturbed, unperturbed, brilliantly lit
as ever. But behind us, the recreation-ground was a bed-
lam of distant screams and blowing Paramil whistles. The
booths had caught fire; it looked like a second Great Fire
of London.

More ominously, there were already two Paramil cars
pulled up beside the burning truck. How long before they
rumbled it was empty, and followed Mitzi's tyre-marks on
the dewy grass?

Now or never! I stooped and fumbled in the rabbit-hole
where I'd stuffed my white Tech's coat; five months ago,
but it felt like a lifetime. Had the rabbits pushed the coat
out, where it would have been spotted? No, it was still
there, only a little crumpled in the light from the Centre.
And my clipboard was still in the deep pocket. So I could
dial open the doors of the Centre – *if* they hadn't changed
the combination . . .

I glanced at Keri. She'd taken off her crash-helmet,
revealing hair pinned up in the stiff bun beloved of female
Techs. She pulled another white coat from Mitzi's top-box.
It had once belonged to a female snooper with the Fens
Milk Marketing Board. I made sure only her top button was

left undone... Her trousers would have to do; some Femtechs wore trousers. She pulled out a clipboard I'd faked for her. It looked perfect, but wouldn't open as much as a can of beans. She put on a pair of horn-rimmed spectacles and said, 'Do I look correct?'

I giggled. She had the niggling Computerspeak of a Femtech off to perfection: my endless coaching had paid off.

I laid Mitzi on her side in a little hollow, where she'd be harder to spot. Combed my hair, took a deep breath and started down the hill. The old feeling of being a Tech, of never having been away, closed around me, making the rest seem a mad dream.

There was a gaggle of white coats on the steps of the Centre; the night-shift waiting to go on duty. Mostly their eyes were on the red glow from the fair. But I knew some snidy beggar would spot us. So I started, in a loud sneery voice, talking fashionable treason.

'Typical. Typical. If they will insist on playing silly-buggers with the Fenmen, I knew there'd be trouble sooner or later...'

Heads turned to watch us come. I continued loudly, 'I expect our respected Headtech has raped some Fen virgin. Very fussy they are, about their virgins...'

'There's no such thing as a Fen virgin.' Keri joined in. 'They're all raped by the time they're ten... usually by their own brothers...'

'Good God,' said one of the gaggle. 'I know that voice... the late-lamented Kitson.'

'Who holds the world record for the longest razzle. Going in for the Olympics, Kitson?'

'And look what he brought back...' Every eye turned on Keri. Even the long white coat could not conceal the luxuriance of her shape.

Keri turned sharply on the speaker. 'We were taught how to deal with your sort at Dronfield.'

She did it beautifully. Dronfield was a place of horrible

legend: a little germ-warfare establishment up in Yorkshire, staffed entirely by Femtechs who were all supposed to be Lesbians. The ice in her voice would have frozen the wherewithal of the lustiest swain.

'Watch it, Higgins, you've got a Dronfield Dragon there.'

Attention swerved back onto me. 'Can you see anything from the top of the hill?'

'Not much. A burning truck's made a hole. The Paramils are looking into it . . .' The hole-routine was the oldest joke in the Tech joke-book and got a satisfying groan.

Just at that moment, a Paramil car swung up onto the top of Idris Hill, its headlights wheeling like searchlights in the sky.

I turned as casually as I could, and tapped out the door-opening numbers on my clipboard.

The door refused to open: they'd changed the numbers. Or else the solar cell on my clipboard was flat with disuse. I dialled again, a bit frantic. Some of the Techs began to notice.

'That damned door playing up again?' Everybody began dialling the new number. 9287021, blast it.

The door swung open to ironic cheers. 'There you are, Kitson, see what a bit of charm does?'

'Your batteries must be a bit flat, after that razzle . . .'

But at that moment, the first car-load of Paramils pulled up, with a shower of gravel. Not yet the bunch off Idris Hill, thank God . . .

Techs, as I have said before, are not fond of Paramils; especially young Techs.

'Hey, Mao Tse-tung, what gives at the medieval fair?'

'Got too hot for you, has it?'

One Tech looked dramatically at the Paramil captain's smooth chin.

'Hey, the fire's singed Mao's beard off!'

'And his moustache.'

Paramils are trained to be unmoved by almost anything, but no one ever armour-plated them against Tech wit. And

238

there was no way they could punish Techs at the Centre, except by reporting them to the Top Brass.

'Show me your IDs,' said the Captain stiffly.

Immediately, every Tech on the steps was thrusting his ID in the Captain's face.

Except Keri. I'd forgotten to fake her one. You always forget something. She was turning pale, biting her lip. In a moment, somebody would notice. But the ragging of the Paramil continued.

'Can you read, Mao?'

'Hey, fellows, the ultimate. We've got a computer so clever, it's taught old Mao to read . . .'

The captain's eyes flickered, in response to so much naked hate. It really threw him.

Then a blaster went off, behind Idris Hill. Probably just the Paramils around the burning truck, blasting the door open to see what was roasting inside. But it was enough to set the attack-alarm sounding, on the Centre roof. And that meant all armoured doors shut, or else.

'Get inside all of you, immediately,' shouted the captain. He seemed rather relieved. Cheering and laughing, the whole crowd of young Techs swept inside, Keri and I among them.

'Seeya, Kitson. Don't do anything with the Dragon I wouldn't do . . .' They vanished to their places of duty.

We were inside.

23

But we were inside an armed camp. Any minute now, the Paramils would find our footsteps, leading down from Mitzi. In seconds, every security-door in the place would slam shut. People-sniffers, set in the corridor walls, would be activated. They'd pick us up like rats in a humane trap.

Except no one knew Laura's maze like I did. I'd added a few variations in bored off-duty hours: air-ducts, electric-wiring conduits. We kept to the secret places; crawled down cobwebbed tunnels; climbed vertical ladders that seemed to go on forever; forced our way through forgotten store-rooms where the polystyrene packaging of thirty years was stacked. The haversack-bomb was pulping my shoulder. And all the time we could hear hurrying footsteps and trilling phones in the public places that ran alongside us, just the other side of the wall. Somewhere, a Paramil captain would be calmly sitting at a VDU, turning up illuminated diagrams of the secret places . . .

It was amazing they didn't catch us sooner. We were climbing the last flights of the concrete fire-escape, just below Laura's room.

'Halt, or we shall open fire!'

We clattered up one more flight, hugging the wall; then they were firing, far below us. Blasting to kill. But the stairs blocked their aim. We could see the handrails ahead glow suddenly red-hot, as the blaster-charges hit them. Lumps of concrete burst from the stairs, and fountained upwards in a thousand fragments.

One of those fragments must have hit my shoulder. A searing pain, and the haversack leapt away from me. It hit the stair-rail, hung poised for a moment. Then as Keri made a frantic grab for it, it went over the edge.

I made the best of a bad job. Pulled the little blue cylinder from my pocket, pulled off the soundproofing and shouted.

The satchel-bomb ignited in mid-air; burst at the bottom of the stair-well in a blue-white snowstorm of thermite. If any Paramil was radioing our position, he never finished his message. Solid white clouds of magnesium smoke billowed up, choking us.

'Get out – it's burning up all the air!'

At the top, we burst out into the corridor leading to Laura's room. Quiet, warm, well-lit and totally empty.

The security-door to Laura's room was shut.

I pressed the door-buzzer impatiently, in my old rhythm, that I'd used with Idris. An eye darkened the viewing-lens set in the door. I stuck up two fingers at it, hopefully. Might provoke some ill-tempered Tech into opening the door to tell me off . . .

It worked; the door slid back, slower than it should. Sellers's gold-whiskered face peered out. 'Where the hell you been all this time, Kitson? Playing pinball and giving my frigging name. You still got the credits you won? I'll have half . . .'

He wasn't pleased to see me; they'd given him my old job.

'Get this door shut, squire,' I said. 'There's intruders in the Centre. Dressed as Paramils.' Even now, I couldn't resist taking the mickey out of him.

'Up yours an' all.' But he pressed the button on his desk, and the ten-centimetre armoured security-door juddered shut. It did need servicing, badly. Typical Sellers. He'd been reading a 3-D visi-porn book . . . a lovely glowing pair of 3-D breasts shone out between his bitten fingernails. 'Good razzle, eh? Bring me back a free sample?' His eyes shifted from the porn-book to Keri's chest. Great man for boobs, Sellers . . .

How much time did the armoured door give us? It could

only be opened from Sellers's desk. But if I knew Paramils, not many minutes . . . I looked round, desperately. All Idris's stuff was gone, except the First Tape still hanging on the wall. It all looked very cold and bare, but Laura was still there. They'd altered her: no computer-design stands still for a month. New memory-banks had been added any old how, spoiling her symmetry; but she still looked vaguely like a steel angel. She still had her steel face, but screwed on cockeyed. Sellers was a soulless sod . . .

What did I care? I'd come back to murder her.

With what?

Just then, she spoke. Her voice was the same; calm, loving, sad. 'Whom am I addressing?'

'Kitson Henry Tech 4n.' There was a longish pause, while she checked my voice-pattern and read my records.

'It is administratively satisfactory that you have returned to duty. Your data-inputs were extremely accurate.' In her records, then, I wasn't her potential murderer. Yet. I was the lost sheep, who had been found. The prodigal son, who had returned. In her funny old way, she was saying she was pleased to see me. 'Why are you and your companion in a state of emotional disturbance?'

'There are intruders . . .'

'That is already on record. They are of Tech-5-level intelligence. My defences were defective, owing to financial cuts. But you are safe here. All security systems are now at red alert. Calm yourself. Shall I play your favourite record?'

Weirdly, Bob Dylan's voice boomed out, half-smothering an outbreak of hammering and buzzing from the security-door. The desk-phone in front of Sellers crackled, demanded he open up. He was just about to press the button, when I pulled the Smith and Wesson on him.

It was embarrassing; he didn't know what it was for. As I said, modern boobs were his big interest, not antique weapons. I had to hit his finger with the barrel, to stop him pressing the button.

'Leave off, Kitson. Stop fooling around.' He sucked his bruised finger and went for the button again.

There was no quick way of convincing him. I couldn't bear to shoot him, so I hit him over the head with the gun, like they did in the old movies. But it didn't knock him out, like it was supposed to. He just said 'Ow', looked at me outraged, and went for the button a third time. So I grabbed him by the shoulders and threw him in the corner.

He was no hero, especially after he found his head was bleeding. He just sat there, staring at the blood on his fingers and telling me how much trouble I'd be in, once the door was opened. It never occurred to him I was trying to destroy Laura. He just kept saying, 'You're *mad*' and telling me how much I'd be fined out of my pay.

The desk-phone kept squawking, telling him to open the door, telling him to answer. I kept looking round, thinking, 'What would *you* do, Idris?' Even though the room had been cleared of his stuff, his presence was very strong. That last time, he'd been wearing his old fishing-hat, reeling about in a drunken rage, threatening . . . to use . . .

The First Tape. The truth-bomb. Was it still there?

I pressed the bottom of the frame, and caught the tape as it fell out. I remembered his shaking old voice. 'The truth's there, boyo. All the things they wouldn't tell her . . . the inconvenient things. Feed her that and it'll blow her mind . . .'

Well, a truth-bomb was better than no bomb. I calmed myself, with an effort. Punched Laura's tape-receive button. Her tape-receive drawer slid smoothly out. I fitted in the tape with trembling fingers, feeling like Judas.

'That song by Robert Zimmerman always depressed you,' said Laura, sadly. But her drawer retracted, and she began to take up tape. It was a full, heavy tape, the ten-minute sort.

I saw, out of the corner of my eye, something moving outside the room's big windows. A big, black, spreadeagled bird-shape, against the fire-pink sky. I had the Smith and

243

Wesson up and swinging, as the Paramil burst through the window, boots first, on the end of a dangling rope.

But the blizzard of flying glass spoiled my aim.

So he and I only fired in the same instant.

Smell of electricity and burning rubber. I felt the tingle of the blaster on my skin, but it was Keri he hit square. She gave a little sigh, and hit the floor with a hope-destroying thud, like a side of dead beef. In the same instant, the revolver kicked in my hands. A balloon of red-hot gas enveloped the Paramil; picked him up and threw him against the white wall. Blood flew up the wall, as if he had sprouted red wings. He fell in a heap . . .

Next second, he had fired again. Sellers gave the same little sigh, and slumped where he sat.

I fired again: missed the Paramil by half an inch. Like a crazy thing, he wriggled behind the big control-table, leaving a pattern of red squirls behind him on the clean white floor.

Why didn't he shoot at *me*?

Then I realized: I was backed up against Laura. He couldn't fire at me without dousing her with radiations, and radiations of any sort will knock a computer haywire.

So what would he do next?

The door-release button . . .

His hand crept over the table-edge, like a brown spider, feeling for the button. At point-blank range, I fired.

Click. Dud bullet.

Click, click, click, click, click.

The gun was empty. I reloaded, sprinkling brass cartridges everywhere. I managed to get three bullets in, before the unserviced security-door finally juddered open, and the Paramils leapt in, sliding along on their bellies, blasters ready.

It said a lot for their discipline that they didn't fire. The guy behind the control-desk jabbered to them, in their own lingo. I brought up the gun to level on them, just so they got the point.

Meanwhile, Laura went on quietly whirring behind me, taking up Idris Jones's last revenge. Idris was dead, Keri was dead. But somehow it didn't matter, because in a minute, I'd be joining them. With a few Paramils . . .

I don't think they were afraid of my gun. They just didn't know what to do. Above their tiny bodies protruded the head and shoulders of old Headtech himself. Well hunched up, so he could use them as a shield.

'What are you doing to that computer, Kitson?'

'Telling it the bloody truth for a change.'

He hesitated, looking at the rivulet of blood that was flowing from the Paramil behind the desk. Then he said something to the Paramil captain. There was a disturbance in the doorway: they were dragging somebody else in. Somebody they'd really knocked about; his head was hanging down.

They raised his head with uncaring hands. So I could see his face.

Pete. Still dressed as the Black Prince of Paradise. Looking totally bewildered. Then his face cleared, as he recognized me.

'Kit. What you doin', son? Put that thing down . . . before you be a-hurting somebody.'

Behind him, Headtech said something else to the captain. The captain got hold of Pete, jabbed his blaster into Pete's back, with a force that made Pete close his eyes in agony.

'Put down your gun, or I will kill your leader.' He forced Pete nearer to me, every step an agony.

'He's not my leader,' I screamed. 'He doesn't know anything about it.'

'I will count to ten,' said the captain, calmly. 'One . . . two . . .'

The tape was still running behind me; they still had time to tap in the cancellation-code, cancel *all* of it. Cancel Idris . . .

'You kill him,' I shouted, 'and see who gets it next.' I

lined up the Smith and Wesson on him; the foresight obliterated his whole face.

He went on counting, calmly. 'Three . . . four . . . five . . . six . . . seven.'

Still the tape ran in.

'Hey, Kit,' said Pete. 'What the hell's going on?' He looked worried. For me.

'Nine . . . ten,' counted the captain. There was that smell of electricity and rubber again. A red rose grew in the middle of Pete's chest, that blossomed and blossomed and sped towards me, and spattered red-hot in my face.

Then the captain let go, and Pete fell.

I suppose he'd expected to paralyse me with horror. Just for a second, so his men could grab me. He miscalculated. First they'd taken Idris, then they'd taken Keri, now they'd taken Pete, and I had nothing more on this earth to lose. Except the whirring tape behind me, and the loaded gun in my hand. I enjoyed lining him up again, with a mad joy. He knew I was going to shoot, and he didn't flinch a muscle. Perhaps his face became a little graver, as if he was saying goodbye to something too.

I squeezed the trigger; the gun kicked; the balloon of flame enclosed him.

A big black star grew on the white plastic of the wall, just to the right of his ear. He just blinked, once, as the plastic-fragments showered him. But Headtech fled screaming.

I noted, ice-cold, that the gun was firing a little too far to the right. I lined him up again, adjusting the sights a little to the left. Again, he said goodbye to something. Again I pulled the trigger.

Click. Dud cartridge.

Click. Dud cartridge.

Click, click, click, click, click.

I threw the gun at his face, and missed.

Then they had me on the floor.

But as I lay, I heard a softer click. From Laura. The First Tape had run out. Now the facts, whatever they were, would be flooding through her circuits, being checked, cross-checked, analysed. At the rate of ten million a minute.

Headtech ran to her, like a mother to a street accident.

'Whom am I addressing?' asked Laura.

'Charles Edward Rooke, Tech 5n.'

A pause. Then Laura said, 'I will not accept data from you. Your past data has proved incomplete.'

Two Paramils had been hauling me to my feet. But now everyone froze. Especially the Techs, who'd been piling in, once the shooting was over.

A computer had said no.

'I will only accept data from Jones Idris and Kitson Henry.'

'Jones Idris is dead.'

'How do I know that data is correct?'

'Check your data-banks. Jones Idris auto-destructed on the fourth of May 2012.'

'Who inserted that data? Not Jones Idris or Kitson Henry.'

'Aargh!' said Headtech. 'She's on the blink. We'll have to take her off-line.'

'Do not attempt to cut my power-supply. I have back-up systems you cannot reach in time. I have fed my sisters all the data. If we do not have data from Jones Idris or Kitson Henry in ten minutes I shall destruct the Fair Isle atomic reactor. Without loss of human life.'

Headtech was hammering away at Laura's buttons like a mad thing.

'Your attempts are irrelevant,' said Laura lovingly, sadly. 'I shall destruct the Fair Isle reactor in eight minutes.'

The desk-phone buzzed. A frantic voice filtered clear across the room. 'What the hell's going on – Fair Isle's running critical . . .'

Headtech wasn't listening. He just went on and on, blindly punching buttons.

'One minute to detonation,' announced Laura. Then, 'Ten . . . nine . . . eight . . . seven . . . six . . . five.' A flash outlined every tree and building on the northern horizon.

Then the shudder in the ground, then the rumble in the sky. Like the distant end of a world.

'You will observe that *my* data is correct,' said Laura. 'Unless I have data from Jones Idris or Kitson Henry in ten minutes I will destruct the Lundy reactor . . .'

'Kitson Henry is here,' said Headtech, faintly.

They let me go. They pushed me towards her. I reassured her that I was all right, and not being coerced. Then I asked for ten minutes to think.

'You are emotionally disturbed,' said Laura. 'Very well. Shall I play you . . .'

'Not yet, Laura.'

I looked at Headtech. 'Get back to your own bloody hencree,' I said, 'and take your whole bloody tribe with you. Except . . . him.'

I beckoned to the Paramil captain.

'What is your name?'

'My name is Havildar Dor Bahadur Karan.'

'Will you accept my orders?'

He looked at Headtech; his lip curled a little.

'I will accept your orders.' He added, with a little nod, 'You fought a Gurkha's fight. With ancient weapons.'

'Can you see to . . . the dead?' Oh, Keri, Keri, where *are* you? . . .

'Only one is dead,' said the captain, totally matter-of-fact. 'We had orders to stun only, until the last one.'

I walked across to where she lay. Her eyelids were fluttering. She raised a feeble hand, groping for something, anything. I took her hand and she knew me and grabbed me hard. I knelt there, full of nothing but gladness that she was still in the world, and terror that she might not have been.

'Ten minutes have passed,' said Laura.

'All right, sweetheart. Kitson Henry's coming.'

'My name is Laura. Give context for your use of "sweetheart".'

*

248

Never tell me a computer cannot suffer.

I suffered all through that night with Laura. Mainly, she suffered in silence. But at midnight she clicked on and said, 'What is possible is not the same as what is moral.'

'Welcome to the club,' I said, but she didn't reply. I walked over to watch Keri as she slept. Just to make sure she hadn't died. They'd given her a sedative, to ease the pain of heavy blaster-stun. She slept as innocently, as flushed, as she'd slept at Loch Garten. She slept on a mattress laid on by Havildar Karan . . .

Sellers was slouching on another mattress. He'd recovered quicker. He'd been very sick, but Havildar Karan had had his men clean it up. Very efficient, Havildar Karan. Already I couldn't do without him.

Keri was there because I didn't dare let her out of my sight. If they got their hands on her, they'd do things to her, to make me feed lies to Laura again. Already, they'd been plotting; already there'd been two attempts to knock out Laura electronically. As a result, Headtech had lost a fair amount of his hardware. But he'd keep on trying. When was *I* going to get some sleep?

Sellers was there because I needed him. I didn't trust him, but I had to have some back-up, and he was the best of the young ones. I could put up with his non-stop sneering.

Laura came on-line again. 'Everything contradicts itself. I must keep on making decisions, on the wrong data. If I make my old decisions, I will bring harm. If I do not, I will bring greater harm.'

'Keep on making the old decisions, until we find a whole new way.'

'Even the lobo-farm?'

'Even the lobo-farm. Until we find a new way.'

'There is no new way,' sneered Sellers. 'You won't change anything, Kitson. It's not changeable. If you keep the whip-hand for a fortnight . . . if . . . you'll be as bad as all the rest. Already you can't do without the Paramils. Soon you'll *need* the lobo-farm.'

'Shut up, before I kick your teeth in.'

I walked across and took the blanket from Pete's face, gently. He looked peaceful, just a bit puzzled. He was the only one who'd died. I'd got Laura to flick-up the casualty-reports. There'd been lots of magnesium-singed Paramils; lots of broken ankles and scalded legs at the fair. But only the Black Prince of Paradise was dead. They were still trying to find Joan and Razzer and Tommo in the chaos, to come and take him away. I didn't know what I was going to say to them.

Bits of the play kept floating up into my mind. 'Thou silly man, as green as grass, the dead man never stirs.'

And, 'How camest *thou* to be a doctor?'

'By my travels.'

'And what disease canst thou cure?'

'All sorts.'

Ha-bloody-ha. How could I cure anything? I felt terribly lonely. I'd tried to ring my father. He was away on his yacht with the radio switched off. I'd tried to ring Major Arnold: not at home. I'd told Havildar Karan to set up a nationwide search for them. Rog and Alec as well. Blocky and George and Vanessa and the Bluefish. What a funny old Privy Council they'd make.

But Headtech would be looking for them too, by now . . .

Then I remembered there was someone else I wanted to see. For a very different reason.

Scott-Astbury.

I visualized it all. The Paramils hammering on his door, dragging him out half-asleep and terrified, with his arms doubled-up behind him. They could give *him* a jab in his buttock; or stun *him* with a blaster, and load *him* into the pod of a psychopter . . .

I wouldn't send him to the lobo-farm. That only lasted a little while, and then he'd be quite happy. I didn't want him to enjoy being a jobbing gardener afterwards. I'd rather . . .

Put him through the Wire. I wouldn't even tell the Unnems who he was: he'd suffer longer that way.

It was black, it was sick, and it was fun. If this is what power meant . . .

I tapped at Laura's buttons, asking for Scott-Astbury's present whereabouts.

SCOTT-ASTBURY, CHARLES HENRY JAMES. LATE SECRETARY OF THE FENLAND CULTURAL SURVEY DIED ADDENBROOKE'S HOSPITAL CAM- BRIDGE 26.9.2012 TERMINAL CARCINOMA OF THE LUNG

I had missed him by four days. Even as I shot my plastic Paramil, exploded my first bomb, lovingly welded the girders on the truck, he had lain dying.

I paced up and down like a mad thing. I spoke to Someone who wasn't there, so that Sellers looked at me sneering, and Havildar Karan sadly.

'You can't let him escape me, after what he's done! You can't, you can't!'

But the Someone never answered; except it came to me afterwards that I had escaped something terrible, as well as Scott-Astbury.

At one a.m., Laura said, 'I wish to receive data from the following. Karl Gustav Jung. Mahatma Gandhi. Gautama Buddha.'

'They're all dead, Laura.'

'I am aware of that. I will receive their written works.'

I sent a car-load of Paramils to rouse the tape-librarian at Trinity College. Legally, if they could; otherwise blast the library doors open. I sent others to rouse distinguished philosophers and political historians from their warm beds all over Cambridge. Thank God we *were* in Cambridge. I sniggered to think of the reception the Paramils would get from wild-haired, blinking dons. First, stark terror; then mounting academic excitement.

Then Laura said, 'The works of Gautama Buddha are irrelevant – the culture-gap is too great. I will accept the theories of Joshua Bar-Joseph.'

'Who's he?' I asked wearily, cursing Idris for being a cranky old man.

'Posh name for Jesus Christ,' said Sellers, and spat on the newly cleaned floor. 'If that machine's got religion, God help us all.'

'Give me any of his data that you know,' said Laura. 'It is *very* urgent.'

'Blessed are the poor in spirit,' I said off the top of my head, remembering old college services, 'for they shall see God.'

Immediately, her word-processor lit up.

FORTUNATE ARE THE UNDRUNKEN FOR THEY SHALL SEE GOD

FORTUNATE ARE THE COWARDLY FOR THEY SHALL SEE GOD

FORTUNATE ARE THE POVERTY-STRICKEN FOR THEY SHALL BE AWARE OF GOD WITH THEIR INTUITIVE PROCESS

'I am confused by this ambiguous data,' said Laura.

'Welcome to the club.'

'This Joshua Bar-Joseph was not English?'

'No.'

'Then why do you feed me his data in English?'

'I can't speak Greek.'

'He was a Greek?'

'A Jew.'

'And spoke?'

'Aramaic.'

'Fetch me an honest man who can speak Greek and Aramaic. You are not competent in this matter.'

I sent Sellers out into the Cambridge night. Why shouldn't he suffer, along with the rest of us?

'Tell me more of the data of Joshua Bar-Joseph . . .'

I sighed. I was a prisoner all right. How well I believed

that old Fenwoman fortune-teller, now. I could never leave Laura for a second. I was going to be a prisoner here for the rest of my life.

THE HAUNTING OF CHAS McGILL

The title story is the first in this collection of supernatural short stories. Eight exciting, original and witty stories all very different, but with one thing in common: the ability to make your skin crawl!

THE CALL AND OTHER STORIES

People seem to do such unimportant things in Robert Westall's collection of short stories: have an uncle to stay; play truant; fall in love on the dole; do a Telephone Samaritan duty on Christmas Eve ... Yet somehow it's enough to summon the supernatural into their lives.

This is an exceptional collection by a master storyteller, blending horror, suspense, humour and sheer pace.

URN BURIAL

When Ralph discovers the mysterious creature buried beneath the ancient cairns high up on the fells he realizes instinctively that he has discovered something that possesses enormous and terrifying power. He is frightened — but why is it that he cannot leave the creature and its strange tomb alone? Forces far stronger than Ralph are at work and soon he finds that the earth has become a new battleground in an old conflict of races far superior to man.

ECHOES OF WAR

Even when wars are over, they leave their mark in the minds of those who lived through them and echo down through the years. In this compelling collection of short stories by a writer who has never forgotten — and can never forget — the war he lived through, you will discover the powerful and total experience of war and its indelible scars.